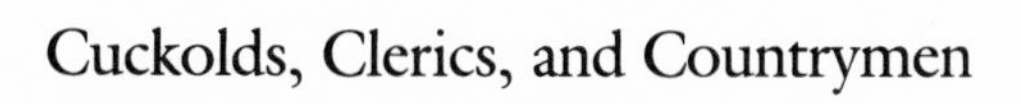
Cuckolds, Clerics, and Countrymen

Cuckolds, Clerics, & Countrymen

MEDIEVAL FRENCH FABLIAUX

Translated by John DuVal

Introductions, texts, and
notes by Raymond Eichmann

THE UNIVERSITY OF ARKANSAS PRESS

FAYETTEVILLE, 1982

The University of Arkansas Press, Fayetteville, Arkansas 72701
Printed and bound in the United States of America

Library of Congress Catalog Card Number 81–14731

Library of Congress Cataloging in Publication Data
Main entry under title:
Cuckolds, clerics, and countrymen.
English and French.
Contents: Du bouchier d'Abevile-The butcher of Abevile—Brunain, la vache au prestre-Browny, the priest's cow—Des trois boçus-The three hunchbacks—[etc.]
Bibliography: p. 125
1. Fabliaux. 2. Fabliaux—Translations into English. 3. English literature—Translations from French. I. DuVal, John, 1940– . II. Eichmann, Raymond, 1943–

PQ1308.E6C8 841'.1'08 81–14731
ISBN 0–938626–06–X AACR2

Thanks to Kay
for love and a good life.
Whatever of mine that is good
is dedicated to her.

JD

For my wife,
Linda,
and for my children,
Leslie and Justin.

RE

Acknowledgments

I wish to express my thanks to the University of Arkansas, whose generous grant in 1979 allowed me to initiate my research for this work. Several persons have played an important role in the realization of this work and deserve the expression of my gratitude: Susan Stiers and Debbie Wilson for their competent help and unfailing patience in preparing the manuscript; Ethel Simpson, whose graceful and expert assistance has made my work in the University of Arkansas Library efficient and, yes, pleasant; Professor Lewis A. M. Sumberg, whose constant encouragements have kept me moving ahead; my colleagues in the Department of Foreign Languages, particularly Professor James F. Ford, Chairman, for graciously allowing me time away from my teaching duties in order to bring this project to fruition. Special thanks are due to Professor Miller Williams, Director of the University of Arkansas Press, for his continuous sound advice and support and for making, I am sure, this book better than it would otherwise have been.

These fine people should share in whatever satisfaction this book will provide but should, in no way, be responsible for any of its shortcomings.

R.E.
Fayetteville, Ark.
November 1981

Several of these translations were composed with much good advice and support from Miller Williams and students in his translation workshop at the University of Arkansas. Thanks very much to them.

Thanks to Victor Miller for his friendship and for the title of this book.

Thanks are due to the editors of the following publications, in whose pages some of these fabliaux first appeared: *Intro 7, Lazarus,* and *Publications of the Missouri Philological Association*.

J.D.
Albany, Ga.
November 1981

Contents

Abbreviations

CH.——Cooke, Thomas D., and Benjamin L. Honeycutt, eds. *The Humor of the Fabliaux: A Collection of Critical Essays.* Columbia: University of Missouri Press, 1974.

JO.——Johnston, R. C., and D. D. R. Owen, eds. *Fabliaux.* Oxford: Basil Blackwell, 1957.

MR.——Montaiglon, Anatole de, and Gaston Raynaud, eds. *Recueil général et complet des fabliaux des XIIIe et XIVe siècles.* 6 vols. Paris, 1872–1890; rpt. New York: Burt Franklin, n.d. (All references to a fabliau are to this text and are cited by volume and page number.)

N.——Nykrog, Per. *Les Fabliaux: Etude d'histoire littéraire et de stylistique médiévale.* Copenhagen: Munksgaard, 1957. We have used Nykrog's siglum classification outlined on pp. 310–11 of his work in order to refer to the various manuscripts in which our fabliaux are located.

R.——Rychner, Jean. *Du Boucher d'Abevile: Fabliau du XIIIe siècle. (Eustache d'Amiens).* Geneva: Droz, 1975.

Introduction

I. Definition of the Fabliaux

To define a genre with some degree of precision is not an easy task. To define a medieval genre is even more difficult. Medieval writers did not share our modern preoccupation for neatly categorizing artistic works according to genre. The medieval manuscript collectors placed the fabliaux alongside epics, courtly romances, and saintly narratives without fear of artistic incongruity. In addition, medieval vocabulary and orthography were still in an unsettled state and one genre could have several names. Beside the seminal Old French term *fablel,* we also find the dialectal term of the Parisian region, *fableaus.* In the Picard dialect of northern France, where most of the fabliaux were composed, the word was *fabliaus,* from which our modern term is derived. These words derive from *fable,* of course, which has a variety of meanings: it can be an instructional *exemplum,* the raw material of a tale, or a fictionalized, untrue tale.

To complicate matters even further, other terms such as *dit* (a humorous narrative, lacking action), *aventure, conte, exemple,* and *fable* are often used as titles or descriptions of works that are also expressly called *fabliaux* by their authors or by other fabliaux writers. To rigidify a genre by giving it a specific, narrow definition would not only be difficult but would also probably be a deliberate violation of supple processes by which medieval authors named, defined, and categorized works. Joseph Bédier's almost century-old definition of the fabliaux has the merit of being flexible: "contes à rire en vers" (verse tales meant for laughter). This definition is broad enough to take account of the genre's malleable character yet specific enough to separate it from other narrative pieces.[1] Per Nykrog's rule that the tale must confine itself to the narration of a single episode and its immediate consequences further narrows the definition without destroying its flexibility.[2]

Other attempts at defining the fabliaux, while precise, fail to improve on Bédier's. Knud Togeby has built an elaborate table of narrative genres wherein most medieval works are categorized according to levels, length, and attitudes.[3] The fabliau for him is a "nouvelle de niveau bas du XIIIe siècle" (low-level thirteenth-century short story). Thomas Cooke, while very comfortable with Bédier's definition, adds to our understanding of the nature of the fabliaux by arguing that what unites the disparate fabliaux is the artistic preparation for the climax and the reader's enjoyment at finding his anticipation fulfilled.[4] Cooke does not insist on defining the genre on the basis of this characteristic, because it is not a feature unique to the fabliaux (*Old French,* pp. 15–16). His characterization has the advantage of not excluding some tale because it happens to be outside the definition's boundaries. Most attempts at definition result in the exclusion of many poems that were considered fabliaux during the Middle Ages or that modern scholars and anthologists have generally accepted as fabliaux. For instance, as Cooke noted, Clem Williams's characterization of the fabliau as a narrative whose ending is chaotic and fragmented is invalid since "there are simply too many fabliaux in which the main action ends in a complete and satisfying resolution."[5] Consequently, Williams had to exclude some tales from his corpus. The safest attempt at definition is that by M. J. Schenck, who uses only tales expressly called fabliaux during the Middle Ages and extracts ten Proppian functions common to each of them.[6] Such an interesting endeavor unfortunately has the obvious disadvantage of extending the definition to unmanageable proportions. In addition, there is no absolute assurance that these functions would not be found in narratives different from the fabliaux. But all definitions must begin with the thing being defined, and the poems themselves, anthologized here, tell what a fabliau is better than even the best definition.

II. Nature, Origins, and Transmission of the Fabliaux

Some 150 fabliaux have come down to us, a very small selection from an obviously popular genre. Almost all of these, plus a few poems that obviously do not fit even Bédier's definition, are anthologized in the six-volume *Recueil général . . . des fabliaux,* edited by Anatole de Montaiglon and Gaston Raynaud.[7] With the exception of one fabliau in the Montaiglon-Raynaud corpus, all fabliaux are written in octosyllabic couplets. They vary in length, from eighteen to thirteen hundred lines, but most average around two hundred and fifty lines.

Where does this elusive yet very popular genre come from? Because of striking resemblances between some fabliaux and Oriental tales, Theodor Benfey advocated that these narrative elements were imported en masse from India by way of the crusaders or the Spanish Moors.[8] In 1874, Benfey's theory of the Oriental origin of the fabliaux was restated by Gaston Paris, who, from there on out, was to carry the brunt of subsequent attacks. Bédier, in 1895, masterfully destroyed the theory, demonstrating decisively that to attempt to discover a common geographical source for all tales was futile and that those tales were part of the legacy of mankind. According to Bédier, it was the specifically Gallic genius that molded the raw material into its artistic form. This form was the creation of a single social class, the bourgeoisie, written by them and for them, despite evidence that the aristocracy also had quite a taste for the fabliaux. Indeed, the genre flourished concomitant with the rise of the middle class in medieval France. Charles Muscatine disagreed and, on the basis of vocabulary analyses, found evidence that the fabliaux have a rural, not a burgher character. He concluded that, in view of the nonhomogeneity of medieval social classes, the fabliaux are not the property of one lone class.[9]

In 1957 the Danish scholar Per Nykrog launched a severe attack on Bédier's thesis, aiming particularly at his inconsistency with regard to his choice of audience for the fabliaux. Echoing Jean Rychner's advice to equate style with audience, Nykrog maintained that the fabliau was an aristocratic genre, written for the aristocracy and, possibly, for the highest order of the bourgeoisie. After all, courtly literature emerged during the same epoch as the bourgeois class did (pp. xl–xli). In returning the fabliaux to the aristocracy, he rehabilitated them. Whereas Bédier had hastily judged them unworthy of consideration and without artistic merit, the medieval manuscript collectors, Nykrog pointed out, deemed them worthy to be placed alongside highly artistic romances and epics. These tales were therefore considered valuable enough to be preserved, and, indeed, careful, unprejudiced readings support Nykrog in that opinion. The fabliau, for him, is "très souvent une parodie de la courtoisie, mais loin de viser l'aristocratie, cette parodie se moque des classes qui lui sont inférieures" (very often a parody of courtliness, but far from being aimed at the aristocracy, this parody makes fun of the inferior classes) (N, p. 104). In Nykrog's estimation (N, p. 74), the nobility amused themselves at the expense of "la courtoisie des vilains" (the courtliness of the commoners). Knud Togeby agreed and expanded his definition to include parody of courtly, serious genres (CH, pp. 8–9).

As early as 1924, the noted classicist Edmond Faral argued that the dramatic nature of ancient Latin comedies by Plautus and Terence had been totally misunderstood by medieval authors who had transformed them into narrative fiction.[10] The fabliaux, he claimed, had their origin in the written, medieval Latin comedy. But why then, Nykrog correctly objected, do no fabliaux preserve from those Latin comedies any stylistic traits, any stock characters such as the lazy slave, the glutton, or the braggart soldier? A more likely link exists between the medieval drama and the fabliaux, which were often acted out to form what Grace Frank called "représentation par personnages."[11] This confusion of genres led Faral to mistakenly view a clearly dramatic thirteenth-century play such as *Courtois d'Arras* as a fabliau acted out in front of an audience.[12]

R. C. Johnston and D. D. R. Owen, as well as Nykrog, have suggested that the fabliaux might have originated from the fables.[13] Etymologically and thematically, the link between fables and fabliaux can be established, and the disturbing question of the morals in the fabliaux can thereby be explained with some degree of satisfaction. This theory has the merit of not linking the fabliau to a particular social class and of separating the question of the raw material of the fabliau from the question of the nature of the fabliau. Robert Harrison explains:

> It is possible that in the fabliaux we see the emergence into written literature of a body of folklore that has always been with us, living a scurrilous underground life in the bawdy joke and the tavern tale, and constantly being transmitted and enriched by local wags and visiting firemen who, knowing how to make a good story better, keep intact the general theme and punch lines while revising superficial details to suit the local audience.[14]

The universality of fabliau material cannot be overly stressed. The attribution of some fabliau to a certain social class might have its relevance, but such a process cannot be valid overall. Muscatine cautions that social classes were more mobile than Bédier had supposed. France's social makeup was very complex in the Middle Ages, and, outside of Paris, the social distinctions between country people and burghers were often blurred ("The Social Background," pp. 18, 19). Each of the fabliaux must be considered individually in relation to a particular class. No one social class will reveal the secret of their origin.

Joseph Bédier assigned the fabliaux to bourgeois audiences, although he admitted the aristocracy's liking for the genre. Nykrog claimed that since only the upper class was familiar with courtly literature, only the upper class could truly enjoy the "parodic nature of the fabliaux."[15] Both Nykrog and Harrison erred in assuming dogmatically that a certain degree of literary sophistication in a fabliau implies an aristocratic audience.[16] Jean Rychner advised strongly to look at the style, "c'est le style, non le sujet, qui jauge le niveau social d'une oeuvre" (It is the style, not the subject, that indicates the social level of a work).[17] When he examined variant versions of a number of fabliaux, he invariably assumed that the best written one was the first and the one destined for a higher class of audience, whereas the more poorly written ones were intentionally revised and adapted for a less demanding (in other words, bourgeois or popular) public.[18] However, from the tales themselves, we can gather that the audiences were mixed. Some fabliaux must have been recited in taverns, for one jongleur (*Du Povre Mercier,* MR, 2:122) asks, "Done moi boire, si t'agree" (Please pour me a drink!). Others were performed at the house of an individual (*De Boivin de Provins,* MR, 5:52), where it was the custom to have the guest recite a fabliau when invited to stay over, at marketplaces, and in castles. Johnston and Owen state, "It would be as unwise to allot to them one particular public as it would be to ascribe them solely to one class or author" (JO, p. vi). A natural temptation would be to assume that each fabliau is destined for the social class of its most sympathetic character or destined for the class furthest from that of its least sympathetic character, that, for example, because the peasants in *De La Sorisete des Etopes* (MR, 4:158) and *Du Fol Vilain* (Livingston, *Le Jongleur Gautier le Leu,* p. 147) are so pitifully ignorant, those fabliaux are intended for a noble or upper-middle-class audience and that a third version of the same story (*Du Sot Chevalier,* MR, 1:220), which makes the sexual ignoramus a knight, must be intended for a lower class.[19] But such an assumption neglects the fact that most people are able to laugh at themselves and that they can enjoy laughing at the types of people they know best, including the people of their own class.

The tale of the foolish peasant/knight is one of many tales with multiple versions. In fact, since an appreciable percentage of the fabliaux appear in more than one manuscript, it is rare for there not to be differences in wording. However, it requires some stretch of the imagination to accept Harrison's claim that multiple versions were a "literary fact of life."[20] Why literary? Johnston and Owen's explanation that scribes "felt free to abridge, to expand, to alter details on facts, and to improve stylistically on the story they retold" (JO, p. xx) makes much better sense when applied to those who spread the tale orally, the jongleurs. They were the ones who by their handling of the fabliaux were responsible for the constant process of re-creating them from performance to performance. Moreover, a jongleur had a deeper commitment to the poem as *his* poem than any scribe could have. The scribe was putting the work onto paper, but the jongleur was carrying the live material with him. It was his livelihood, and the fabliau had to be the best he could make it in accordance with his abilities as a performer, with what jokes worked best for him, and with what situations most stirred his particular audiences.

"Ce qui frappe d'abord, c'est en effet l'absence de toute prétention littéraire chez nos auteurs" (What is indeed most striking is the absence of all literary pretension among our authors), says Bédier in a superficial chapter on the fabliaux' style. Nykrog, arguing for an aristocratic origin for the tales, could not agree. He pointed out that the medieval manuscript writers and collectors evidently did not consider the fabliaux to be artistically base. In the manuscripts, the fabliaux keep good company alongside "respectable" romances, lays, and moral tales. Rutebeuf, Jean Bodel, Jean de Condé, Philippe de Beaumanoir, and Henri d'Andeli, among others, were prominent poets who did not think it beneath themselves to write fabliaux. Moreover, a close look at some of these poems shows that a great deal of artistic skill often did go into their creation. The octosyllabic rhymed couplet, a verse form of some reputation and tradition, gives the fabliaux a brisk, jaunty rhythm. Since the fabliau is a short narrative and must proceed rapidly to its conclusion, the couplet renders a staccato, uninterrupted rhythm. The ear learns to respond to the couplet rhythm so that the listener is constantly anticipating the second line, and, when it comes, he feels the pleasure of fulfilled expectancy and often discovers there a key word or comment or twist of meaning by the author. In *Du Prestre di abevete,* the priest finishes his assault on the peasant's wife before the husband can understand what has happened and before the listener can dwell on the tale's erotic quality. The verse pattern has compelled the tale to its conclusion and left no time for any response but laughter. When the lady in *Berangier* reveals to her husband who it is who will protect her from him for the rest of her life, the octosyllable allows her to relish the triumph of her revelation: "Bérangier" she says, lingering over the last syllable because it is the end of a line (and rhyming with "dangier"), even though his name is only half the hero's full title. Then "Au lonc cul" comes down hard, abrupt, sudden, and emphatically punctuated by the early caesura at the end of *cul* (vv. 292, 293).

In *Du Bouchier d'Abevile* the conversations between the lady and the servant girl and the priest are more than mere squabbles. However nasty the separate speeches may be, once linked together in the couplet form, they click with Ping-Pong rapidity. This click, which is as pleasurable to the ear of the audience as it is painful to the participants, is a product of the meaning, the meter, the rhyme, and the fact that the dialogue usually shifts at the middle of a couplet.

Even formulas, and the tags so much maligned by Bédier, are used skillfully by storytellers to pick up the pace, for instance, when a character races frantically and breathlessly from one scene to the next.[21] In other places, they are not only a compositional necessity but also provide for plenty of humor, as Benjamin Honeycutt has shown.[22] Clearly the fabliaux have artistic merits that are more and more coming to light under unprejudiced scrutiny.

One praise that Bédier accorded the fabliau was its quality of brevity (*Les Fabliaux,* p. 347). A quality but also a restriction! There is little opportunity to elaborate backgrounds or develop characters in a brief tale. The fableor has to present straightforwardly the necessary elements of his tale. Paul Theiner shows how all other elements are reduced to bare functional necessity as the fabliau concentrates on its single purpose, which is that of amusing its audience;[23] little decorative description can be allowed lest the public's attention be diverted from this purpose. Whatever ornamental richness there is will have to be extended by the procedure of allusion, as, for example, the courtly description of the lady in *Des Trois Boçus.*

Another consequence of the fabliaux' brevity is the lack of opportunity for character preparation and development. The personages are characterized as types, stock figures: they often remain unnamed, as in *Berangier.*[24] While modern writers often juxtapose the most dominant psychological traits of personalities, for instance the dreamer versus the man of action, the fabliau, according to Nykrog, juxtaposes outward features (N, p. 109). The peasant is opposed to the priest, the lover to the husband, the wife to her husband. Medieval writers, lacking specialized vocabularies and psychoanalytical insight, often use allegories as a means of portraying psychological confrontations. Such subtleties are by no means rare in some fabliaux (see our introduction to *Du Bouchier d'Abevile*). Nykrog elaborates a rigorous chart outlining the various possibilities of opposition among characters and leaving the impression that a character's nature and actions are rigidly predictable: a priest, for instance, is punished in two-thirds of his attempted seductions and is never successful when the husband is a knight (N, p. 110). The predictability of the fabliau is easily understandable in view of the oral nature and presentation of the tales, whose success is based on immediate, or near immediate, recognition on the audience's part. Cooke, however, modifies somewhat the impression of rigidity left by Nykrog's figures. Granting that fabliau characters are not as fully developed as those of other genres, he demonstrates (*Old French,* pp. 24–40) that they are more than types: although fableors wish to present them as quickly as possible, they still add many complexities that enrich personalities and situations alike.

The movement of action in the fabliau is essentially binary, contrary to other genres, especially its allied one, the farce, which allows the movement to be spread among additional personages. The reason for the difference is obvious: the farce belongs to a visual genre whereas the fabliau, although probably enhanced by the mimicry of the jongleur, must keep its tension tight. The best and safest way to achieve this is to keep that tension between only two protagonists at a time. Having to play three characters and a narrator would be a real juggler's trick for one jongleur. Nykrog sensed this when he noted (N, p. 111) that in some fabliaux with the adulterous triangle as theme, the lover is often reduced "à l'état d'une simple silhouette" (to a mere profile). In *Du Prestre ki abevete,* on the other hand, it is the passive wife, tersely described (v. 6) as "sage, courtoise et bien aprise" (courtly, wise, and well-bred), who is the silhouette. Without protesting, she lets the priest take his pleasure with her for the general reason that she wants "icele cose / que femme aimme sor toute cose" (that thing which / a woman loves more than anything) (vv. 57–58). The tension in this fabliau is clearly based upon the confrontation between the priest and the husband and upon the trickery perpetrated by the former on the latter. The authors allow few intrusions or ornamentations that would unbalance that delicate tension: no third character is going to be featured too prominently. Consequently, an episode's action will almost always be distributed between only two characters at a time: between the wife and lover, the husband and his wife's lover, or the husband and his wife.

It is worth noting, though, that within a given fabliau the movement of relationships is capable of shifting from scene to scene with the final outcome leading definitely to a balanced situation. The overwhelming majority (75 percent) of the fabliaux are frankly erotic, and sixty-three of them deal with the theme of the adulterous triangle.[25] In these, the sacred institution of marriage is often jolted but never fails to remain intact. The fabliaux in our present edition support that fact: at the end, things may not be Pollyannaishly rosy, but hostilities have ended for the moment, although the truce may be precarious.[26] The character in the tale who has exhibited extreme features capable of tilting the balance of marriage has been duly punished, and the marriage bond is preserved.

III. *The Anti-Clericalism of the Fabliaux*

A clear and ever-present danger to marital equilibrium is the lover or suitor, who is often successful if he is a knight or clerk. If the seducer is a priest, he will arouse audience antipathy. Of the three priests in the collection, the one in *Brunain* is avaricious; the priest who peeked is lecherous, lying, and preys on his parishioners; and the other, in *Du Bouchier,* is proud, rude, inhospitable, fornicating, jealous, and greedy. Such priests must be a little shocking to modern readers, but they are not at all unrepresentative of priests in other fabliaux. As protagonists, the priests are either married (MR, 5:37), have concubines (MR, 5:143; 2:146), or are after other people's wives and daughters (MR, 2:8; 4:11). A priest in *De Constant du Hamel* (MR, 4:166) belongs in two categories. He is married and in hot pursuit of his parishioner's wife.

Through decrees and edicts, popes and church councils since the fourth century had attempted to enforce celibacy on the clergy.[27] Concubinage had never been approved, but the frequent interdictions against it are proof that it was a very difficult practice to stop. The church's attempt to prevent marriage among priests met with more overt opposition, since there was little scriptural support for required celibacy. Earl Sperry quotes one eleventh-century priest who argued that the prohibition against marriage encouraged fornication and adultery and who blamed the higher clergy because "they winked at concubinage and licentiousness while stigmatizing marriage" (*History of Clerical Celibacy,* pp. 23–24). This fear was more than theoretical; by the fifteenth century, despite the fact that clerical marriages had been declared invalid in the thirteenth century, parishioners in Switzerland and in parts of Spain were compelling their priests to marry, "as a safeguard for the virtue of their wives and daughters and as a remedy for the flagitious lives of priests and prelates."[28] Two centuries earlier, in France, these people would have provided sympathetic audiences for the author of *De Connebert* (MR, 5:160), who castigates those priests

Qui sacrement de marriage
Tornent a honte et a putage!

(Who turn the sacrament of marriage
To shame and harlotry!) MR, 5:170

The continuing efforts of popes and church councils to stamp out moral turpitude among priests is evidence that a large population of scurrilous priests really did exist outside the imaginary world of the fabliaux. But the efforts at moral reform also indicate that standards of sexual continence were continually present, confronting and accusing the violators. The reaction of the fabliau public, therefore, would have been one both of recognition and of shock on hearing of priestly actions totally out of keeping with priestly ideals.

The author of *Du Prestre ki abevete* takes a tolerant attitude toward his outrageous priest, blaming the rape on the husband's folly rather than on the priest's viciousness; but the fabliaux are generally much less tolerant of lasciviousness in priests than in members of any other class and are much less likely to award priests with a happy ending. Nykrog informs us that Guerin's priest is one of five who succeed in their attempted adultery; seventeen fail (N, p. 110). This is opposed to 100 percent success by knights, squires, bourgeois, clerks, and men of undetermined social status, and 50 percent success by commoners. Of those priests who fail, some are killed,[29] some are castrated,[30] and some are merely beaten up and humiliated.[31] A priest mentioned in *Du Pescheor de Pont seur Saine* (MR, 3:68) is killed and later castrated, after his body has floated a way downstream. Charles Ray Beach has concluded from his survey that only four out of fifty-six priests can be classified as having been treated in a favorable light.[32] The regular ecclesiastics of both genders—monks, abbots, nuns, and abbesses—fare even worse: out of fifty-seven instances, not a single one is favorably treated. Clearly the ecclesiastics enjoyed the least favor among the fabliaux authors, a fact that Beach claims is due to the authors' resentment at harsh treatment of assumed heretics in northern France during the thirteenth century by church officials, especially the terrible Friar Robert. Such a view would, of course, imply that the fabliaux are more than entertainment and that they satirize with the intent of reforming abusive conditions.[33]

IV. The Antifeminism of the Fabliaux

Aside from priests, the characters most ill-treated in the fabliaux are women, or so it is commonly accepted. Ferdinand Brunetière states angrily that "une telle conception de la femme est le déshonneur d'une littérature" (such a concept of women is the disgrace of a literature).[34] Bédier devotes a whole chapter to the scorn heaped upon women in the fabliaux, which, he claims (*Les Fabliaux,* p. 321), along with the "contes grivois" (licentious tales) of all ages and countries, express "ce fond de rancune que l'homme a toujours eu contre la femme" (a deep-seated grudge which man always has held against woman). But the fabliaux, continues Bédier, go far beyond this universal resentment of man for his wife, and he establishes this as an absolute dogma of the fabliaux (*Les Fabliaux,* p. 321): "les femmes sont des êtres inférieurs et malfaisants" (women are inferior and evil-minded beings). That women were inferior was a commonly accepted opinion in the Middle Ages: philosophically, woman was defined as a "misbegotten male." Nykrog accepts without question the viciousness of women as Bédier sees it in the fabliaux, and instead of modifying the portrait, he sets about proving that Andrew the Chaplain and other "courtly" writers held an equally low opinion of women (pp. 193 ff.). Clem Williams goes so far as to include in his definition of the fabliaux "a tendency in particular to denigrate the character of women and priests" ("The Genre and Art," p. 18).

In some cases, the antifeminism is indeed similar to modern antifeminism. A few fabliaux do show how wrong it is for the wife to try to wear the pants in the family; these end happily with her put into place by the superior force of the husband. In *De Sire Hain et Dame Anieuse* (MR, 1:97), for instance, the husband actually lays his pants on the floor and bids his wife fight for them, which she willingly does. Only after he has severely beaten her does she concede him the right to dominate in their marriage. The author concludes (MR, 1:111) by advising husbands to treat their wives as Sire Hain did, who "li ot/Batu et les os et l'eschine" (beat her bones and her back), advice that Bédier quotes (*Les Fabliaux,* p. 325) as the "meilleur procédé" (best procedure), according to the fabliaux. In other words, husbands should use the one kind of superiority that they undoubtedly have, physical superiority, to keep their wives in check.

But male physical superiority does not extend to sexual matters. As a matter of fact, the most frequent charge that the fabliaux level against women is their sexual insatiability. In *Du Vallet aus douze fames* (MR, 3:186), a bachelor who thought he needed twelve wives to satisfy him, once married, cannot satisfy one. In *De la Damoiselle qui sonjoit* (MR, 5:208), for another bachelor what begins with rape ends with failure to keep his victim satisfied. When he is worn out, she has to get on top. This humiliating posture could not be considered the male wish-fulfillment of a modern antifeminist. A modern antifeminist would be more likely to be portrayed as claiming that *he* can satisfy any woman than that all women are insatiable.[35]

What women are mainly abused for in the fabliaux is their *moral* inferiority, their treachery, and their trickery, characteristics that imply a superior cleverness and that modern antifeminists would therefore not care to admit. There are not many "sweet young things" in the fabliaux. Time after time the women do outwit the men.[36] The antifeminist conclusion that Bédier draws (*Les Fabliaux,* p. 324) from all this feminine cunning is, "Que chascuns se gart de la soe, / Qu'ele ne li face la coe" (Let each guard his own wife / Lest she make the tail for him [cuckold him]).

Often, however, although feminine trickery is a very important part of the story, there is no attitude of condemnation attached to it, and therefore no real antifeminism of any flavor, modern or medieval. If there is any lesson for husbands in the poems translated below, it is just the opposite of the one cited by Bédier. They should not treat women like property; they should not buy them from greedy fathers, and they should not keep them guarded. Guerin in his *Berangier* is too busy being antibourgeois to be antifeminist. The wife is debased by a marriage arranged by her father to a lowborn, cowardly man. Therefore, when she tricks her husband and liberates herself from his power, she merits the praise she gets at the end of the poem: she was neither low nor foolish. She has proved her superiority over her husband in trial by combat, the husband having given up without a fight.

Within the marital relationship, her bold initiatives usually save the marriage. Again, according to medieval views, the responsibility of the direction of the household was placed directly on the husband's shoulders. The abdication of or misuse of that responsibility will endanger the marriage. Woman's function as the helper of man, as defined by St. Thomas Aquinas, is readily and cleverly portrayed in numerous fabliaux where the couple together, or the wife alone, wards off the despicable advances of various suitors. Man, according to Aquinas, has more "of the good of reason"; he is more and better endowed with cognitive powers than woman.[37] Therefore, he has more responsibilities, and, when he fails, the disgrace is so much the more apparent. The wife's maneuvers and actions (see *Les Trois Boçus*) are therefore praiseworthy inasmuch as her craftiness has caused that marital balance to be preserved again (see *Berangier*).

Sometimes, too, despite a superficial antifeminism, the sympathies are for the tricky wife. The author of the *Borgoise d'Orliens* may comment (vv. 86, 87) with an antifeminist proverb, "Par lor engin sont deceü / Li sage des le tens Abel" (Wise men have been deceived by their women's trickery since the time of Abel), and Bédier may cite this as he enumerates the womanly vices in the fabliaux (*Les Fabliaux,* p. 324), but the story is from the wife's point of view. We sympathize with her, we do not accuse her, we want her to get away with her deception. As for the husband, we learn at the beginning of the poem that he is a hard, tight-fisted man who does not let go of a single thing he gets. This characteristic is illustrated with one "thing," his wife. The poem is about her freeing herself from his tight fist. And she has our sympathy.

Many of the fabliaux do share the modern antifeminist position that a woman should be subordinate to her husband. But the prevalent fabliau view of the wife as cleverer than her husband is miles away from the smug assumptions of intellectual superiority among modern male antifeminists.

V. The Humor in the Fabliaux

"Tales meant for laughter," claimed Bédier. Are they satirical? With the exception of a few fabliaux, one must answer negatively because satire implies serious, heavier overtones. In the fabliaux, everything is subservient to laughter, even "serious" lessons. Johnston and Owen characterize the fabliaux' sense of humor as macabre (JO, p. ix): the audience is made to laugh at physical deformities (hunchbacks), infirmities (blindness), or corpses that are made to travel from one site to another. For Bédier, the comic in them is superficial and easily achieved (*Les Fabliaux,* p. 313). This notion has been severely shaken by modern critics who have shown that fabliau humor is often complex and its climax artistically prepared.[38] Humor is achieved by conscious ploys on the author's part either by establishing distance between public and fabliaux characters or events (Theiner, Lacy, and Cooke in CH) or by the openly parodic and burlesque. The ironic vision that fableors give the audience is a device to arouse laughter that most essayists in that collection have analyzed (Nykrog, Cooke, Lacy, and Honeycutt in CH). The importance of these essays is that they demonstrate the sophistication of the comic devices and rehabilitate the genre to place it on an artistic level equal to other medieval works.

If indeed Norris Lacy is correct in pointing out that humor is primarily achieved by a technique of distancing that frees the public from any dangerous sympathetic attachment to or identification with the characters, then we can begin to accept the "macabre" elements and the curious, often shocking morality of the fabliaux. Bédier (*Les Fabliaux,* p. 311) believed that the morals concluding the fabliaux are useless, "la morale n'est qu'accessoire" (the moral is only an appendage). Nykrog called them an insipid literary habit (N, p. 102). Like Nykrog, Johnston and Owen see the moral as a substantial link between the fabliaux and the more serious fable: two thirds of the fabliaux in the MR collection contain some kind of moral (JO, pp. xiii–xvi). The moral would then be a residual element left over from the transfer from one genre to another. Lacy, on the other hand, believes the morals to be more often than not recited tongue in cheek, because this procedure creates the distance that "enables the reader or audience to suspend moral judgment" and allows for uninhibited laughter (CH, p. 117).

Cooke argues that many morals have a justification in that they have a "comic dimension" (*Old French,* p. 43). A generalization about them would be impossible because they are part of a fableor's private technique and special effects: each has a special meaning relating to the faliau's individual preparation and development. The moral of *Brunain* is humorous and quite apropos in view of the back-and-forth movement of the cows. The one of the *Vilain Asnier,* "stick to your nature," as Cooke has observed (*Old French,* p. 42), is humorously ambiguous: as a narrative's ending it advises the peasant to stay close to his manure but as a lesson to the audience it could be implying, with the appropriate voice inflection, that it applies likewise to them. The proverb that ends

Berangier alludes again, by its anatomical crudeness, to the highlight of the fabliau: the misdirected kiss. Some fabliaux, such as *La Borgoise,* end abruptly without a moral, while others conclude with a device of courtly poets, that of a request for judgment by the audience, as in *Bouchier.*

In sum, the moral can be seen as an integral part of the fabliau and as a further example of the author's art: "the right delivery, of course, is important: if spoken in a serious manner, they [the morals] would sound false and inept, if spoken with the right inflection and tone, their irony would be clear."[39]

Why did the fabliaux disappear in the fourteenth century? It is not a coincidence that jongleurs and fabliaux faded away concurrently. According to Edmond Faral,[40] the early jongleur was not only a poet; he was an acrobat, an animal trainer, a dancer, an actor, a juggler, a fire-eater. These talented and versatile performers were often violently condemned by the Church because of the dissolute lives they were leading, the scabrous material they were presenting, or the temptations into which they were leading others (including clerics). Traveling around the country, they were held in great favor during the thirteenth century by audiences of all levels. Later, when their numbers increased, their availability was too great and the demands for them slackened. Those particularly gifted and fortunate found a steady patronage among the nobility and were called minstrels (*minister:* servant at court). In this more servile function, they had to specialize in the more noble type of endeavors: some became men of letters while others, according to Harrison (*Gallic Salt,* pp. 30–34), specialized in other artistic functions, as actors, singers, or musicians. It was the jongleurs, with their versatility and their unattachment, who were instrumental in spreading the fabliaux. Once they disappeared, the fabliaux were replaced by prose tales such as *Les XV Joies de Marriage, Les Cent Nouvelles Nouvelles.* The often anonymous jongleurs were replaced by writers of such renown as Marguerite de Navarre and Nicolas de Troyes. The common fund of stories from which materials were drawn never exhausted itself, and the fabliau enjoyed a brief and momentary revival with Jean de La Fontaine in the seventeenth century. It will certainly never die in spirit: a good story is as eternal and as prevalent as the air we breathe (probably as polluted too). The raw material continues to exist; but the art of rhyming has unfortunately been neglected. That neglect is one of the reasons for the present edition.

In selecting the fabliaux we have tried to choose tales that are as representative of the genre as possible. Our edition mirrors the variety that exists among the fabliaux. These tales are short as well as long, subtlely humorous or coarsely slapstick, strictly literal or with allegoric levels. Our characters come from all social levels: burghers, peasants, aristocrats, and clergymen perform in situations that vary from the innocuous to the licentious and even to the frankly obscene. Some characters, such as the hunchback's wife, earn our sympathy; others, such as the priest of *Du Bouchier,* only draw our scorn. We admire some characters' ingenuity while we are appalled at the stupidity of others. The tales' aim may be to entertain, to parody, to teach, or all of these. They are varied but never boring. *Du Bouchier* and *Guillaume au faucon,* our longest tales, are good examples of rich fabliaux that lend themselves well to allegorical interpretations. Eustache d'Amiens's tale, in a burgher setting, is praiseworthy for its narrative technique. Eustache exploits its theme to the ultimate by dividing the tale into a series of conflicts, pitting in succession one protagonist against the other. Meanwhile, at the castle, Guillaume is helped in his passage to maturity by the lady who is also skillful in shifting linguistic levels of meaning. While the lady wonders at the power of words with the poise expected of one of her social rank, the peasant couple in *Brunain* rejoices loudly when they discover a literal outcome of a symbolic promise. *Des Trois Boçus* is an admirable representative of the unwanted corpse cycle in the fabliaux. Our *Du Prestre ki abevete* is one of many versions of similar tales in Western and Eastern literatures, where wife and lover take their pleasures in the presence of the husband, who is made to believe that he is the victim of an optical illusion. In *De la Saineresse,* as Larry Benson and Theodore Andersson point out,[41] the deception is aural rather than ocular, since the husband is told with daring precision what occurred, but he is not intelligent enough to understand. In that, the burgher is similar to the aristocratic husband of *Guillaume au faucon*. *Berangier* not only is an example of the application of the misdirected kiss motif, but it stands also as an effective parody of courtly literature. The ultimate message of this fabliau is a warning against those unworthy social climbers who will eventually bring about the degeneracy of an entire lineage. Much more succinctly, but not less eloquently, the *Vilain Asnier* advocates social immobility: no peasant can ever escape his nature, and it is wrong for him to try. Both *Des Tresces* and *De la Borgoise d'Orliens* depict nicely the skill of the wife who gets out of the trouble she is in when she is discovered with her lover. In the first tale, the husband is led to believe that his vision is distorted and is subsequently dispatched to a pilgrimage, while in the second tale the cuckold is beaten but happy, convinced (mistakenly) of his wife's fidelity.

A Note on the Text

To establish our text, we have used photocopies kindly furnished by the duplication services of the Bibliothèque Nationale of Paris and the Bürgerbibliothek of Bern, to whom we express our thanks. For the B.N. 837 (*A*), we have used its reproduction published by Henri Omont, *Fabliaux, dits et contes en vers français du XIII siècle; Fac-similé du manuscrit français 837 de la Bibliothèque Nationale* (Paris: 1932; rpt. Geneva: Slatkine, 1973); and for the B.N. 19152 (*D*), the facsimile edition by Edmond Faral, *Le Manuscrit 19152 du fonds français de la Bibliothèque Nationale* (Paris, 1934).

In establishing the text, we have followed in their general lines the editorial recommendations of Alfred Foulet and Mary Blakely Speer, *On Editing Old French Texts* (Lawrence: The Regents Press of Kansas, 1979), pp. 57–85. Thus we have consistently kept the future and conditional tenses of *avoir* and *savoir* with a *v* rather than a *u,* and have retained the numbers as written in the manuscripts except for *un* since it doubles as an article. The graphy *x,* as in *Diex, beax, fox, cox, ax* standing for *us, Dieus, beaus, fous, cous,* and *aus,* has been kept faithfully (Foulet and Speer, p. 63). The main diacritical marks have also been kept: the cedilla under the *c,* the acute accent on the tonic *e* and on past participles. Whenever advisable, we have added grave accents to differentiate homographs (*à, où,* and so forth). The diaeresis has been added when there is a difficulty in determining the syllable count in a hiatus in a line of verse or in a word itself. Brackets indicate that we have added a word to the text. In our notes, *vv.* refers to the Old French text and a † symbol to our translation.

1.

Du Bouchier d'Abevile
(The Butcher of Abbeville)

Eustache d'Amiens's only known work is perhaps the most admired of the medieval French fabliaux. The five extant manuscripts of the poem attest to its popularity in Eustache's day. In our own time, as recently as 1975, Jean Rychner has reaffirmed the poem's worth by publishing all five manuscript versions, along with his own edited version, in a single book (R). Roy J. Pearcy praises Eustache as a "polished artist" whose lone work is to be admired for "tightness of . . . plot, . . . excellent character portrayal, enhanced by lively dialogue" (CH, p. 186).

His artistic polish is evidenced not only by his skills in presenting a good, comic tale, but also in the way in which he gives the poem a weight and power usually lacking in the fabliaux. Howard Helsinger (CH, pp. 98–103) shows us that the pastor, in his pride, his inhospitality, his luxuriousness, and his neglect of duty, is a perfect model for the bad priest or bad shepherd, in contrast to Jesus' model of the good shepherd. In this light, the butcher, aptly named David, arrives like a divine scourge upon the priest.[1] The priest has been privileged with material comfort as well as with the honor of belonging to a religious elite. Both privileges are well encapsuled in the old lady's statement that the priest has "the only *wine* around for miles" (v. 46). He has let his own moral being, his household, and his parish fall into a state of dilapidation. The dilapidated barn "whose roof had half caved in" (v. 98) is an exterior sign of his spiritual degradation. Eustache has repeatedly alerted us to the parabolic nature of his tale by, ironically, making references to parables in the Bible: the image of David with a sheep on his shoulders, his request for hospitality on the basis that "God will reward . . . more than double" (v. 60) (see the fabliau *Brunain* in this collection); the fact that he is finally allowed inside by the priest who "liked one thing that was dead / Better than four still living" († 137–38); and the shepherd's search for his lost sheep at the end. More explicit is the priest's neglect of his religious duties. According to Helsinger, the mass performed by the priest is tainted. Pope Urban II's message with regard to the celebration of mass by married men makes this one invalid in view of the celebrant's state of sin. Moreover, David interrupts the mass without any protest on the priest's part.

The serious allegory seems incongruous with the fact that the fabliaux are conventionally thought to be trivial. Helsinger points out that incongruity is the basis and essence of some fabliaux' humor: the fableor parodies the religious intentions and the allegory as a system. Thus the concluding moral, which in the courtly poetic fashion asks the audience to pass judgment as to who actually possesses the fleece, is irrelevant in view of the deeper and more serious overtones of the poem. The question is so preposterously irrelevant that it forces the audience to go beyond the letter of the question and think of the import of the tale. After all, did Eustache not alert us at the very beginning that "any word / Is wasted when it isn't heard" († 5, 6)? Those book-end admonitions and instructions, in the prologue and in the moral at the end of the tale, force us to look for deeper meanings that please us because we have found a "pearl in the swill."

Skillful structuring is one of the main ingredients for a successful fabliau. As Nykrog notices (N, pp. 150, 151), the fabliau could have ended successfully after the butcher's departure, but Eustache's instincts drove him to complete the tale with the punishment of the priest, exploiting this theme to the very end. The dramatization of the revenge is essential. Thomas D. Cooke observed that if the revenge were absent or minimally presented, we would feel cheated because our expectancy had been raised.[2] A chancy or accidental punishment would not have satisfied the public either: from the moment the butcher sells the priest's own fleece to the priest and leaves the scene, the priest has been punished materially for refusing hospitality to a stranger, but the audience's desire for retribution is unsatisfied until the priest has been punished intellectually for the proud words with which he turned the stranger away. He must acknowledge that he has been bested by the man he has humiliated. The last 245 lines can be divided into three scenes: the lady's conversation with the servant, described by Nykrog as mounting from crescendo to furioso (N, p. 151), which shows the order and peace of the household disintegrating; these two characters' interview with the priest, who, through his own searching and questioning, is forced to learn of matters better left unknown; and lastly, the priest's interrogation of the shepherd, where the priest admits utter defeat and the local degradation is spread to the community. This ending is quite reminiscent of the scenes of recognition or of discovery in Molière's comedies that portray a dramatically slow and painful unveiling of the deception.

The butcher is portrayed very sympathetically indeed: his initial generosity and honesty have been emphasized on several occasions (vv. 11, 13, 14, 89, and especially † 41, 42: "I think it's better / Not to be someone else's debtor"). "We admire the butcher and excuse his actions," says Cooke very aptly (*Old French*, p. 37); his revenge is absolutely justified. His speech with the priest is as admirably correct ("for the love of God," † 58) as it will be cunning with the three members of the household later on.

The complexity of the priest's character is revealed by his fall from pride. That he *is* proud puts him in a complex position to begin with, for, as Andrew the Chaplain points out,[3] no one has more reason to be proud than a priest, in his holy office. Yet since pride is the worst of sins, in a man of God it is a worse abomination than in a layman, and the priest who is proud deserves to be shamed more than any other man. The shame of the priest is to be cuckolded and fleeced. His shame is compounded by the fact that he never should have had a concubine to be cuckolded of, nor should he have had such an interest in material goods that a fleecing should have mattered to him. And his shame is doubled: his first shame is to be outwitted; his final shame is to be shown that he was. This is no cuckold "beaten and content" as in *De la Borgoise d'Orliens* and its variants. He pursues his disgrace with a relentlessness and intelligence comparable to Oedipus' pursuit of a more serious one. The clever servant girl does not fool him for a minute, and his cross-examination of the lady is devastating. If he does not blind himself when he discovers her infidelity, he is at least blind with rage, a rage that is transferred to the innocent shepherd. But after the final revelation, that he has been fleeced as well as cuckolded, rage gives way to mortification —admiration for the butcher's cleverness and despair over his own folly. But the emotions find their bitterest expression in the "De ma . . ." metaphorical proverbs: "De ma mance m'a ters mon nés" (With my sleeve he wiped me my nose), and "De ma paste m'a fait tortel" (With my dough he made me a roll). Sandwiched between these proverbs is another proverb († 543–46): "On puet cascun jor molt aprendre" (One can learn something every day). With this proverb he makes an effort at philosophical resignation, but mortification takes over again with the second "De ma . . ." proverb. His emotional vacillation is comic, but it is the comedy of a real man in a situation with which he cannot cope, not just a cardboard cuckold.

The lady's pride is also in opposition to David's initial wise and humble demeanor. Like the priest's, her pride is paradoxical; however, hers is paradoxical because it is based on an illegitimate relationship and therefore rests on an extremely flimsy foundation. She also is disgraced twice: once by the maid and once by the priest himself.

It is she who begins the last act of the poem (v. 320) as lovely as a lady in a romance. Only the fact that she cinches her waist very tightly *par orgueil* (out of pride) indicates that her interior may not be worthy of her exterior. Her disgrace begins immediately when, out of greed and overbearing pride, she allows herself to haggle with the servant girl over a sheepskin. Once again she is like the priest. Because of his pride and stinginess, he has tried to send a man in need away into the night. She, out of overbearingness and greed, wants to throw the girl out of the house and out of a job. The girl touches her mistress at a vulnerable point when she threatens to tell the master. The word of the lady, despite her overbearing ways, is not final in this house. With that reminder and a possible fear that the servant may be threatening to tell about more than a sheepskin, the lady's dignity crumbles. She is able to reply in nothing but abuse, the lowest form of conversation (v. 374). Her last insult, *"bastard,"* leaves her wide open to the servant's implication that the lady's children are bastards, that her entire relationship with the priest is illegitimate, and that, consequently, so is her position as mistress of the house and mistress to the girl.

Logically, the lady is defenseless. There is no further reply she can make other than to descend from abuse to violence (vv. 382–83), further disgracing herself. The poet's picture of her has changed remarkably in a few lines.

At the end of the poem, the lady returns to the bedroom where she is ordinarily confined when the priest has a guest (vv. 186–87), deeper into the house where she is now more securely than ever a prisoner. The priest, crushed and in a state of paralysis, simply sits down (v. 501). The maid, who has not left, despite her threats and the lady's command, will continue to remind priest and lady both of their inability to govern their house. How the mighty have fallen!

Du Bouchier d' Abevile		The Butcher of Abbeville
Seignor, oiez une merveille,[4]		Listen, my lords, to what I say.
Onques n'oïstes sa pareille,		Never have you, until today,
Que je vous vueil dire et conter.		Heard such a wonder as I shall tell.
Or metez cuer à l'escouter.	4	Gather round and listen well.

Parole qui n'est entendue,
Sachiez de voir, ele est perdue.
A Abevile ot un bouchier
Que si voisin orent molt chier.
N'estoit pas fel ne mesdisanz,
Mes sages, cortois et vaillanz
Et loiaus hom de son mestier,
Et s'avoit sovent grant mestier
Ses povres voisins soufraitex:
N'estoit avers ne covoitex.
Entor feste Toz Sains avint
Qu'à Oisemont au marchié vint
Li bouchiers bestes achater,[5]
Mes ne fist fors voie gaster.
Trop i trova chieres les bestes,
Les cochons felons et rubestes,
Vilains et de mauvés afere.
Ne pot à els nul marchié fere:
Povrement sa voie emploia,
Onques denier n'i emploia.
Aprés espars marchié s'en torne,[6]
De tost aler molt bien s'atorne;
Son sorcot porte sor s'espee,
Quar pres estoit de la vespree.
Oiez comment il esploita:
Droit à Bailluel li annuita;
En mi voies de son manoir
Quar tart estoit, si fist molt noir,
Penssa soi plus avant n'ira,[7]
En la vile herbregera:
Forment doute la male gent
Que ne li toillent son argent,
Dont il avoit à grant foison.
A l'entree d'une meson
Trueve une povre fame estant.
Il le salue et dist itant:
"A il en ceste vile à vendre[8]
Riens nule où l'en peüst despendre
Le sien, por son cors aaisier,
C'onques n'amai autrui dangier?"
La bone fame li respont:
"Sire, par Dieu qui fist le mont,
Ce dist mon baron, sire Mile,
De vin n'a point en ceste vile,
Fors noz prestres sire Gautiers.

You know, my lords, that any word
Is wasted when it isn't heard.
A butcher lived in Abbeville
8 Whose neighbors bore him much good will.
He wasn't evil-tongued or cold,
But wise, well-mannered, courteous, bold,
Dedicated to his trade,
12 Considerate and quick to aid
His neighbors who were poor and needy,
He wasn't miserly or greedy.
Near All Saints' Day this butcher went
16 To the marketplace at Oisement
To buy livestock. It wasn't long
Before he wished he hadn't gone.
The animals were far from cheap.
20 The goats were scrawny, so were the sheep.
The pigs were low grade, tough and poor,
Not worth his while to bargain for.
His time was wasted. He had spent
24 Most of the day, and not a cent.
Now that the day was almost gone,
He threw his outer jacket on
Above his sword and left at last
28 From Oisement market, walking fast.
Now hear what happened. Evening fell
As he was going through Balluel,
Just halfway home from where he'd been.
32 He thought he'd have to find an inn
And put up there until the dawn.
Now that the dark was coming on,
He started dreading an attack
36 By prowlers out to get his sack,
Which still was full. He saw a poor
Woman standing by her door,
And asked her, "Ma'am, could you suggest
40 A place to sleep. I need some rest.
I'll gladly pay. I think it's better
Not to be someone else's debtor."
The woman courteously replied,
44 "By God, who for us sinners died,
According to my husband, Giles,
The only wine around for miles
Is what belongs to our parish priest.
48 He brought two vats of it at least
From Nogentel a week ago.

A .II. tonniaus sor ses chantiers
Qui li vindrent de Noientel.
Toz jors a il vin en tonel: 52
Alez à lui por ostel prendre."
—"Dame, g'i vois sanz plus atendre,"
Dist li bouchiers, "et Diex vous saut![9]
—"A foi, sire, Diex vous consaut!" 56

Atant s'en part, n'i vout plus estre,
Venuz est au manoir le prestre.
Li doiens seoit sor son sueil,
Qui molt fu plains de grant orgueil. 60
Cil le salue, et puis li dist:
"Biaus sire, que Diex vous aīt!
Herbregiez moi par charité,
Si ferez honor et bonté." 64
—"Preudom," fet il, "Diex vous herbert!
Quar, foi que doi à saint Herbert,
Lais hom ceenz ja ne girra.[10]
Bien ert qui vos herbregera 68
En cele vile là aval.
Querez tant à mont et à val
Que vous puissiez ostel avoir,
Quar je vous faz bien asavoir 72
Ja ne girrez en cest porpris.
Autre gent i ont ostel pris,
Ne ce n'est pas coustume à prestre
Que vilains hom gise en son estre." 76
—"Vilains! sire, qu'avez vous dit?
Tenez vous lai homme en despit?"
—"Oīl," dist il, "si ai reson.
Alez en sus de ma meson. 80
Il m'est avis ce soit ramposne."[11]
—"Non est, sire, ainz seroit aumosne,
S'anuit mes me prestiez l'ostel,
Que je n'en puis trover nul tel. 84
Je sai molt bien le mien despendre;
Se rien nule me volez vendre,
Molt volontiers l'achaterai,
Et molt bon gré vous en saurai, 88
Quar je ne vous vueil rien couster."
—"Ausi bien te vendroit hurter
Ta teste à cele dure pierre,"
Ce dist li doiens; "par saint Piere![14] 92
Ja ne girras en mon manoir."
—"Deable i puissent remanoir,"

In my opinion you should go
To the rectory for board and bed."
—"I'll go there now," the butcher said,
"May God in heaven be with you."
—"Faith, Sir," she said, "God bless you too."

This parish priest, puffed up with pride,
Was sitting on the step outside.
The butcher said, "God grant you grace.
For the love of God, give me a place
To sleep tonight and for your trouble,
God will reward you more than double."
The priest replied, "God lodge you then,
For by the saints and holy men,
The laity may not lie here.
You'll find a good room fairly near,
Somewhere or other in the town.
Go search the village up and down
Till you find lodgings, and sleep there,
Not on my premises; I swear
I'll never let you come inside.
What's more, the rooms are occupied.
For priests to have to entertain
Common folk goes against my grain."
—"Common, Sir! Do you mean to be
Contemptuous of the laity?"
—"Indeed I do, boy, and why not?
Enough of this. Get off my lot.
This strikes me as impertinence."
—"No, Sir, but it's beneficence
To let me sleep here. You must know
There's nowhere else for me to go.
I don't mind spending what is mine.[12]
If you should like to sell some wine,
You'll have my lasting gratitude.[13]
I'll pay you though: my money's good.
It wouldn't cost you anything."
—"You might as well be battering
This heavy rock against your head,
For by St. Peter," the priest said,
"In my abode you'll never sleep."
The butcher said, "The devil keep
Your house, vile priest. To Hell with you—
Frivolous fool, and common, too!"

Dist li bouchiers, "fols chapelains!
Pautoniers estes et vilains."
Atant s'en part, ne volt plus dire,
Plains fu de grant corouz et d'ire.
Oiez comment il li avint!
Quant il fors de la vile vint,
Devant une gaste meson
Dont cheü furent li chevron,
Encontre un grant tropé d'öeilles.[15]
Por Dieu, or escoutez merveilles.
Il demanda au pastorel,
Qui mainte vache et maint torel
Avoit gardé en sa jonece:
"Paistres, que Diex te doint leece!
Cui cist avoirs?" —"Sire le prestre."
—"De par Dieu," fet il, "puist ce estre?"
Or oiez que li bouchiers fist:
Si coiement un mouton prist
Que li paistres ne s'en perçut;
Bien l'a engingnié et deçut.
Maintenant à son col le rue;
Par mi une foraine rue[16]
Revient à l'uis le prestre arriere,
Qui molt fu fel de grant maniere,[17]
Si comme il dut clorre la porte,
Et cil qui le mouton aporte
Li dist: "Sire, cil Diex vous saut,[18]
Qui sor toz hommes puet et vaut!"
Li doiens son salu li rent,
Puis li demande isnelement:
"Dont es tu?" —"D'Abevile sui.
A Oisemont au marchié fui;
N'i achetai que cest mouton,
Mes il a molt cras le crepon.
Se anuit mes me herbregiez,
Que bien en estes aaisiez,
Je ne sui avers ne eschars:
Anuit ert mengié la chars
De cest mouton, por qu'il vous plaise,
Quar aporté l'ai à malaise."
Li doiens pensse qu'il dit voir,
Qui molt goulouse autrui avoir:
Miex aime un mort que .IIII. vis,[19]
Dist ainsi, comme il m'est avis:
"Oïl certes, molt volentiers;

At that he left. What more to say?
96 Heart full of wrath he stormed away.

Now hear what happened. During the night
100 Just outside town the butcher caught sight
Of an old dilapidated building
Whose roof had half caved in—and milling
Around the walls, a flock of lambs.
104 The shepherd was one who used to keep
Large herds of cattle in his day.
"Shepherd," he asked, "whose sheep are they?"
—"Good Sir, the priest owns all of them."
108 —"Is that so?" said the butcher, "Hmm."

Listen to what the butcher did:
112 Protected by the night, he hid
A sheep so slyly in his coat
That the old shepherd took no note.
Once out of sight, he shouldered the load
116 And went back by another road,
To where the crude and haughty pastor
Was shutting his door. "May the great Master
And Judge of men be good to you,"
120 Said the man with the sheep, "how do you do?"
The priest replied, "Where'd you come from?"
"From Abbeville, but I've just come
From Oisement Market where I sought
124 Some high-grade meat. All that I bought
Was this one sheep, but what a buy!
He's heavy in the flank and thigh.
If you would let me lodge here, please,
128 For your advantage and your ease,
I promise you, I won't be cheap:
Tonight we will enjoy this sheep
For dinner, Sir, if you agree.
132 Its weight has been too much for me.
He's got enough fat, tender meat
For everyone in the house to eat."
Deceived, the priest, who never rued
136 Eating someone else's food
And who liked one thing that was dead
Better than four still living, said,
"Yes, willingly, I do agree.

Se vous estiez ore vous tiers, 140
S'auriez vous ostel à talent.
Ainz nus hom ne me trova lent
De cortoisie et d'onor fere.
Vous me samblez molt debonere; 144
Dites moi comment avez non?"
—"Sire, par Dieu et par son non,
J'ai non David en droit baptesme,
Quant je recui et huile et cresme. 148
Traveilliez sui en ceste voie;
Ja Dame Diex celui ne voie,
A foi, cui ceste beste fu;
Tans est huimés d'aler au fu." 152
  Atant s'en vont en la meson
Où le feu estoit de seson.
Lors a sa beste mise jus,
Puis a regardé sus et jus; 156
Une coingnie a demandee
Et on li a tost aportee,
Sa beste tue et puis l'escorce;
Sor un banc en geta l'escorce,[20] 160
Puis le pendi, lor iex voiant:
"Sire, por Dieu, venez avant;
Por amor Dieu, or esgardez
Com cis moutons est amendez, 164
Veez comme est cras et refais,
Mes molt m'en a pesé li fais,
Que de molt loing l'ai aporté.
Or en fetes vo volonté! 168
Cuisiez les espaules en rost;
S'en fetes metre plain un pot[21]
En essau avoec la mesnie.
Je ne di mie vilonie: 172
Ainz mes plus bele char ne fu,
Metez le cuire sor le fu!
Veez comme est tendre et refete:
Ainçois que la saveur soit fete 176
Ert ele cuite voirement."
—"Biaus ostes, fetes vo talent;
Sor vous ne m'en sai entremetre."[22]
—"Fetes donques la table metre." 180
—"C'est prest; n'i a fors de laver
Et des chandoiles alumer."
  Seignor, ne vous mentirai mie;
Li doiens avoit une amie 184

You're welcome here. If there were three
Of you, my house would be sufficient.
Never have I been found deficient
In courtesy or honest dealing.
You're a gentleman, I have a feeling.
Tell me, I pray, what is your name?"
—"David, in truth. The name's the same
As I received it in baptism
From parish priest with oil and chrism.
This trip's been hard," he told the priest;
"May he who owned this heavy beast
Never see the light of Heaven.
And now let's put him in the oven."
  This time the butcher was invited
Into the house. A fire was lighted.
The butcher put his burden down,
Took a hasty look around,
And told the parson that he ought
To have an ax, so one was brought.
He killed the sheep and dressed it too.
The thick and heavy fleece he threw
Across a beam before their eyes.
"Come here," he said, "Sir, what a prize
This sheep is! Will you take a look!
There's grade-A mutton on the hook.
This fellow grew up big and stout—
Too big, in fact, for I'm worn out
From having to carry him for hours.
Do with him what you like. He's yours.
Roast the shoulders. Put the rest
Into a kettle for the best
Lamb stew your household ever ate.
All other meat is second rate.
There's never been more tender flesh.
Look how it's succulent and fresh.
Just put it on the flames to heat.
It will be done enough to eat
Before you can prepare the sauce."
—"Good guest, you do it. I'm at a loss.
Compared with you, I am unable
To manage this." —"Then set the table."
—"It's set. I'll have the candles lit.
Let's wash. We'll eat when you see fit."
  I can no longer, lords, ignore
The presence of a paramour

Dont il si fort jalous estoit,		For whom the priest was so possessed
Toutes les nuiz qu'ostes avoit,		By jealousy that when a guest
La fesoit en sa chambre entrer.		Would visit, he would make her stay
Mes cele nuit la fist souper	188	Inside her room; but on that day
Avoec son oste liement.		At his command the lady joined
Servi furent molt richement		Them at the table. He made a point
De bone char et de bon vin.		Of treating her with great affection.
De blans dras, qui erent de lin,	192	When they had dined to their satisfaction,
Fist on fere au bouchier un lit.		The lady had her servants spread
Molt ot leenz de son delit.		Some fresh white sheets on her guest's bed.
Li doiens sa meschine apele:		The pastor called the maid, "My dear,
"Je te commant," fet il, "suer bele,	196	Attend to our guest while he is here.
Que noz ostes soit bien et aise,		Make sure Sir David takes delight
Si qu'il n'ait rien qui li desplaise."		In everything done for him tonight.
Atant se vont couchier ensamble		Do nothing counter to his whim,
Il et la dame, ce me samble,	200	Since we have profited by him."[23]
Et li bouchiers remest au fu.		They went to bed together then,
Ainz mes si aaisiez ne fu,		The lady and the priest, I mean;
Bon ostel ot et biau samblant:[24]		The butcher rested by the fire.
"Bele suer," fet il, "vien avant!	204	There wasn't a thing he could desire.
Trai te en ça, si parole à moi,		He had a roof and a warm bed.
Et si fai ton ami de moi:		"Come over here, my dear," he said
Bien i porras avoir grant preu."		To the servant girl, "Let's talk this over.
—"Ostes, tesiez, ne dites preu![25]	208	Kindly let me be your lover.
Ja n'apris onques tel afere."		I promise you you'll profit by it."
—"Par Dieu, or le te covient fere		—"Good guest! What folly, please be quiet!
Par tel couvent que je dirai."		That's the worst thing I ever heard."
—"Dites le dont, et je l'orrai."	212	—"You'll do it, though. You can't afford
—"Se tu veus fere mon plesir		To refuse an offer such as this one."
Et tout mon bon et mon desir,		—"Let's hear it then," she said, "I'll listen."
Par Dieu, que de vrai cuer apel,		—"If you would do my will tonight
De mon mouton auras la pel."	216	And do my joy and my delight,
—"Biaus ostes, jamés ce ne dites!		As God's my witness, you may keep
Vous n'estes mie droiz hermites,		The fleece I stripped from off my sheep."
Qui tel chose me requerez.		—"Now don't go saying that to me.
Molt estes de mal apenssez;	220	You're not a holy hermit, I see,
Dieu merci, com vous estes sos!		Coming here with this request.
Vo bon feïsse, mes je n'os:		You certainly are a naughty guest.
Vous le diriez demain ma dame"		Glory to God, what a fool you are.
—"Suer, se ja Diex ait part en m'ame,	224	I'd do your will, but I don't dare.
En ma vie ne li dirai		You'd tell my mistress all tomorrow."
Ne ja ne t'en encuserai."		—"May God condemn my soul to sorrow
Dont li a cele creanté		If ever I give a hint or clue
Qu'ele fera sa volenté	228	Of this affair or tell on you."
Toute la nuit, tant que jors fu,		The maid believed in what he said,

Dont se leva et fist son fu,
Son harnois, et puis trest ses bestes.

Lors primes s'est levez li prestres.
Il et son clerc vont au moustier
Chanter et fere lor mestier,
Et la dame remest dormant.
Et ses ostes tout maintenant
Se vest et chauce sanz demeure,
Quar bien en fu et tans et eure.
En la chambre, sanz plus atendre,
Vint à la dame congié prendre;
La clique sache, l'uis ouvri;
Et la dame si s'esperi,
Ses iex ouvri, son oste voit
Devant s'esponde trestout droit.
Lors li demande dont il vient[26]
Et de quel chose il li sovient:
"Dame," fet il, "graces vous rent;
Herbregié m'avez à talent
Et molt m'avez biau samblant fait."
Atant vers le chevés se trait;
Sa main mist sor le chavecuel
Et tret arriere le lincuel;
Si voit la gorge blanche et bele,
Et la poitrine et la mamele:
"E! Diex," dist il, "je voi miracles!
Sainte Marie, saint Romacles,
Comme est li doiens bien venuz
Qui o tel dame gist toz nuz!
Que si m'aït sainz Onorez,
Uns rois en fust toz honorez!
Se j'avoie tant de loisir
Que g'i peüsse un poi gesir,
Refez seroie et respassez."
—"Biaus ostes, ce n'est mie assez
Que vous dites, par saint Germain!
Alez en sus, ostez vo main!
Mesires aura ja chanté;
Trop se tendroit à engané
Se en sa chambre vous trovoit;
Jamés nul jor ne m'ameroit,
Si m'auriez mal baillie et morte."
Et cil molt bel la reconforte.

So that she did his will in bed
All night until the night was done
232 Then got up with the rising sun,
Built up the fire and fed the beasts.
Soon afterward arose the priest,
Who went together with his clerk
236 To church to sing and do their work.
The lady stayed in bed and slept.
Her guest, however, straightaway leapt
From bed, put on his shoes and dressed:
240 Time to be up; no time to rest.
He went upstairs to bid farewell
Now to the parson's demoiselle.
He quietly undid the lock
244 And opened the door. The lady woke,
Opened her eyes, turned her head,
And saw him standing by her bed.
She asked where he had come from, Sir?
248 What did he have to do with her?
"My Lady, thanks," he said, "Last night
I lodged with you to my delight."
He moved toward the pillow, stood above her,
252 And gently pulled away the cover,
And there she lay. The lady's guest
Beheld her snow-white throat and breast.
"What miracle do my eyes feast
256 Upon? St. Romalcus! This priest
Leads a charmed life—and Lord! what charms—
Naked in such a lady's arms!
St. Honoré salvation bring!
260 She would do honor to a king.
I wish to God someone would let
Me lie a little here and get
Refreshment, comfort, ease from pain!"
264 —"Oh, no!" she answered him, "it's plain
You don't ask much. Sir! I command
You leave this room. Remove your hand!
The pastor's singing should be done.
268 He'll think there's something going on!
If he should see me with a man,
He'll never care for me again.
You'll be the death of me for sure."
272 The butcher calmed her down and swore,
"Lady, by Mary full of grace,
I am not moving from this place,

"Dame," fet il, "por Dieu merci,
Jamés ne mouverai de ci
Por nul homme vivant qui soit.
Nes se li doiens i venoit,
Por qu'il deïst une parole
Qui fust outrageuse ne fole,
Je l'ocirroie maintenant.
Mes or otroiez mon commant
Et fetes ce que je voudrai,
Ma piau lanue vous donrai
Et grant plenté de mon argent."[27]
—"Sire, je n'en ferai noient,
Que je vous sent si à estout
Que demain le diriez partout."
—"Dame," dist il, "ma foi tenez
Tant com je soie vis ne nez,
Ne le dirai fame ne homme,
Par toz les sainz qui sont à Romme."
Tant li dist et tant li promet
La dame en sa merci se met,
Et li bouchiers bien s'en refet.
Et, quant il en ot son bon fet,
D'iluec se part, n'i volt plus estre,
Ainz vint au moustier où le prestre
Ot commencié une leçon
Entre lui et un sien clerçon;
Si comme il dist: *Jube, Domne,*[29]
Ez le vous el moustier entré.
"Sire," fet il, "graces vous rent,
Ostel ai eü à talent,
Molt me lo de vo biau samblant.
Mes une chose vous demant
Et vous pri que vous le faciez,
Que vous ma pel achatissiez,
Si m'auriez delivré de paine;
Bien i a .III. livres de laine;
Molt est bone, si m'aït Diex;
.III. sols vaut, vous l'aurez por .II.,
Et molt bon gré vous en saurai."
—"Biaus ostes, et je le ferai
Por l'amor de vous volentiers.
Bons compains estes et entiers,
Revenez moi veoir sovent."
Sa pel meïsme cil li vent;
Congié demande, si s'en va.

Not for any man alive,
276 Not if the pastor should arrive,
For if he did, and said one word
That was outrageous or absurd,
I'd kill the man. Now hear my offer:
280 If you consent to be my lover
And do my will, then you'll receive
My wooly sheepskin when I leave.
It's worth more money than I could pay."
284 —"I wouldn't dare! What would people say?
I think you're mad. You wouldn't lose
A minute before you spread the news."
—"Lady, he said, "you must have faith.
288 As long as I have life and breath,
By all the Saints in Rome I swear
I'll tell nobody anywhere."
The butcher urged and pled until
292 The lady yielded to his will,
And for the sheepskin he would owe her[28]
She put her body in his power,
Which the butcher took advantage of.
296 And after he had had enough,
He left. He had no need for staying.
He went to church. The priest was praying
The lesson with his acolyte.
300 The butcher didn't hesitate.
Right at the *Jube Domine*
He came into the church. "Good day,"
He told the priest, "last night you lodged
304 Me comfortably. I'm much obliged.
Your hospitality is the best.
However, I have one request.
This is the last of my demands.
308 Please take my sheepskin off my hands
And make my journey light today.
Three pounds the wool alone must weigh.
It's a good fleece, I promise you.
312 It's worth three sous. Take it for two.
I'd be most grateful if you'd have it."
—"I will indeed, for your sake, David,
Most willingly for love of you.
316 You're a good friend, loyal and true.
Come back as often as you please."
The butcher sold the priest's own fleece
Then said good-bye and off he went.

Et la dame lors se leva, 320
Qui molt ert jolie et mingnote;
Si se vest d'une verde cote
Molt bien faudee à plois rampanz.
La dame ot escorcié ses panz 324
A sa çainture par orgueil:
Cler et riant furent si oeil;
[Bele, plaisans ert à devise,
En le caiere s'est asise.] 328
Et la baissele, sanz atendre,
Vint à la pel, si la vout prendre,
Quant la dame li desfendi.
"Di va," fet ele, "et quar me di: 332
Qu'as tu de cele pel à fere?"
—"Dame, j'en ferai mon afere;
Je la vueil au soleil porter
Por le cuirien fere essuer." 336
—"Non feras, lai le toute coie,
Ele pendroit trop sor la voie,
Mes fai ce que tu as à fere."
—"Dame," dist el, "je n'ai que fere; 340
Je levai plus matin de vous,
A foi, maugré en aiez vous![30]
Vous en deüssiez bien parler!"
—"Trai te en sus, lai la pel ester, 344
Garde que plus la main n'i metes
Ne que plus ne t'en entremetes!"
—"En non Dieu, dame, si ferai,
Toute m'en entremeterai: 348
J'en ferai comme de la moie."
—"Dis tu donques que ele est toie?"
—"Oïl, je le di voirement."
—"Met jus la pel, va, si te pent 352
Ou tu ailles en la longaingne.
Certes or ai je grant engaingne
Quant tu deviens si orguilleuse.
Pute, ribaude, pooilleuse, 356
Va tost, si vuide ma meson!"
—"Dame, vous dites desreson,
Qui por le mien me ledengiez:
Se vous seur sainz juré l'aviez, 360
S'est ele moie," —"Toute voie.[31]
Vuide l'ostel, va si te noie!
Je n'ai cure de ton service,
Que trop es pautoniere et nice. 364

The lady, who was elegant
And beautiful, arose and dressed
In a green gown that had been pressed
In neatly folded pleats. She laced
It very tightly at the waist
To satisfy her vanity.
She was as pleasing as could be.
Her eyes were lively, bright, and clear.
She came and sat down in a chair.
Just then the serving girl came in
And was about to take the skin,
When the lady stopped her: "Wait, my girl.
Inform me please, who in the world
Told you to take that fleece from there?"
—"Madam, this fleece is my affair.
It's too much in the way inside.
I'll leave it out until it's dried,
Hanging in the sun and air."
—"Well don't," she said, "Just leave it there.
Go do the work you're paid to do."
—"Ma'am, I rose earlier than you
And did my work, though I admit
I haven't had much thanks for it.
You shouldn't mention work to me."
—"Get out, and let the sheepskin be.
Just keep your fingers off the hide.
Don't meddle with it." The maid replied,
"I will, by God, in spite of you.
I'll meddle with this skin. I'll do
What I want with what belongs to me."
—"You think the skin is yours, I see?"
—"That's what I think and what I know."
—"Well put it down!" said the lady, "Go!
Get out. Go hang yourself or drown
In the outhouse hole. You make me frown
At you. You've gotten much too big
For your own britches, hussy! Pig!
You leave my house at once. Get out!
—"But ma'am, abusing me about
What's mine is foolish. You may swear
By all the saints that ever were—
The skin's still mine." —"In any case
Get out of my sight. Go drown someplace.
Your service is no longer needed.
You've bungled here too long—and cheated.

Se mesires juré l'avoit,
Ceenz ne te garantiroit,
Si t'ai je ore cueilli en hé."
—"Par mi le col ait mal dehé 368
Qui jamés jor vous servira!
J'atendrai tant que il vendra,
Et puis aprés si m'en irai;
De vous à lui me clamerai." 372
—"Clameras? Pute, viex buinarde,
Pullente, ribaude, bastarde!"
—"Bastarde? Dame, or dites mal!
Li vostre enfant sont molt loial, 376
Que vous avez du prestre eüs?"
—"Par la passïon Dieu, met jus
La pel, ou tu le comparras."
—"Miex vous vendroit estre à Arras,[32] 380
Par les sainz Dieu, voire à Coloingne!"
Et la dame prent sa quenoille,
Un cop l'en done, et ele crie:
"Par la vertu sainte Marie, 384
Mar m'i avez à tort batue!
La pel vous ert molt chier vendue
Ainçois que je muire de mort."
Lors pleure et fet un duel si fort. 388
A la noise et à la tençon
Entra li prestres en la meson.
"Qu'est ce?" dist il, "Qui t'a ce fet?"
—"Ma dame, sire, sanz mesfet." 392
—"Sanz mesfet, voir, ne fu ce mie
Qu'ele t'a fet tel vilonie."
—"Par Dieu, sire, por la pel fu
Qui là pent encoste ce fu. 396
Sachiez que vous me commandastes
Ersoir, quant vous couchier alastes,
Que nos ostes sire Davis
Fust aaisiez à son devis, 400
Et je fis vo commandment,
Et il me dona vraiement
La pel, sor sainz le juerrai,
Que molt bien deservie l'ai." 404
Li doiens ot et aperçoit
Aus paroles qu'ele disoit,
L'avoit ses ostes enganee:[33]
Por ce li ot sa pel donee. 408
S'en fu corouciez et plains d'ire,

Whatever my lord may have decreed
You job here isn't guaranteed.
Today you've earned my lasting hate."
—"Plague take the woman who would wait
On you again. I'll stay until
The master comes, and then I'll tell
On you and tell what's going on,
And after that, good-bye, I'm gone."
—"Is that right, now? You'll tell the master?
You stinking slut, whore, pig, bitch, bastard!"
—"Bastard? Ma'am! Come now, admit
Exactly how legitimate
Your children by the priest have been?"
—"By God's passion! Drop that skin!
Don't, and I'll make you wish you did!
You'll wish you were living in Madrid,
Cologne, by God, or Switzerland."
She took the distaff in her hand
And struck the girl. The girl exclaimed,
"By Mary Queen of Heaven, shame!
Oh what a woeful blow you've dealt!
Believe me though, you'll buy this pelt
At a high price before I die!"
She started to weep and wail and cry.
The priest, who heard the noise and fuss,
Came in to see what the matter was.
—"What's going on? Who dared assault you?"
—"The mistress, Sir. She had no call to."
—"Without some call, I'm sure your lady
Wouldn't have beaten you so badly."
—"Sir, she did it for that hide
That's hanging by the fireside.
Last night before you went to bed
You gave me orders, Sir, and said
I should give comfort to our guest,
Sir David, just as he thought best.
I did just as you ordered, Sir.
He gave the skin to me, not her.
May my immortal soul be burned
If it's not mine. It's what I earned!"
The priest concluded that the maid
Had earned the skin by getting laid;
Despite his wrath he didn't dare
Accuse her of it then and there.
"Lady," he said, "I clearly see

Mes son pensser n'en osa dire.
"Dame," fet il, "se Diex me saut,
Vous avez fet trop vilain saut: 412
Petit me prisiez et doutez,
Qui ma mesnie me batez."
—"Ba! Qu'ele veut ma pel avoir!
Sire, se vos saviez le voir 416
De la honte qu'ele m'a dite,
Vous l'en renderiez la merite,
Qui voz enfanz m'a reprovez,
Mauvesement vous en provez, 420
Qui soufrez qu'ele me ledange
Et honist toute par sa jangle.
Je ne sai qu'il en avendra,
Ja ma pel ne li remaindra: 424
Je di qu'ele n'est mie soie."[34]
—"Qui est ce donques?" — "Par foi, moie."]
—"Vostre" —"Voire!" —"Par quel reson?"[35]
—"Nostre ostes jut en no meson[36] 428
Sor ma coute, sor mes linceus;
Que mau gré en ait sainz Aceus
Si volez ore tout savoir."
—"Bele dame, or me dites voir: 432
Par cele foi que me plevistes,
Quant vous primes ceenz venistes,
Cele pel doit ele estre vostre?"
—"Oïl, par sainte patrenostre." 436
Et la baissele dist adonques:
"Biaus sire, ne le creez onques!
Ele me fu ainçois donee."
—"Ha! Pute, mal fusses tu nee! 440
On vous dona la passïon!
Alez tost hors de ma meson,
Que male honte vous aviegne!"
—"Par le saint Signe de Compiegne, 444
Dame," fet il, "vous avez tort."
—"Non ai, quar je le haz de mort,
Por ce qu'ele est si menterresse,
Cele ribaude larronnesse." 448
—"Dame, que vous ai je emblé?"
—"Ribaude, mon orge et mon blé,
Mes pois, mon lart, mon pain fetiz.
Certes, vous estes trop chetiz 452
Qui ceenz l'avez tant soufferte!
Sire, paiez li sa deserte;

You haven't been doing right by me.
Beat my servant, and you neglect
To offer me my due respect."
—"Bah! She wanted my fleece. My Lord,
It served her right. If you had heard
The way she kept insulting me,
You'd tell me I did well. Why she
Insinuates that I bear shame
For your own children. You're to blame.
You keep on letting her besmatter
My reputation with her chatter.
She may dispute the fact for years,
But my fleece never will be hers."
—"Your fleece?" —"Yes!" —"May I ask why?"
—"Your guest in my house slept on my
Clean sheets last night and on my cot,
By St. Acheus, if you've got
To question all I say to you."
—"My lady, come now, tell me true,
By the faith you promised me and swore
When first you entered through this door,
This fleece, should it indeed be yours?"
—"Yes! By all the saints, of course!"
The servant girl broke in: "My Lord,
Don't you believe a word you've heard.
The skin was given me before
It was to her." —"Damn you, you whore,
Hot pants is all that you were given.
Get out of my house before you're driven,
And may misfortune be your guide."
"Now by the cross," the priest replied,
"Lady, I say you're in the wrong."
—"Oh no, I'm not. My anger's strong
Enough to kill the girl. In brief,
I hate the lying little thief."
—"What have I ever stolen, ma'am?"
—"Slut! My barley, peas and ham—
She steals my fresh baked bread, my flour—
Why you continue to allow her
To make her home here I don't know.
Pay her wages, let her go,
And be well rid of her at last."
—"Lady," he answered, "not so fast.
What I still want to know is this:
Whose property the sheepskin is,

Por Dieu, si vous en delivrez!"
—"Dame," fet il, "or m'entendez: 456
Par saint Denis je veuil savoir
Laquele doit la pel avoir.
Cele pel, qui la vous dona?
—"Nostre ostes, quant il s'en ala." 460
—"Vois, por les costez saint Martin.
Il s'en ala des hui matin
Ainz que fust levez li solaus.
Diex! Com vous estes desloiaus 464
Qui jurez si estoutement!"
—"Ainz prist congié molt bonement
Avant qu'il en deüst aler."
—"Fu il donques à vo lever?" 468
—"Nenil, adonc je me gisoie;[37]
De lui garde ne me donoie,
Quant je le vi devant m'esponde.
Il estuet que je vous desponde. . . " 472
—"Et que dist il au congié prendre?"
—"Sire, trop me volez sorprendre. . .
Il dist: A Jhesu vous commant.
Adonc s'en parti à itant, 476
Ainz plus ne parla ne ne dist,[38]
Ne nule rien ne me requist
Qui vous tornast à vilonie.
Mes vous i chaciez boiserie. 480
Onques ne fui de vous creüe,
Et si n'avez en moi veüe,[39]
Grace Dieu, se molt grant bien non,
Mes vos i chaciez trahison. 484
Si m'avez en tel prison mise
Dont ma char est tainte et remise;
De vostre ostel ne me remue;
Mise m'avez muer en mue;[40] 488
Trop ai esté en vo dangier
Por vo boivre, por vo mengier."
—"Ahi!" fet il, "fole mauvaise;
Je t'ai norrie trop aaise, 492
Pres va que ne te bat et tue.
Je sai de voir qu'il t'a foutue,[41]
Di moi, por quoi ne crias tu?
Il t'estuet rompre le festu;[42] 496
Va, si vuide tost mon ostel
Et je irai à mon autel,
Maintenant deseur jurerai

And if it's yours, then say who gave it."
—"Our guest did when he left, Sir David."
—"Now by the holy Eucharist Cup,
This guest you talk about was up
And gone before the break of day.
There's no believing what you say,
The way you swear to God and lie."
—"But he politely said good-bye
Before he left," the lady said.
—"While you were getting out of bed?"
—"No." —"Well when?" —"While I was still
Asleep. I didn't notice till
He stood beside my pillow. I mean,
My Lord, I think I should explain—"
—"What sort of farewell did he use?"
—"Sir! You're trying to confuse
Me now. He said, 'Peace of the Lord—'
And left without another word,
Not a request, not a suggestion,
Nothing was done. There was no question
Of any blemish or affront
To your good name, but you must hunt
For ruses to accuse me of.
You're never satisfied. You love
To hunt deceit, but find in me
Nothing, thank God, but honesty.
You've kept me in this house imprisoned
Until my flesh is pale and wizened.
You've closed me up inside a cage
To molt and wilt until old age.
I've let my nature be subdued
By you too long for drink and food."
—"Too long indeed, ungrateful cheat,
I've let you take your ease and eat!
You've got a beating coming to you!
I know the truth. You let him screw you!
Why didn't you scream? This time we're through.
I'm going to have to break with you.
Get out of my house! Go! Leave it now!
I'm going to my church to vow
Upon the bones of the holy dead
Never again to share your bed!"
Infuriated, filled with grief,
He sat down, shaking like a leaf.

amés en ton lit ne girrai.”	500	
ar molt grant ire s'est assis,		
orouciez, tristes et penssis.		
Quant la dame aïré le voit,		The lady realized that the pastor
orment li poise qu'ele avoit	504	Wouldn't hear reason. He was mastered
encié ne estrivé à lui;		By rage. She wished that she'd kept silence.
olt crient que ne li face anui:		Fearing that he might do her violence,
n sa chambre s'en va atant.		She turned and went back to her chamber.
t li paistres tout maintenant,[43]	508	The shepherd, who had found the number
Qui ses moutons avoit contez		Of sheep he had was short by one,
rsoir l'en fu li uns emblez,		Came to the house at a terrible run,
l ne set qu'il est devenuz.		Not knowing where it could have been.
rant aleüre en est venuz,	512	He reached the door and tramped on in,
rotant ses hines, en meson.[44]		Looking in corners everywhere.
i prestres ert sor sa leson		The priest was sitting in his chair,
Molt corouciez et eschaufez:		Simmering with indignation.
“Qu'est ce? Mal soies tu trovez,	516	“What's this? What's going on? Damnation
Mauvés ribaus, dont reviens tu?		Take your soul. Where'd you come from?
Qu'est ce, comfet samblant fez tu![45]		Where are your sheep, you no-good bum?
ilz à putain, vilain rubestes,		Son of a bitch! You're playing some trick.
r deüsses garder tes bestes,	520	I ought to beat you with my stick.
Pres va ne te fier d'un baston.”		You should be tending to your herd.”
—“Sire, n'ai mie d'un mouton,		—“Sir! One of the sheep has disappeared,
Tout le meillor de no tropé;		The prize of all your flock, the chief!
Je ne sai qui le m'a emblé.”	524	He's gone, and I can't find the thief.”
—“As tu donques mouton perdu?		—“I understand. You've lost a sheep.
On te deüst avoir pendu;		You're paid to guard them, not to sleep!
Mauvesement les as gardez.”		A hanging's what you ought to get.”
—“Sire, fet il, or m'entendez:	528	—“Listen, Sir. Last night I met
Ersoir, quant en la vile entrai,		A man I never chanced to meet
Un estrange homme i encontrai		In town, in fields, or on the street
Que onques mes veü n'avoie		Until just then. I saw him look
En champ, n'en vile, ne en voie,	532	Long and hard, Sir, at my flock.
[Qui molt mes bestes esgarda,[46]		He asked whose sheep they were. Of course
Et molt m'enquist et demanda		I answered, Sir, that they were yours.
Cui cis biaus avoirs pooit estre,		It's him who stole it, I suggest.”
Et je li dis: ‘Sire no prestre!']	536	—“By God, that must have been our guest,
Cil le m'embla, ce m'est avis.”		David. Here's where he spent the night.
—“Par les sainz Dieu, ce fu Davis,		He made a fool of me all right,
Noz ostes, qui ceenz a jut;		Screwed everyone in the rectory
Bien m'a engingnié et deçut	540	And sold my own damn skin to me.
Qui ma mesnie m'a foutue;		He wiped my nose with my own sleeve.
Ma pel meïsme m'a vendue:		I'm born to be deceived and grieved,
[*De ma mance m'a ters mon nés;*[47]		Letting that trickster get away—
En mal eure fuisse jou nés.	544	Well, live and learn from day to day.

Quant je ne m'en seuch garde prendre!		He rolled me out in my own dough!
On peut cascun jor molt aprendre:]		Is this your sheep's pelt, would you know?"
De ma paste m'a fet tortel.		—"Yes, Sir," the shepherd told the priest,
En connoistroies tu la pel?"	548	"I'd recognize my own sheep's fleece.
—"Oïl, sire, foi que vous doi,		For seven years I've been its master."
Bien la connoistrai, se la voi,		He took the sheepskin from the pastor,
Je l'ai eü. VII. anz en garde."		Examined head and ears and chin
Cil prent la pel, si la regarde;	552	And knew it was his own sheep's skin.
Aus oreilles et à la teste		—"Alas the day that I was born, he
Connut bien la pel de sa beste:		Is the one, Sir. That's old Horny,
"Harou! Las," dist li pasturiaus,		The animal I loved the best,
"Par Dieu, sire, c'est Cornuiaus,	556	The finest, fattest, wooliest.
La beste que je plus amoie!		By good St. Vincent, Sir, there wasn't
En mon tropé n'avoit si coie;		A better sheep among ten dozen.
[Foi que je doi à saint Vincent,		A better couldn't have been at all."
N'avoit si cras mouton en cent,]	560	—"Come here, my Lady," the pastor called,
Mieudres de lui ne pooit estre."		"And answer me as I command.
—"Venez ça, dame," dist le prestre,[48]		And you, my girl, come here and stand
"Et tu, baissele, vien avant,		And answer when I tell you to.
Parole à moi, je te commant,	564	You claim this skin belongs to you?"
Respont à moi quant je t'apel:		—"Yes, Sir, as I'm a loyal maid,
Que claimes tu en ceste pel?"		I claim it all," the servant said.
—"Sire, trestoute la pel claim,"		—"Fair Lady, you, whose shall it be?"
Dist la meschine au chapelain.	568	—"By God, that skin belongs to me.
—"Et vous, que dites, bele dame?"		It should be mine and mine alone."
—"Sire, se Diex ait part en m'ame,		—"It won't be either's. It's my own,
Ele doit estre par droit moie."		Bought with my money. I maintain
—"Ele n'ert ne vostre, ne soie.	572	It's mine and mine it should remain.
[Je l'acatai de mon avoir,[49]		He sold it to me at my altar
Ele me doit bien remanoir.		As I was reading in my psalter.
Il m'en vint priier au moustier,		And by the true apostle Peter,
Là ù ge lisoie men sautier.	576	It won't be hers or your skin either
Par saint Pierre, le vrai apostre,		Without a judgment by the courts."
Ele n'iert ne soie ne vostre,]		
Se par jugement ne l'avez."		
Seignor, vous qui les biens savez,[50]	580	My lords, Eustache d'Amiens exhorts
Huistaces d'Amiens vous demande,		And urges and beseeches you,
Et prie par amors, et mande		Who understand what's just and true
Que vous faciez cest jugement.		To give the judgment. Which of these
Bien et à droit et lëaument,	584	By law and right should have the fleece,
Chascuns en die son voloir		The pastor or the pastoress
Liquels doit miex la pel avoir,		Or the saucy little servant lass?
Ou li prestres, ou la prestresse,		
Ou la meschine piprenesse.	588	

2.

De Brunain, la vache au prestre (Browny, the Priest's Cow)

This short, seventy-two-line fabliau stands as a good example of the compact character a narrative can have and of the artistry that such an economical structure requires. Most fabliaux whose humor rests on a verbal basis, a misunderstanding or a misapplication of what somebody has heard, are short. Fabliaux whose humor is essentially situational can afford the luxury of ornamentation, whereas the verbal ones cannot, lest the connection between the actual understanding and the expected one (much more fragile in its retention in our consciousness) be made less keen. Here, the characters are neither named nor described: the peasant, his wife, and the priest are all that is needed for this tale. The setting is unspecified. Yet the author profits from this conciseness: the fabliau shows how literal application can, as quickly as adding one plus one, bring about an unexpected result: two. With the prospect of reward, people tend to act quickly and unpredictably. The priest, elated at such a stroke of luck, dispatches the peasant ("Va t'en," v. 33) and immediately (". . . en oirre," v. 38) has the cow led away lest he change his mind. When the fableor stresses the rapidity of the couple's decision, "Que ne firent plus longue fable" (v. 21), he is also expressing his own desire not to dwell on the background of the couple or on the motives behind their decision, but to move forward to the climax of his tale.

This fableor has been identified as Jean Bodel, the author of the *Jeu de St. Nicolas,* the *Chanson des Saisnes,* the *Congés,* and seven other fabliaux. Nykrog (N, p. 165) and Togeby (CH, p. 11) cautiously propose that he may have been the inventor of the genre, at least one of its first composers.[1] Whether he composed the eight fabliaux and whether he was the same Jean Bodel who wrote the *Congés* have been mildly argued (Bédier, *Les Fabliaux,* pp. 483–86; Nykrog, N, pp. 268–71). Nykrog wisely proposes that this attribution and identification can be reasonably presumed but not stated with scientific certainty. That a Jean Bodel wrote *Brunain* is certain, but that this fabliau is our *Brunain* cannot be affirmed with full assurance in view of the multiplicity of fabliaux versions in existence, a caution that Johnston and Owen repeat (JO, p. 94).

A feature that appears to be common to Jean Bodel's fabliaux is his use of understatement, as Nykrog points out (N, p. 165). In the midst of the heartiest laugh, Bodel likes to insert a discreetly human touch. For instance, when the peasant, in wonderment, sees his hopes fulfilled in the form of Brunain dragging home another cow, he comments that now the shed will be too small (v. 63). When the couple, with seeming piety, decides on the praiseworthy sacrifice of their only possession to the priest, the peasant declares that their cow gives little milk anyway (v. 17). His wife hastens to agree, in view of such good reasoning, "par tel raison" (v. 19).

Contrary to most fabliaux, Bodel's have no truly hateful characters. Whether this pleasant feature is due to Bodel himself or to his time is not known, but throughout his works he does seem to give us portraits of fairly happy couples. He does not despise his peasants. Indeed, we look upon their stroke of good luck with great sympathy, especially since it was achieved without inflicting physical injury to anybody. Whether the peasant acted with malice or with the simple hope of an unspecified future reward is conjectural, although the latter is more likely. Nevertheless, he is presented to us as a humble fellow, politely addressing the priest in a pious pose, "à mains jointes" (with folded hands) (v. 26). One has, however, the feeling throughout the fabliau that the peasant is more astute than first glance would reveal: the resolution with which he sets things in motion after he hears of the scriptural quotation (almost as if he had luckily stumbled on a loophole assuring him of a windfall profit), with which he convinces his wife to go along with the idea, with which he sets out for the priest's house, with which he slaps the reins of his cow into the priest's hand as if afraid the latter would retract the Scripture's vital interpretation, and with which he gives his unsolicited oath (v. 29) that the cow represents all his possessions, as if to ensure that he has kept his part of the bargain to the letter (compare v. 9)—all these do make us pause and wonder about his motives. With all the firmness and straightforwardness the peasant exhibits, Jean Bodel tells us, in a nicely rhythmic line, that he still was full of amazement and disbelief at first when the promise was actually fulfilled ("Li vilains garde, si le voit," v. 56, and also v. 59: "Voirement est Diex . . .").

Even the priest is not the hateful cleric of other fabliaux. The earlier characterization of him as "sages et cointes" (v. 25) must be ironic in view of the further precision that he was always ready to take something (v. 32). In his elation, he cannot hide his greedy, calculating instincts, thinking like the peasant that he has uncovered a lucrative system and that if all his parishioners were as "wise" (v. 34) as the peasant he would soon have a very sizable herd (v. 36). Such portrayal of greed is too good-humored to embitter the audience against the priest.

Helsinger chooses this fabliau to project his thesis that the humor in the fabliaux can originate from the allegorical system being turned inside out when the figurative becomes literal. Jean Bodel seems to be mocking the allegorical procedure by making literal-mindedness successful: "In . . . *Brunain* . . . the letter does not kill; it instead nourishes" (CH, p. 94). Indeed, the double allusion to biblical verses, in the prologue (v. 8) and in the moral at the end (v. 67), would seem to suggest that we search for symbols in a tale where literal interpretation wins over. Thus are to be understood the numerous appeals to reason in this fabliau (vv. 7, 19, 34; "c'est or del mains," v. 69): it is not the philosophical, abstract reason that prevails, but the peasant's concrete, pragmatic understanding. Yet when all is said and done, it is not either interpretation but rather good fortune that causes the peasant to own two cows ("eür," a fact that Bodel stresses in vv. 69, 70).

The moral, therefore, is also ambiguous. Amidst a heavy sententious tone of expressions such as "example" (v. 64), "fols est . . . " (v. 65), "Cil a le bien cui . . . " (v. 66), "C'est or del mains" (v. 69), "Tels cuide . . . " (v. 72), a very simple truth emerges: "He who thinks he is progressing, is actually regressing!"

De Brunain la vache au prestre

D'un vilain cont[e] et de sa fame,[2]
C'un jor de feste Nostre Dame
Aloient ourer à l'yglise.
Li prestres, devant le servise,
Vint à son proisne sermoner,
Et dist qu'il fesoit bon doner
Por Dieu, qui reson entendoit;[3]
Que Diex au double li rendoit,
Celui qui le fesoit de cuer.
"Os," fet li vilains, "bele suer,
Que noz prestres a en couvent:[4]
Qui por Dieu done à escïent,
Que Diex li fet mouteploier.
Miex ne poons nous emploier
No vache, se bel te doit estre,
Que pour Dieu le donons le prestre.[5]
Ausi rent ele petit lait."
—"Sire, je vueil bien que il l'ait,"
Fet la dame, "par tel reson."
Atant s'en vienent en meson,
Que ne firent plus longue fable.
Li vilains s'en entre en l'estable,
Sa vache prent par le lien,
Presenter le vait au doien,
Li prestres ert sages et cointes.
"Biaus Sire," fet il à mains jointes,
"Por l'amor Dieu Blerain vous doing."[6]
Le lïen li a mis el poing.
Si jure que plus n'a d'avoir.
"Amis, or as tu fet savoir,"
Fet li provoires dans Constans,
Qui à prendre bee toz tans.
"Va t'en, bien as fet ton message.
Quar fussent or tuit ausi sage
Mi paroiscien comme vous estes:
S'averoie plenté de bestes."
Li vilains se part du provoire.
Li prestres commanda en oirre
C'on fasse por aprivoisier
Blerain avoec Brunain lïer,
La seue grant vache demaine.
Li clers en lor jardin la maine,

Browny, the Priest's Cow

Once, on blessed Mary's day,
A peasant took his wife to pray
And celebrate the mass in town.
4 Before the office, the priest came down
And turned to the people to deliver
His sermon: Blessed be the giver
Who gives for love of God in heaven.
8 God will return what has been given
Double to him whose heart is true.
"My wife!" the peasant said, "Did you
Hear what the parson up there said?
12 Whoever gives for God will get
The gift returned and multiplied?
What better use could we decide
For our cow, Berny, than to give her
16 To God through the priest? Besides, she never
Did give much milk. She's not much good."
"Well," said the wife, "I guess we should,
Since that's a fact. Let's take that cow
20 And give her to the parson now."
They rose at once and left together.
When they got home, the farmer tethered
His cow and led her from the shed
24 And took her back to town and said
To the priest, whose name was Constant, "Sir,
Here's my cow Berny. I'm giving her
To you because I love the Lord."
28 He handed him the tether cord
And swore that she was all he had.
"That's wise indeed," the parson said,
Who night and day kept careful watch
32 For any handout he could catch.
"Well done, my son. In peace depart.
If all my parish were as smart
And sensible as you, there'd be
36 Plenty of animals for me."
The farmer left and made his journey
Home to his wife. The priest gave Berny
To one of his clerks to be secured
40 To *his* cow, Browny, till they were sure
She felt at home. The clerk pulled hard
And brought the cow to the backyard

Lor vache trueve, ce me samble,		And got the priest's fat cow and tied
An .II. les acoupla ensamble.	44	Berny and Browny side by side,
Atant s'en torne, si les lesse.		Then turned around and left the cows.
La vache le prestre s'abesse,		The parson's cow preferred to browse,
Por ce que voloit pasturer,		And bent her head to keep on chewing,
Mes Blere nel vout endurer,	48	But Berny balked: no, nothing doing.
Ainz sache le lïen si fors,		She pulled the tether good and hard,
Du jardin la traïna fors.		Dragging her out of the priest's yard,
Tant l'a menee par ostez,		Past houses and hemp fields, over bridges,
Par chanevieres et par prez,	52	Through meadows and hedges, hills and ditches
Qu'ele est repereie à son estre		Till home she came to her own backyard.
Avoeques la vache le prestre,		The parson's cow, who held back hard
Qui molt à mener li grevoit.		The whole long way, came dragging after.
Li vilains garde, si le voit;	56	The farmer looked outside, and laughter
Molt en a grant joie en son cuer.		Filled his heart. He gave a cheer.
"Ha," fet li vilains, "bele suer,		"Hey!" he shouted, "Look, my dear!
Voirement est Diex hom doublere,[7]		See how the good Lord multiplies.
Quar li et autre revient Blere;[8]	60	Here's Berny back and Berny twice—
Une grant vache amaine brune,		Only the second's brown, and bigger!
Or en avons nous .II. por une:		That's two for one the way I figure.
Petis sera nostre toitiaus."		And now our barn's not big enough."
Par example dist cis fabliaus	64	My lords, this fabliau is proof
Que fols est qui ne s'abandone;		It's foolish not to give all you own.
Cil a le bien cui Diex le done,		The good things come from God alone.
Non cil qui le muce et enfuet;		They are not buried in the ground.
Nus hom mouteploier ne puet[9]	68	Nothing ventured, nothing found,
Sanz grant eür, c'est or del mains.[10]		And nothing multiplied. That's how
Par grant eür ot li vilains		God blessed the man who risked his cow:
.II. vaches, et li prestres nule		Two for the peasant, none for the priest,
Tels cuide avancier qui recule.	72	And those who have the most, get least.

3.

Des Trois Boçus (The Three Hunchbacks)

As a result of an odd series of circumstances, three bodies are together in one house. A person, very much compromised by their presence, calls for a porter, shows him only one body and asks him to get rid of it. When the porter returns, he is shown the second body and is tricked into believing that the first has come back. He carries the second body away, and the scene is repeated. Finally, the porter will kill a passer-by who resembles the corpse, because he is so angry that it had kept coming back.

Such is Bédier's synopsis (*Les Fabliaux,* p. 245) of this tale's fourteen versions, which have spread over Europe and the Middle East. All fourteen have a communality of essential traits but do differ in ornamental features such as the circumstances surrounding the presence of the bodies in the house. In six tales out of fourteen, they are the wife's lovers, actual or intended, and meet their deaths under various circumstances. In the remaining eight, they are all hunchbacks, either brothers of the avaricious husband whom the lady feeds because she feels sorry for them, or minstrels, as in our fabliau, invited in because they had common infirmities (v. 68) and for the purpose of providing entertainment (v. 99). Consistent with his thesis of native origin and his disapproval of the Orientalists' theory of origin, Bédier maintained that the tales that included the hunchbacks were the earlier of the two categories. It was, according to him, by the vague process of contamination of tales that the second category, where the dead bodies were lovers, came into being. As an example of such a process, Bédier elaborated the following hypothesis. The author of one of the tales in the second category, during his composition, faced with the prospect of having to get rid of three suitors who had made advances to some man's wife, remembered the fabliau *Des Trois Boçus* and chose to have them killed and have the bodies dispatched in the same manner as in our fabliau. Likewise, Bédier continued, the Armenian storyteller who reworked the *Roman de Sept Sages* liked the story of the recalcitrant dead but could not have integrated it into the framework of the *Roman* because the woman of the tale he knew (*Estormi,* MR, 1:198, a variant of our fabliau) was portrayed too sympathetically for the storyteller who wanted to present an example of the perversity of women. Thus the storyteller changed his tale accordingly. These intricate explanations of course conveniently supported Bédier's insistence that the French tales were the models of all others. Why not vice versa? Well, Bédier claimed that the hunchback tales represent the better of the two categories and that *Des Trois Boçus* is the best among them: the others include clumsily borrowed and modified ornamental details to fit their particular frameworks. Johnston and Owen, however, are not convinced and point out that the theory of Eastern derivation is not without merit, as was plausibly shown by Alfred Pillet and Walther Suchier (JO, p. 89). Nevertheless, our tale is "une étrange histoire, sans dates et sans géographie" (a strange story, undatable and unlocatable) (Bédier, *Les Fabliaux,* p. 248).

That our tale is excellent is undeniable. The popularity of the general plot is attested by several other fabliaux reminiscent of ours: *Constant du Hamel* (MR, 4:166), *Estormi, Des IIII Prestres* (MR, 6:42), and several other stories with the unwanted corpse theme. The humor of our tale lies in its incongruity and in its repetitive elements, the "absurdity of mistaking a live hunchback for a dead one" and the pacing of the story (Cooke, *Old French,* p. 47). For Thomas Cooke, the humor arises from the comic repetition "of the same act three times, each done with mounting exasperation," which "establishes the pattern that makes inescapable the disposal of the husband who shares an important accidental characteristic with the three minstrels" (*Old French,* p. 125). The fabliau *Des IIII Prestres,* quite inferior to ours, also tries, but clumsily, to present that inescapability of death by having a fourth, totally innocent passer-by be killed, instead of one related to the core of the story. As Cooke points out, in our fabliau "there is an inevitability in his [the husband's] return, and in these circumstances an inevitability in his death . . . it startles us with its appropriateness, whereas the chance appearance of the fourth priest astonishes us with its coincidence" (*Old French,* pp. 125–26). Bédier (*Les Fabliaux,* p. 246) had seen correctly the quasi-mathematical, equationlike, series of macabre events: "Tout le conte parait imaginé pour cet épisode final, si imprévu, si logique pourtant" (The whole tale seems to have been created for this surprising, yet so logical, final episode).

Johnston and Owen's sensitivities are somewhat offended by "the macabre sense of humor displayed in this tale" (JO, p. 89). They characterize this mocking as an indelicate habit of medieval social behavior because there is no sympathy displayed for the minstrels who died unjustly and for the husband "whose only vice was jealousy" (JO, p. 89). These objections, we believe, are unfounded. First, the husband, in addition to being jealous, is possessive, grasping (vv. 57–59), inhospitable (v. 56), and ill-tempered (vv. 83–88). Moreover, his jealousy is much more overpowering than usual (compare with *De la Borgoise d'Orliens,* below): it keeps him awake (v. 55), he literally sequesters his wife by locking his door continually (v. 56), and he periodically comes back to his house for no apparent reason except to check on his wife (vv. 121–23). It is his mania for unexpected returns that actually causes the death of the minstrels.

The impact of their death, tragic as death may be in reality, is somewhat weakened for two reasons: the requirement of artistic economy in the fabliaux and the emphasis laid on the tragic plight of the lady. The economical nature of the fabliaux need not be restated. Suffice it to say that the three minstrels are deprived of all narrative life, except in that brief scene where they depart happily from the house because they have had a good day. Any sympathies bestowed on them would have detracted from the ones we should give the lady. The fact that they are mere silhouettes is, therefore, de rigueur.

Clearly, the story is to be examined from the pitiable position of the lady. We are told, in a description reminiscent of the heroines in the courtly romances (see Cooke, *Old French,* pp. 83, 84), that she was of extreme beauty (vv. 16–26). This portrait is immediately contrasted with the hideous description of the hunchback (vv. 27–45). As Cooke notes (p. 84), the contrast is especially enhanced by the presence in both portraits of the technique of *diminutio:* the claim that someone's appearance is beyond description (see vv. 21–26; 37–39). Since she was apparently given away in marriage without her consent (vv. 49, 50), it is easy to imagine the lady's feelings of freedom, of escape from the prison of her marriage when the husband dies (vv. 280–85). The author places his tale at Christmastime, a time for generosity, for laughter, and for feasting. But none of these pleasures is for her: her husband is grasping, unpleasant, and not known for his generosity. Evidently she was not even present at the assembly of hunchbacks (vv. 68, 69). Only the husband and the minstrels are mentioned (v. 65; vv.76, 77). Most likely, because of his jealousy, she was made to stay in another room from where she heard them sing and carry on merrily (vv. 98, 99). This would explain why she is driven to call the minstrels back, to hear them in person (v. 101). She is also shown exhausted after having dragged a body out of the *escrin* (vv. 164–66) in a scene that contrasts her daintiness with the burliness (vv. 148, 195) of the dullard porter who disdainfully calls the burden a dwarf (v. 170), stuffing the body in a sack (vv. 154, 184, 213: *bouter*) and slinging it around his strong neck (vv. 155, 185, 214: "A son col fierement le rue"). This contrast is a clear case of brains versus brawn where we are presented with the humorous repetitive scenes in which the porter each time stuffs his sack, throws it on his shoulders, curses the bodies and calls them devils (vv. 220, 177, 181), and superstitiously declares (v. 237) that he has been hexed (vv. 224, 237). We are amused at his constant running up and down the stairs. The stairs are perhaps the most important element of Durand's scenery. He is constantly reminding us of their existence (vv. 71, 125, 148, 156, 217, 231, 232, 260). Up and down them the porter goes, fast and furiously getting nowhere until the grotesque and hilarious climax where he slays the husband on the steps (v. 249)—then one more race to the river and back up the stairs to get his pay, and he and the lady are free. The macabre element in this last action is somewhat diluted because of its expected nature: not only is it equationally justified, but the husband has ironically suffered the same fate that he threatened the minstrels with if they ever were to come back (vv. 86–88).[1]

The poem ends with a moral directed against greed and seemingly against women. This antifeminism sounds oddly out of keeping with the sympathies developed for the lady throughout the narration. One is tempted to suppose that the moral is accidental to the poem, that someone named Durand took the narration as we have it now and tacked on a moral without giving much thought to its application to the story, or that the poem as we have it is a recomposition of an earlier poem that developed less sympathy for the lady. (Durand has repeatedly mentioned that he is telling a story, *aventure,* not of his own composition, vv. 5, 44.) But the moral is too closely integrated with the rest of the poem to allow such a solution. Line 294 in the moral ending, "La dame qui tant bele estoit" (the lady who was so beautiful), contrasts with and echoes v. 282 in the narration, "son mari, qui tant ert lais" (her husband, who was so ugly). The contrast between the ugly man and the beautiful woman echoes the contrasting physical descriptions at the beginning of the narration, both of which note the work that Nature put into these separate creations and both of which end with a claim that the beauty or ugliness of the character is beyond description.

Since the very sound of the line, "La dame qui tant bele estoit," puts the moral into the context of the narration, the moral is no tacked-on afterthought, and it is best to look for the meaning of the moral in the narrative context also. The statement that there never was a woman whom money could not buy, standing by itself, is as antifeminist as it could be, but in this poem, it is aimed at certain men, presumably the friends of the girl's father, for it is they who have sold her for the hunchback's wealth. She certainly has not sold herself.

The poem ends with an attack on the *man* who "lives for money" and "puts it first." The word for *man, hons,* echoes the word for *shamed, honiz:* "Honiz soit li hons. . . ." Thus both words, as well as the link between them, are emphasized. The shame applies to every man in the poem, the father, the husband, the friends, even the porter. The only character who is not out for money is the lady. The antifeminist cliché thus becomes antimale in a context where men sell and buy women.

Des Trois Boçus

Seignor, se vous volez atendre[2]
Et un seul petitet entendre,
Ja de mot ne vous mentirai,
Mes tout en rime vous dirai
D'une aventure le fablel.
Jadis avint à un chastel,
Mes le non oublié en ai,
Or soit aussi comme à Douay.
Un borgois i avoit manant,
Qui du sien vivoit belemant.
Biaus hom ert, et de bons amis.
Des borgois toz li plus eslis,
Mes n'avoit mie grant avoir;
Si s'en savoit si bien avoir[3]
Que molt ert creüz par la vile.
Il avoit une bele fille,
Si bele que c'ert uns delis,
Et, se le voir vous en devis,
Je ne cuit qu'ainz feïst Nature
Nule plus bele creature.
De sa biauté n'ai or que fere
A raconter ne à retrere,
Quar, se je mesler m'en voloie,
Assez tost mesprendre i porroie;
Si m'en vient miex tere orendroit
Que dire chose qui n'i soit.
En la vile avoit un boçu,
Onques ne vi si malostru;
De teste estoit molt bien garnis,
Je cuit bien que Nature ot mis
Grant entencïon à lui fere.
A toute riens estoit contrere.
Trop estoit de laide faiture.
Grant teste avoit et laide hure,

The Three Hunchbacks

My lords, if you will linger here
A little while and lend an ear,
I will relate a fabliau
4 Of something that happened long ago.
It's true, and furthermore it rhymes.
A burgher lived in former times,
I don't recall exactly where,
8 Douay perhaps, or near to there,
Who lived in luxury and ease
By selling off his properties.
He was a man men liked to know.
12 Although his cash was getting low,
He always knew where he could get it:
Rich bourgeois friends would give him credit;
Soon he was everybody's debtor.
16 He had a very lovely daughter,
So beautiful it was a sin.
Indeed, I think there's never been
Created since the dawn of nature
20 A more exquisite, perfect creature.
I don't know how—and no one does—
To say how beautiful she was,
So I'll say nothing. It won't do
24 For me to say what's less than true.

A humpback lived there in the town.
28 An uglier wretch could not be found.
His head was almost half his height.
Nature must have worked all night
To fashion him exactly wrong,
32 For no two parts seemed to belong
Together; all was ugliness.
His head was big, his scalp a mess;

Cort col, et les espaules lees,		His neck was short, his shoulders wide—
Et les avoit haut encroëes.[4]	36	They hugged his ears on either side.
De folie se peneroit		I'd be a fool to waste the day
Qui tout raconter vous voudroit		Trying and failing to convey
Sa façon: trop par estoit lais.		His ugliness. His life he'd spent
Toute sa vie fu entais	40	Collecting interest and rent,
A grant avoir amonceler,		And if the story is correct,
Por voir vous puis dire et conter,		This hunchback managed to collect
Trop estoit riches durement.		Much too much money. They didn't come
Se li aventure ne ment,	44	Richer than he; and that's the sum
En la vile n'ot si riche homme.		Of him and how he worked and lived.
Que vous diroie? C'est la somme		The father's friends agreed to give
Du boçu, comment a ouvré,		The daughter in the bloom of health
Por l'avoir qu'il ot amassé	48	To the hunchback for his wealth.
Li ont donee la pucele		But from the minute they were married,
Si ami, qui tant estoit bele;		The hunchback husband fumed and worried
Mes, ainz puis qu'il l'ot espousee		Because of the beauty of his wife.
Ne fu il un jor sanz penssee,	52	Jealousy controlled his life.
Por la grant biauté qu'ele avoit,		Night after night he hardly slept.
Li boçus si jalous estoit		All day the door to his house he kept
Qu'il ne pooit avoir repos.		Tight shut. He sat there doing sentry
Toute jor estoit ses huis clos;	56	Before the door, refusing entry
Ja ne vousist que nus entrast		To all who came, unless they'd come
En sa meson, s'il n'aportast,		To pay him money or borrow some;
Ou s'il emprunter ne vousist.		Until one Christmas afternoon
Toute jor à son sueil seïst,	60	There came to him to ask a boon
Tant qu'il avint à un Nöel		Beneath the landing where he rested
Que troi boçu menesterel		Three hunchback minstrels who requested
Vindrent à lui où il estoit;		That they might share his Christmas meal,
Se li dist chascuns qu'il voloit	64	For nowhere else could these three feel
Fere cele feste avoec lui,		So comfortable; here they might find
Quar en la vile n'a nului		Festivity with their own kind,
Où le deüssent fere miex,		Because he had a back like theirs.
Por ce qu'il ert de lor pariex,	68	He brought them up the outside stairs
Et boçus ausi comme il sont.		To the front door and let them in.
Lors les maine li sire amont,		Dinner was ready to begin.
Quar la meson ert à degrez.		A place was set for every guest.
Li mengiers estoit aprestez;	72	The master, it must be confessed,
Tuit se sont au disner assis,		Served them a very hearty feast.
Et, se le voir vous en devis,		He wasn't tight, not in the least,
Li disners ert et biaus et riches.		But made them welcome to partake
Li boçus n'ert avers ne chiches,[5]	76	Of peas and bacon, capons, cake.
Ainz assist bien ses compaignons.		When they had eaten, before they left,
Pois au lart orent et chapons.		He gave them each a handsome gift

Et, quant ce vint aprés disner,
Si lor fist li sires doner
Aus trois boçus, ce m'est avis,
Chascun .XX. sols de parisis,
Et aprés lor a desfendu
Qu'il ne soient jamés veü
En la meson, ne el propris;
Quar, s'il i estoient repris,
Il auroient un baing cruel
De la froide eve du chanel.
La meson ert sor la riviere,
Qui molt estoit granz et pleniere.
Et, quant li boçu l'ont oï,
Tantost sont de l'ostel parti
Volentiers, et à chiere lié,
Quar bien avoient emploïé
Lor journee, ce lor fu vis.
Et li sires s'en est partis,
Puis est deseur le pont venuz.
La dame, qui ot les boçuz
Oï chanter et solacier,
Les fist toz .III. mander arrier,
Quar oïr les voloit chanter;
Si a bien fet les huis fermer.
Ainsi com li boçu chantoient
Et o la dame s'envoisoient,
Ez vous revenu le seignor,
Qui n'ot pas fet trop lonc demor.
A l'uis apela fierement.
La dame son seignor entent,
A la voiz le connut molt bien;
Ne sot en cest mont terrïen
Que peüst fere des boçuz,
Ne comment il soient repus.
(Un) chaaliz ot lez le fouier[6]
C'on soloit fere charriier;
El chaaliz ot .III. escrins.
Que vous diroie? C'est la fins.[7]
En chascun a mis un boçu.
Ez vous le seignor revenu,
Si s'est delez la dame assis,
Qui molt par seoit ses delis;[8]
Mes il n'i sist pas longuement;
De leenz ist, et si descent
De la meson, et si s'en va.

Of twenty Paris-minted sous,
80 And bidding them sincere adieus,
He warned them solemnly and swore
That if they ventured anymore
Within his house or in his yard
84 And they were caught, they'd find it hard
To have to bathe outside and shiver
In the cold waters of the river.
(The hunchback's mansion stood beside
88 A river that was deep and wide.)
When they had heard what he had to say,
Immediately they went away
Most willing, and well content,
92 Considering that they had spent
A profitable evening there.
The lord went down the outside stair
Out to the bridge for a little walk.
96 His wife had heard the minstrels talk
And merrily sing in the room below.
She got a servant girl to go
And fetch them back to sing some more.
100 When they came in, she locked the door.
But as the guests stood entertaining
The lady with their glad refraining,
Here came the husband, who didn't care
104 To be too long away from there.
He tried the door and found it locked,
Called out her name and loudly knocked.
And by his voice she knew him well,
108 But for the world, she couldn't tell
What to do or how provide
A place for three hunchbacks to hide.
Over in a corner stood
112 A bed of heavy oaken wood,
And in the bed three wooden chests.
What shall I say? You'll hear the rest.
In each, a hunchback had to hide.
116 And when the master came inside,
His wife, who knew his every whim
Felt obliged to sit by him.
It wasn't very long before
120 The husband rose, went out the door
And left the house. She wasn't sorry.

A la dame point n'anuia 124
Quant son mari voit avaler.
Les boçus en vout fere aler,
Qu'ele avoit repus es escrins,
Mes toz .III. les trova estins, 128
Quant ele les escrins ouvri.
De ce molt forment s'esbahi,
Quant les .III. boçus mors trova.
A l'uis vint corant, s'apela 132
Un porteur qu'ele a avisé;
A soi l'a la dame apelé.
Quant li bachelers l'a oïe,
A li corut; n'atarja mie. 136
"Amis," dist ele, "enten à moi!
Se tu me veus plevir ta foi
Que tu ja ne m'encuseras
D'une rien que dire m'orras. 140
Molt sera riches tes loiers:
.XXX. livres de bons deniers
Te donrai, quant tu l'auras fet."
Quant li porteres ot tel plet, 144
Fiancié li a volentiers,
Quar il covoitoit les deniers
Et s'estoit auques entestez.[9]
Le grant cors monta les degrez. 148
La dame ouvri l'un des escrins:
"Amis, ne soiez esbahis,
Cest mort en l'eve me portez,
Si m'aurez molt servi à grez." 152
Un sac li baille, et cil le prant;
Le boçu bouta enz errant,
Puis si l'a à son col levé,
Si a les degrez avalé; 156
A la riviere vint corant;
Tout droit sor le grant pont devant,
En l'eve geta le boçu.
Onques n'i a plus atendu, 160
Ainz retorna vers la meson.

La dame a ataint du leson
L'un des boçus à molt grant paine. 164
A poi ne li failli l'alaine,
Molt fu au lever traveillie.
Puis s'en est un pou esloingnie.
Cil revint arriere eslessiez: 168

She was, however, in a hurry
To reassure her hunchback guests,
Who still were hidden in the chests,
And let them out; but she discovered
A hunchback minstrel had been smothered
In every chest she looked inside.
She was completely horrified
To find that all of them were dead.
Out of the door the lady fled
And cried to a porter passing near
And beckoned him and called, come here!
When he had heard, as fast as he could,
The young man ran to where she stood.
"My friend," she said, "listen to me.
If you will pledge me fealty
And swear to keep what I say to you
In confidence between us two,
I guarantee your fortune's made:
Thirty pounds you will be paid
When you have carried out my order."
When he had heard her pleas, the porter
Didn't hesitate to take
Her offer, for the money's sake
And for his eagerness and pride.

He raced the stairs and came inside.
"My friend," she said, "do not be nervous.
If you would do me loyal service,
Take this corpse to the river for me."
She raised a lid for him to see
And handed him a burlap sack.
He stuffed it with the dead hunchback,
Shouldered the sack and quick as a hare,
Ran out the door and down the stair,
Then up along the water's edge,
And halfway out across the bridge,
And dropped the hunchback in the water.
Not taking any time to loiter,
Back to the hunchback's house he hustled.
The lady there at last had wrestled
A second corpse from the bed of death
And was completely out of breath
From the hard work that she had done.
She moved from where she'd put him down.
Elated now, the man returned:

"Dame" dist il, "or me paiez!		"Pay me," he told her, "what I've earned.
Du nain vous ai bien delivree."		Your dwarf is carried off and sunk."
—"Por quoi m'avez vous or gabee,"		—"Sir Dolt," she said, "you must be drunk.
Dist cele, "sire fols vilains?	172	You can't pull wool over my eyes.
Ja est ci revenuz li nains;		The dwarf's not taken. Here he lies.
Ainz en l'eve ne le getastes;		You stopped at the street, emptied the sack,
Ensamble o vous le ramenastes.		Then brought both sack and hunchback back.
Vez le là, se ne m'en creez!"	176	Look over there if you think I'm lying."
"—Comment, cent deables maufez.		—"What the devil? Well for crying—
Est il donc revenuz ceanz?		How did that dead man climb the stairs?
Por lui sui forment merveillanz.		Somehow he took me unawares.
Il estoit mors, ce m'est avis.	180	That man was dead; that I could tell.
C'est un deables antecris!		This is some Antichrist from Hell.
Mais ne li vaut, par saint Remi!"		But by St. Ralph, his tricks won't work!"
Atant l'autre boçu saisi,		He seized the hunchback with a jerk,
El sac le mist, puis si le lieve	184	Shoved him headfirst in the sack,
A son col, si que poi li grieve.		Hoisted him upon his back
De la meson ist vistemant:		And down the steps to the river ran.
Et la dame tout maintenant		The lady dragged the third dead man
De l'escrin tret le tiers boçu,	188	Out of the chest where he had died
Si l'a couchié delez le fu;		And set him by the fireside
Atant s'en est vers l'uis venue,		Then went to wait above the street.
Li porterres en l'eve rue		The porter grabbed the hunchback's feet
Le boçu la teste desouz:	192	And hurled him headlong in the river.
"Alez! Que honis soiez vous,"[10]		"Be gone!" he shouted, "Damn your liver
Dist il, "se vous ne revenez!"		If you return here anymore."
Puis est le grant cors retornez,		He hurried back to the lady's door,
A la dame dist que lit pait.	196	Demanding that he get his pay
Et cele, sanz nul autre plait,		Without excuses or delay.
Li dist que bien li paiera.		She said she'd gladly pay his hire,
Atant au fouier le mena,		Then led him upstairs to the fire
Ausi com se rien ne seüst	200	As if she didn't know about
Du tiers boçu qui là se jut.		The third hunchback, whom she'd laid out.
"Voiés," dist ele, "grant merveille![11]		"Look!" she exclaimed, "What a surprise!
Qui oï ainc mes la pareille:		A miracle before our eyes.
Revez là le boçu où gist!"	204	That hunckback's lying there again!"
Li bachelers pas ne s'en rist,		The young man wasn't laughing then
Quant le voit gesir lez le fu.		At the hunchback by the fireplace.
"Voiz," dist il, "por le saint cueur bu![12]		"Look here," he cried, "God's holy face!
Qui ainc mes vit tel menestrel?	208	This minstrel really takes the cake.
Ne ferai je dont huimés el		Will all I do today be take
Que porter ce vilain boçu?		This cursed hunchback to the river
Toz jors le truis ci revenu,		And find him here again whenever
Quant je l'ai en l'eve rué."	212	I come upstairs to get my cash?"
Lors a le tiers ou sac bouté;		Into the sack he had to stash

A son col fierement le rue;
D'ire et de duel, d'aïr tressue.
Atant s'en torne ireement,
Toz les degrez aval descent;
Le tiers boçu a descarchié,
Dedenz l'eve l'a balancié:
"Va t'en," dist il, "au vif maufé!
Tant t'averai hui comporté!
Se te voi mes hui revenir
Tu vendras tart au repentir
Je cuit que tu m'as enchanté;
Mes, par le Dieu qui me fist né,
Se tu viens mes hui aprés moi,
Et je truis baston ou espoi,
Tel te donrai el haterel,
Dont tu auras rouge bendel."
A icest mot est retornez
Et sus en la meson montez,
Ainz qu'eüst les degrez monté,
Si a derrier lui regardé
Et voit le seignor qui revient.
Li bons hom pas à geu nel tient;
De sa main s'est trois foiz sainiez:
"*Nomini* Dame Diex aidiez!"
Molt li anuie en son corage.
"Par foi," dist il, "cis a la rage
Qui si pres des talons me siut
Que par poi qu'il ne me consiut.
Par la röele saint Morant,[13]
Il me tient bien por païsant,
Que je nel puis tant comporter[14]
Que ja se vueille deporter
D'aprés moi adés revenir!"
Lors cort à ses .II. poins sesir
Un pestel qu'à l'uis voit pendant,
Puis revint au degré corant.
Li sires ert ja pres montez:
"Comment, sire boçus, tornez?
Or me samble ce enresdie;
Mes, par le cors sainte Marie,
Mar retornastes ceste part;
Vous me tenez bien por musart."
Atant a le pestel levé,
Si l'en a un tel cop doné
Sor la teste, qu'il ot molt grant,[15]

The third hunchback. Enraged and grieved,
He seized the heavy sack and heaved
216 It to his neck. About he faced
And hot with indignation raced
Down to the riverbank to sink
Another hunchback in the drink.
220 "Go back to Hell, you wretched stiff!
I've carried you so much that if
You venture here again, you'll rue
The moment I catch sight of you.
224 I'm pretty sure you have me hexed,
But by the lord high God, when next
I see you sneaking on my trail,
And I can find a stick or flail,
228 I'll give you such a knock in the head,
The gash you get will be bright red."
The porter, having made this speech,
Left the bridge, but didn't reach
232 The hunchback's doorway with his sack
Before he happened to turn back
And see the husband coming after.
This didn't move the man to laughter.
236 He crossed himself and double crossed:
"*Nomine Patris,* Son and Ghost!"
(He was upset, no *if's* and *maybe's*.)
"Lord help," he said, "this corpse has rabies,
240 Dogging my heels and the livelong night.
He's almost close enough to bite.
Damnation strike me if he doesn't
Take me for a stupid peasant
244 Who doesn't know his way around.
Is his idea of fun to hound
Me everywhere I take myself?"
He ran inside and from a shelf
248 Seized a huge pestle and once more
Came charging out of the front door.
The lord was on the first step then.
"What Mr. Hunchback! Back again?
252 Who would believe it? By St. Nick,
This hunchback takes me for a hick!
Crossing my path again was crazy.
You think I'm recreant or lazy?"
256 He lifted up the pestle, charged,
Hit the lord's head, which was too large,
And gave it such a mighty clout,

Que la cervele li espant;
Mort l'abati sor le degré,
Et puis si l'a ou sac bouté.
D'une corde la bouche loie;
Le grand cors se met à la voie,
Si l'a en l'eve balancié
A tout le sac qu'il ot lïé;
Quar paor avoit duremant
Qu'il encor ne l'alast sivant.
"Va jus," dist il, "à maleür;
Or cuit je estre plus asseür
Que tu ne doies revenir,
Si verra l'en les bois foillir."[16]
A la dame s'en vint errant;
Si demande son paiemant,
Que molt bien à son commant fet.
La dame n'ot cure de plet;
Le bacheler paia molt bien
XXX. livres; n'en falut rien;
Trestout à son gré l'a paié,
Que molt fu lie du marchié.
Dist que fet a bone jornee,
Despuis que il l'a delivree
De son mari, qui tant ert lais.
Bien cuide qu'ele n'ait jamais
Anui nul jor qu'ele puist vivre,
Quant de son mari est delivre.
  Durans, qui son conte define,
Dist c'onques Diex ne fist meschine
C'on ne puist por deniers avoir;
Ne Diex ne fist si chier avoir,
Tant soit bons ne de grant chierté,
Qui voudroit dire verité,
Que por deniers ne soit eüs.
Por ses deniers ot li boçus
La dame qui tant bele estoit.
Honiz soit li hom, quels qu'il soit,
Qui trop prise mauvés deniers,
Et qui les fist fere premiers.
Amen.

The blood and brains came pouring out.
260 There on the step the hunchback died.
The porter put the corpse inside
The sack, securely tied the top,
Then off he ran and didn't stop
264 Till he had dumped the fourth hunchback
Off the bridge, still in the sack
Because he feared the corpse might swim
Back to the bank and follow him.
268 "Begone," he said, "go back to Hell,
And I can honestly foretell
That this time you are gone for good,
Till blossoms spring from a block of wood."
272 He ran to the lady right away,
Demanding that she quickly pay
His money, which he'd worked so much
To earn, nor did the wife begrudge
276 Whatever pay the man demanded.
Thirty pounds, no less, she handed
Over to him and still could feel
She had the better of the deal.
280 And when she paid him, she agreed
He'd done good work, for he had freed
Her from her lord, that ugly dwarf.
All her long life from that day forth
284 Never another care had she
Once widowhood had set her free.
  Durand, who has fashioned this has stated
That never yet has God created
288 A girl whom money couldn't get,
And furthermore, the Lord has yet
To fashion goods, however good,
Which, if the truth were understood,
292 A sum of money couldn't buy.
The hunchback, though the price was high,
Bought him a wife, that lovely girl.
Shame on the man, be he knight or churl,
296 Who lives for money, which is cursed,
And shame on the man who coined it first.
Amen

4.

Du Prestre ki abevete (The Priest Who Peeked)

This tale, where the husband, forced to witness the sporting between the priest and his wife, is persuaded that he is the victim of an optical illusion, has many analogues. Stith Thompson named the entire motif, "The Enchanted Pear Tree."[1] Larry Benson and Theodore Andersson, completing Thompson's list, divided the analogues into two categories. In the first, the victim is persuaded by his wife that the optical illusion is caused by a magical tree. In the second, the husband is jealous and blind; when the lovers cavort in the pear tree, his vision is miraculously restored but his wife quickly convinces him that the restoration is due to her action with the lover. Boccaccio's version in *Decameron,* 7.9, belongs to the first of these two types and Chaucer's "Merchant's Tale" to the second.[2]

Our fabliau holds some resemblances with these tales but also some notable differences. The most obvious one is the disappearance of the element of magic, a disappearance possibly due to cultural reasons and to the down-to-earth nature of the majority of the French fabliaux, from which magic is excluded: the pastoral setting of the analogues is here replaced by the pedestrian dinner table. Another difference is that in the analogues the "magical" explanation comes as an inspired afterthought (inspired by a goddess in Chaucer's tale), whereas the priest's explanation in this tale is prepared for from his first words to the peasant, when he is still locked outside. His excuse for getting into the house and for getting the husband out is the same as his explanation for what he does to the wife after he has gotten in. It is interesting to note that the other old French version of the tale, Marie de France's fable *De Muliere et Proco Ejus* (Benson and Andersson, pp. 258–61), also lacks the supernatural climax and, like our fabliau, emphasizes the stupidity of the peasant. Indeed, in our fabliau the only wonders are the husband's foolishness and the priest's cleverness. Those two features are the only elements that the author, Guerin, wishes to emphasize. It is true that Guerin states that the peasant was confused, deceived, and "bewitched" (*encantés,* v. 80; the only miniscule residue of the magic in analogue tales), but he hastens to add in the next verse that this was done "Et par le prestre et par son sans." In our tale, therefore, magic has nothing to do with the deception. Since the wife, who plays a much more prominent role in the analogues, is here reduced to a mere silhouette, the placing of our fabliau in the first category, as Benson and Andersson do, should only be done with great reservations. The tales of Guerin and Marie de France obviously have different goals than do the other tales: they both emphasize, the former more humorously than the latter, the frailty of human intelligence and reasoning abilities, "qui par veüe . . . foleient" (which so often deceive by appearances) (Marie de France, v. 31).

Guerin, the author of our tale, appears to be a mediocre versifier. Line 52 is awkward: the subject of *ne le prise une bille* should be the closest nominative, namely *li prestres* (v. 50), but it is obviously *li vilains* (v. 48) who did not like being shut out. The line's position, between two other lines of which both subjects are the priest, is unfortunate. Guerin also has a large number of faulty octosyllables (vv. 23, 46, 65, 81, 82). The errors, judiciously corrected by MR, all involve only one syllable either way and might very well be due to a sloppy scribe.

There are five other fabliaux written by a certain Guerin (or Gari(n)s), including our *Berangier au lonc cul*. Benson and Andersson believe they are one and the same (p. 268) but give no reason for that identification. Bédier (*Les Fabliaux,* p. 480) and Nykrog (N, p. 325) are very hesitant because of lack of evidence. What little evidence there is should discourage the attribution of the six to one single Guerin: our fabliau demonstrates some definite Picard dialectical peculiarities (vv. 44, 66, 67, 71, 76) and a propensity for metathesis (vv. 49, 51, 60) while the others, with the exception of *De la Grue* (MR, 5:151, composed by a "Garins," v. 10), which also has a few Picard characteristics, are all from the Île-de-France (Bédier, *Les Fabliaux,* p. 480).[3] Our "Garin," contrary to the Guerin of *Berangier,* is extremely laconic: We know nothing about the household except that the peasant is not very bright and that he neglects his wife (v. 30). The fun lies simply in the deception by the priest of the husband, and everything else in the fabliau, even the characterization and possible motivations of the wife, is subservient to that confrontation.

The poem portrays the quick victory of cleverness over stupidity in a quick, jaunty style. Notice the numerous expressions indicating rapidity of movement: *esmeés* (v. 15), *plus n'i atent* (v. 20), *tous abrievés* (v. 21), *esraumment* (v. 32), *briefment* (v. 34), *sus sali* (v. 48), *maintenant* (v. 54), *en eslepas* (v. 68). For the deception to be effectively carried out, the peasant must not be allowed too much time to think; nor must the audience, lest the trick seem too preposterous to matter. The action must move fast. No sooner does the priest think to talk to the wife than he is off (vv. 14–15). He cannot wait (v. 20). From this moment he does not stop moving, manipulating, and talking. Only once, in the heat of his desire, does he pause to wonder why the peasant is not enjoying his wife's body. And only at the physical and artistic climax of the adventure does the author pause to explain that the priest is doing what women love more than anything (v. 58). There the smooth *m* sounds ("femme aimme": woman loves) contrast with the violence of the action, and the smooth euphemism, at the very point of lovemaking, contrasts with the blunt *foutre,* as it was used earlier to describe what was not happening (v. 38) and later to describe what the peasant thinks is not happening (v. 75). Guerin also runs quickly over background details that can be apprehended by the audience from allusions to situations in other stories. When the lady is said to love the priest, two lines (vv. 10, 11) suffice to remind us of countless other fabliau situations: since such a love affair is not out of the ordinary in those tales, Guerin does not need to explain the whys, whens, and hows of that relationship.

The tale ends with the status quo, the balance has not been violently tilted, the marriage remains intact. No tragic action has occurred, no particular sympathy has been aroused for one character or another; in spite of the reprehensible adulterous act, the audience can laugh without afterthoughts.

)u Prestre
.i abevete

chi aprés vous voel conter,[4]
e vous me volés escouter,
Jn flablel courtois et petit,[5]
i com Garis le conte et dit
)'un vilain qui ot femme prise
age, courtoise et bien aprise;
ìiele ert et de grant parenté.
/Iout le tenoit en grand certé[6]
.i vilains et bien le servoit,
:t [i]ce[le] le prestre amoit;[7]
/ers lui avoit tout son cuer mis.
.i prestres ert de li souspris[8]
'ant que un jour se pourpensa
Que à li parler en ira.
/ers le maison s'est esmeüs,
/Iais ains qu'il i fust parvenus,
'u li vilains, ce m'est avis,
Au digner o sa femme asis.
  Andoi furent tant seulement,
:t li prestres plus n'i atent,
Ains vint à l'uis tous abrievés,[9]
/Iais il estoit clos et fremés;
Quant il [i] vint, si s'aresta[10]
'res de l'uis et si esgarda.
'ar un pertruis garde et si voit
Que li vilains mengue et boit,
:t sa femme delés lui sist;
Au prestre volentiers desist
Quel vie ses maris li mainne[11]
Que nul deduit de femme n'aimme.
:t, quant il ot tout esgardé,
:sraumment un mot a sonné:
Que faites vous là, boine gent?"
.i vilains respondi briefment:
Par ma foi, sire, nous mengons;
/enés ens, si vous en dourons."
—"Mengiés, faites? Vous i mentés,
I m'est avis que vous foutés."[12]
—"Tasisiés, sire, nous faisons voir:
Nous mengons, ce pöés veoir."
)ist li prestres: "Je n'en dout rien,[13]
/ous foutéss, car je le voi bien,

The Priest
Who Peeked

If you will kindly listen well
To my next tale, I'd like to tell
A short and courtly fabliau
4 As Guerin has it. Long ago
There lived a peasant who had wed
A maiden courteous, well bred,
Wise, beautiful, of goodly birth.
8 He cherished her for all his worth
And did his best to keep her pleased.
The lady loved the parish priest,
Who was her only heart's desire.
12 The priest himself was so afire
With love for her that he decided
To tell his love and not to hide it.
So off he started, running hard.
16 As he came running through their yard,
The peasant and his wife were sitting
Together at the table eating.
  The priest neither called their name nor knocked.
20 He tried the door. The door was locked
And bolted tight. He looked around
And up and down until he found
A hole to spy through and was able
24 To see the peasant at the table,
Eating and drinking as she served.
The priest indignantly observed
The way the peasant led his life,
28 Taking no pleasure of his wife.
And when he'd had enough of spying,
He pounded at the doorway, crying,
"Hey there, good people! You inside!
32 What are you doing?" The man replied,
"Faith, Sir, we're eating. Why not come
In here to join us and have some?"
—"Eating? What a lie! I'm looking
36 Straight through this hole at you. You're fucking."
—"Hush!" said the peasant, "Believe me,
We're eating, Sir, as you can see."
—"If you are," said the priest, "I'll eat my hat.
40 You're fucking, Sir. I can see that!
Don't try to talk me out of it.
Why not let me go in and sit?

Bien me volés ore avuler.[14]		You stand out here and do the spying,
O moi venés cha fors ester,	44	And let me know if I've been lying
Et je m'en irai là seoir;		About the sight I'm looking at."
Lors porrés [bien] appercevoir[15]		
Se j'ai voir dit u j'ai menti."		
Li vilains tantost sus sali,	48	The peasant leapt from where he sat,
A l'uis vint, si le desfrema,		Unlocked the door and hurried out.
Et li prestres dedens entra,		The priest came in, turned about,
Si frema l'uis à le keville;[16]		Shut and latched and bolted the door.
Adont ne le prise une bille.[17]	52	However hard the peasant bore
Jusque la dame ne s'areste,		The sight of it, the parson sped
Maintenant le prent par le teste,		To the peasant's wife. He caught her head,
Si l'a desous lui enversee,		Tripped her up and laid her down.
La roube li a souslevee;	56	Up to her chest he pulled her gown
Si li a fait icele cose		And did of all good deeds the one
Que femme aimme sor toute cose.		That women everywhere want done.
Puis a tant feru et hurté		He bumped and battered with such force
Que cele ne pot contresté	60	The peasant's wife had no recourse
Que il fist che que il queroit.[18]		But let him get what he was seeking.
Et li vilains abeuvetoit		And there the other man was, peeking
A l'huis et vit tout en apert		At the little hole, through which he spied
Le cul sa femme descouvert	64	His lovely wife's exposed backside
Et le prestres [si] par desseure.[19]		And the priest, riding on top of her.
Et quist chou: "Se Dix vous sequeure,"		"May God Almighty help you, Sir,"
Fait li vilains, "est che à gas?"		The peasant called, "Is this a joke?"
Et li prestres en eslepas	68	The parson turned his head and spoke:
Respont: "Que vous en est avis?		"No, I'm not joking. What's the matter?
Ne veés vous? Je sui assis		Don't you see: I have your platter.
Pour mengier chi à ceste table."		I'm eating supper at your table."
—"Par le cuer Dieu, ce samble fable",	72	"Lord, this is like a dream or fable.
Dist li vilains, "ja nel creïse,		If I weren't hearing it from you,
S'anchois dire nel vous oïsce,[20]		I never would believe it true
Que vous ne foutissiés ma femme."[21]		That you aren't fucking with my wife."
—"Non fach, sire, taisiés; par m'ame,	76	"I'm not, Sir! Hush! As God's my life,
Austrestel sambloit ore à moi."		That's what I thought I saw you do."
Dist li vilains: "Bien vous en croi."		The peasant said, "I guess that's true."
Ensi fu li vilains gabés		That's how the peasant got confused,
Et decheüs et encantés	80	Bewitched, befuddled, and confused,
[Et] par le prestre et par son sans[22]		By the priest and by his own weak brain
Qu'il n'i ot paine ne [a]hans,		And didn't even feel the pain.
Et, pour ce que li uis fu tuis,		Because of the door, it still is said,
Dist on encor: Maint fol paist duis.[23]	84	"Many a fool by God is fed."
Ci define li fabliaus du prestre.		Here ends the fabliau of the priest.
Explicit: Amen.		The End: Amen.

5.

De Berangier au lonc cul (Bérangier of the Long Ass)

The *Siddhi-kur,* a Mogul collection of tales, contains a story similar to *Berangier,* based evidently on a Sanskrit tale. Felix Liebrecht and Theodor Benfey believed that the Mogul story was the ancestor of our fabliau.[1] Bédier (*Les Fabliaux,* pp. 151–52, 449) convincingly argued against the necessity for accepting the Sanskrit tale as the ultimate source of the French tale since they have in common only their organic traits.

Roy Pearcy offers a source for the two versions of our tale (*A,* anonymous, and *D,* our fabliau by Guerin) in Dagenet of Carlion, a character from the thirteenth-century prose romance *Lestoire de Merlin* who hacks up his own shield to impress his fellow knights with deeds he has not done.[2] Pearcy claims that some narrative *X,* which descends from the *Merlin* episode, but which adds the fabliau motif of marital conflict, is the common source for both Guerin's fabliau and the anonymous version. If this is so, the knight's motivation in *X* is closer to that of the anonymous version, where the knight is out to impress other people as well as his wife. In *Merlin,* there is no wife; in Guerin, there is no one to be impressed except the wife. Thus, Pearcy reasons, the class conflict in the story, which appears with the introduction of the wife, is a late development, and there is no reason to ascribe to Rychner's belief that the anonymous *Bérenger* is not for an aristocratic audience, since it is *not* a watering down of the contentious class consciousness of an earlier poem.[3]

This argument holds only if the narrative in *Merlin* is indeed later than the two fabliaux. Pearcy's claim that it is earlier rests on the fact that each of the fabliaux has a single element in common with the prose narrative that the other fabliau is lacking. In the case of Guerin's fabliau, this element is the oak tree to which the knight attaches his shield before battering it. In the anonymous poem, it is the fact that the knight claims to have killed *two* knights. The oak tree element is a very possible clue to direct influence between two narratives, but it is not proof. An oak tree is as good a place as any in a forest to hang a shield, and the possibility of independent selection of that particular kind of tree for that function cannot be ruled out. The fact that two knights are killed in *Merlin* and in the anonymous *Bérenger* is a much weaker connection. In *Merlin* it is not specifically two knights, but "one or two," an indefinite number of knights killed every time Dagenet goes out. In the anonymous *Bérenger, two* is only the first figure that we hear. The second time we hear of his exploits, the number has multiplied to four dead and three more fled. The third time, he has

> Delivree . . . toute la terre
> De cels qui me fesoient guerre. (MR, 4:65)

A kind of Falstaffian multiplication is going on. "Two knights defeated" is the first claim, because one victim is not enough to establish more than common valor. Three might be too much for his wife to accept. "Four plus three" removes this knight from the natural world and puts him in the context of the heroes of romance and chanson de geste, and it is this claim that the wife does doubt. The claim that he has delivered "all the earth / Of those who were making war on me," made after this coward has been forced to kiss his wife's behind, moves from the realm of romance to the realm of the grotesque. The choice of the number *two* as the first of the knight's false statistics is therefore dictated by rhetorical expedience more than by a need to imitate a source.

If either of these two weak connections (the oak tree in Guerin or the *two knights* in the anonymous poem) is coincidental, then there is no reason to assume that the Dagenet episode precedes either or both of the fabliaux, that there ever was a common source *X* to these poems, that either fabliau is not a direct source for the other, or that one of the fabliaux might not have been a source for the Dagenet author, who found the chivalric, but not the marital, aspects of the comedy useful in his book.

The value of Pearcy's work is that it offers a believable alternative to Rychner's also believable explanation. A third possibility is that Guerin might have heard the anonymous version and decided to improve the poem by giving the knight more definite motivation. A work is at least as likely to be improved by a better artist as corrupted by a worse. If this third possibility is correct, Guerin's creative process was about the same as Pearcy describes it with Guerin working from *X*. As Pearcy aptly points out, Rychner has committed "the fallacy of assuming that the history of redaction is likely to be a history of corruption and degradation" ("Relations," p. 177).

In the anonymous *Bérenger* (*A:* MR, 4:57), the aristocratic snobbery is missing. Also missing, as Rychner points out, is the sharply drawn motivation for the husband's false knight errantry, which in our poem is a direct reaction to his wife's contempt. However, without this version, it is possible that no one would have noticed the lack of motivation in the anonymous version. Playing at knight errantry, after all, sounds like fun, and post-Cervantian readers might easily assume that this peasant's son has steeped himself in enough chivalric literature to want to imitate it. Despite the contempt that Guerin pours on his protagonist, he does not altogether suppress the fun of riding out to the woods, banging on a shield, and coming back a hero. One good touch in the anonymous version that is lacking in Guerin's version occurs when the husband returns home after his humiliation by "Berangier." He has still not quite learned his lesson; he is already boasting of new chivalric triumphs—before his final humiliation by his wife.

In truth, version *A* is weaker: it lacks the opposition between classes presented by Guerin, his tight structuring of the narrative, and his artful descriptions of the husband's excursions. The motivations for the excursions of the husband in *A* are unclear, whereas Guerin shows him going into the woods to avenge the affront he feels is blemishing his lineage. His wife follows him because she wants to verify his prowess, the suspected lack of which is the source of the scorn she holds for him. Motivations in *D* are tight and well presented, and the class conflict gives the fabliau an extra dimension without which it would merely be a tale whose theme deals with the eternal question of domestic domination.

According to Rychner, *D* and *A* are not independent because too many connections exist between the two tales in the form of *rencontres textuelles* (textual similarities shared by two or several versions and used to establish a relationship among them). The value of these textual similarities has come under attack because they are relatively few and often inconclusive as proof of a close filiation among the tales.[4] Often the resemblances are essential (the descriptions of the part of the anatomy to be kissed by the husband, or his boast that he is a splendid knight); they are organic to the story and their coincidence is only natural. That these two tales are related is undeniable, but whether, on the basis of some apparent textual similarities, and because of its weaker motivation and structuring, version *A* is a fabliau adapted from *D* for the benefit of a bourgeois audience is conjectural, as we have already discussed.

Guerin (vv. 15–33) harangues against the mixing of classes through marriage. Nykrog (N, p. 123) argues that a bourgeois public would not have taken kindly to hearing this condemnation of mismarriages in which its own class was being maligned ("Se marient bas. . . ," v. 27). Guerin is, however, speaking of a particular member of the middle class, the usurer (v. 17), who is nobody's favorite, and our author is directing his wrath especially toward noblemen who bind themselves to such people for their money (v. 27, also vv. 32, 33). A lower-class public could have easily accepted the possibility of a coward knight: peasants knowledgeable of the importance of keeping the breeding stock as pure as possible could relate to Guerin's genetic conclusion (vv. 30–31) regarding ill-based unions that "Li chevalier mauvais et vill / Et coart issent de tel gent" (Evil and vile cowardly knights issue from such people). Nykrog (N, p. 123), however, contends that Guerin's explanation that the story occurred in Lombardy where the folk are none too brave (vv. 11, 12) is clearly intended to tactfully spare the feelings of the nobility and would have been wasted on a public other than noble. It had to be an aristocratic audience: "Les contes de *Bérangier* sont indubitablement faits pour les nobles, et pourtant ils comptent parmi les plus stupidement obscènes de tous les fabliaux" (The *Berangier* tales are undoubtedly destined for the nobles, yet they are among the most stupidly obscène of all the fabliaux).

If Nykrog's hypothesis is correct, it is interesting to note that an aristocratic audience could laugh at such obscene tales. This obscenity makes our fabliau a parody, a burlesque of the noblemen's genre par excellence, the chivalric romance. Benjamin Honeycutt (CH, pp. 90–91) points out that laughter in this fabliau is "provoked as a result of flagrant violations of the knight's preestablished proper image" (developed in other literary genres). To accept the tale as a parody of romances would enhance our appreciation of it, but it must be emphasized that the fabliau can be appreciated without knowing the object or intent of its parody. Thomas Cooke is correct in declaring that "fabliaux do make sense in themselves without a knowledge of courtly literature. Most important, however, is that they are not absolutely dependent upon their parody for their humor" (*Old French,* p. 145). Quite so. If parody had been Guerin's unique intention, he might have stopped the tale after the humiliating "misdirected kiss," which would have left the narrative on the jousting field, in the world of burlesqued chivalry. The episode of the final humiliation of the husband who is forced to witness, angrily put powerlessly, the romping of his wife with the perfunctorily sketched lover, throws the tale back to the favorite locus of the fabliaux, the bedroom, and allows it to reacquire that particular essence, which belongs to the fabliaux, not the courtly tale.

Guerin operates at three distinct emotional speeds: after the grave, sermonizing tone of the opening lines (vv. 1–35), he shifts to the hearty, parodic laughter of the middle of the tale (vv. 36–262), then finally he shifts into the grotesque in the last episode, which ends with the well-known scatological proverb expressing disdain for the husband and uniting this last humiliation to his earlier one by referring to the part of the anatomy common to both scenes. The shifts in moods show how well Guerin has command of his narrative art and of his main characters. The husband is presented at first as a mere object and has not come to life yet since he is still an abstract figure within Guerin's moral and sociological discourse. When he does come to life, he is ridiculous. His transformation from villein to knight reflects no inner change. He still prefers tarts and hot custards (v. 46) to noble deeds. He might have been a pitiable character were it not for his thoughtless and impetuous tongue. It is only after he has bragged about himself and about the superiority of his lineage and after he has himself armed and readied for combat that he suddenly realizes the predicament in which he has placed himself and that he now must find a way out (vv. 87–88). He has lived in a narrow world of custards and tarts, a very comfortable world with plenty of everything (vv. 16–20) where problems are solved by money. Money is the means by which he has acquired a beautiful wife and an honorable standing in life, and money will be the first thing he will think of to get himself out of trouble: when challenged by Bérangier, he will immediately offer to buy himself out of the combat (vv. 215, 216). Commenting on the cramped setting of the fabliaux, which lack the "sweep of the epic universe and the extensive travels of long journeys in the world of romance," Thomas Cooke notes that when the husband rides off on an adventure "he goes no farther than the woods behind his home, a geographical limitation that suggests a psychological one" (*Old French,* p. 197, see v. 91).

Believing more and more in his own fantasy and invigorated by the exercises in the woods, the husband kicks aside his wife, who has, in a very courtly manner and as a show of respect, come to hold the stirrup to help him get down from his horse. Not content with proving himself her equal, he reviles her lineage (v. 141). That insult seems to have been the last straw, "Dont el nel tenoit pas à saige" (which she did not think was a wise thing to do) (v. 142). Lacking moderation and intelligence, he does not know when to stop and continues his bragging until she has to be suspicious, especially since he has not bothered to back up his tales with an appropriately battered appearance (vv. 146–57). Nevertheless, he carries out his sorties with great conviction and plays his role with an energy that astounds even his wife when she follows him (vv. 193–94).

At the first sign of trouble, namely the jousting challenge issued by his disguised wife, he reverts to his true nature. She gives him a choice between two repulsive actions (v. 230): to fight or to kiss her behind. While he clearly would prefer to kiss her behind, he cannot bring himself to articulate that preference and simply declares in a delightful litotes that he will not choose the first option, to fight Bérangier (v. 234). This cowardly choice seems to deny him any further substance as a character. He becomes a completely grotesque figure in an episode where he ceases to have a life of his own and turns into a stock fabliau character, *le mari battu, cocu et content* (the beaten husband, cuckold but happy).

The lady, on the other hand, suffers as a character at the beginning and continues to be overshadowed and dominated until she grasps the initiative when she disguises herself as Bérangier. She has been patient for ten years (v. 42) all the while well aware of the unworthiness of her husband (vv. 48–50). Catching the brunt of his bragging and insults, she is at first confused, angry, and speechless (vv. 128, 132, 136, 137). Guerin's favorite term to describe her reactions to the astonishing and unexpected transformation in her husband is *esbahie* (amazed) (vv. 128, 194). At the encounter in the woods, the roles are reversed. Upon witnessing the truth, the banging on the shield, she is "Esbahie et esperdu" (v. 194), and Guerin sarcastically uses the same line, "Esbahiz fu et esperdu" (v. 208), to describe the husband's state of shock on discovering her presence. Clearly, the leadership and initiative have at that moment shifted to the lady.

Even when first convinced of her husband's deceit, she toys with him and teases him by requesting that he take a few men with him on the next expedition (vv. 170, 171). It is when she sees with her own eyes the absolute farce that is the basis of his boasts that she becomes a hard, driving force that not only will teach him a lesson but also will annihilate him in his position as leader in the household. In the woods, after the humiliation, when he pitiably asks his opponent's name, she replies in words reminiscent of his earlier boasts "De mes parax n'en est il nul" (nobody is my equal, v. 259; compare with v. 68). The same biting sarcasm was also evident when she, as Bérangier, gave him the unacceptable option, a scene she must have particularly enjoyed playing (see the insistence on the word *geu,* game, vv. 220, 231). Then, in rapid, choppy lines she completes the final humiliation (vv. 262–68). Her tone from there on is one of full confidence in her powers. She is "she who feared him little" (v. 270). She orders her lover to stay (v. 272) in spite of her husband's presence and loudly and authoritatively demands obedience from her husband (vv. 281–93).

The typical fabliau expression (v. 298) "Et cele fait sa volenté" (and she does her will) is often an euphemism for the sexual act. This line would end the tale in the well-known fabliau situation in which the husband is left holding the candle. This case, however, will become the norm. He will be left to stand by and watch while she enjoys herself for the rest of his life. She will do what she wants; she is now the leader of the household.

In any case, she earns Guerin's respect (v. 299): "Qui ne fu sote ne vilaine" (who was neither foolish nor common).

De Berangier au lon[c] cul		Bérangier of the Long Ass
Tant ai dit contes et fableax[5]		For two years I've been telling so
Que j'ai trouvé, viez et noveax!		Many fine tales and fabliaux
Ne finai passez sont dui an,		Which I've discovered or made up
Foi que ge doi à seint Johan,	4	That by St. John, it's time to stop
Ne cuit que g'en face mais nul		And tell no more except this last
Fors de Berangier au lonc cul.		Called Bérangier of the Long Ass,
N'avez vos mie oï encore,		The likes of which you haven't heard,
Mais, par mon chief, g'en dirai ore,	8	But if you'd like you'll hear it word
Ne cuit que ge targe mais gaire.		For word this minute, no delay.
Oiez que Guerins velt retraire!		Hear it good people! Guerin will say
Quë il avint en Lonbardie,[6]		What happened once in Lombardy,
Où la gent n'est gaires hardie,	12	Where men aren't known for bravery,
D'un chevalier qui ot pris feme,		To a knight errant who'd been wed

Ce m'est vis, une gentil dame,		To a fine lady, purely bred
Fille d'un riche chastelain.		And daughter to a landed earl.
Et cil estoit filz d'un vilein,	16	The young knight's father was a churl
D'un usurier riche et comblé,		Who'd gotten rich by usury.
Et assez avoit vin et blé;		His cellars were full; his grainery
Brebis et vaches, et deniers		Held all it could. He had cows and goats,
Ot à mines et à setiers.	20	Dollars, deniers, marks, sous, and groats.
Et li chastelains li devoit		And the earl was deeply in his debt
Tant que paier ne le pooit,		With nothing left to pay, except
Ainz dona à son filz sa fille.		To give the rich man's son his daughter.
Ainsi bons lignaiges aville,	24	That's how good blood thins down to water,
Et li chastelain et li conte		How counts and earls and all their race
Declinent tuit et vont à honte;		Decline and finish in disgrace.
Se marient bas por avoir,		If people wed to get out of debt,
Si en doivent grant honte avoit,	28	Disgrace is what they ought to get.
Et grant domaige si ont il.		The harm they do cannot be told:
Li chevalier mauvais et vill		From those who covet silver and gold
Et coart issent de tel gent,		More than nobility, a race
Qui covoitent or et argent	32	Of foolish, good-for-nothing, base
Plus qu'il ne font chevalerie:		And chickenhearted knights descends.
Ainsi est noblece perie.		Thus chivalry declines and ends.
Mais, à ce que ge ai apris,		But here's the gist of what I heard
De chief en chief com l'ai conquis,	36	From start to finish as it occurred.
Li chevaliers sanz demorer		Not wasting any time, the earl
Fist sa fille bien atorner,		Put wedding garments on the girl
Si la maria à vilain.		And married her to the young peasant,
Sil fist chevalier de sa mein,	40	Then dubbed him knight for a wedding present.
Si l'enmena, si com moi sanble.		The young man went home with the maid.
Plus de .X. ans furent ensanble		For more than ten years, there they stayed.
Li chevaliers amoit repos;		This new knight valued relaxation,
Il ne prisoit ne pris ne los,	44	Not valiant deeds or reputation:
Ne chevalerie .II. auz;		The code of chivalry could go hang.
Tartes amoit et flaons chauz,		He loved pie, custard, and meringue,
Et molt despisoit gent menue.		But the common people he despised.
Quant la dame s'est parceüe	48	Now when the lady realized
Que ses sires fu si mauvais,		How utterly her husband lacked
Ainz pire de li ne fu mais		Virtue, how he was in fact
Por armes prenre ne baillier,		Useless for tournaments or war
Mielz amast estrain empaillier	52	And liked to fill a straw bed more
Que manoier escu ne lance,		Than wield a lance or grasp a shield
Dont set ele bien sanz doutance		(From which it clearly was revealed
A ce qu'il estoit si parliers		To her that though the man was quite
Qu'il n'estoit mie chevaliers	56	A talker, he was not a knight
Atrais ne de gentil lignaige.		Worth talking of, but born and raised
Donc li ramentoit son lignaige[7]		A commoner), that's when she praised

Où tant a vaillanz chevaliers:
"As armes sont hardiz et fiers,
A sejorner n'amoient rien."
Li chevalier entendi bien
Qu'ele nel dit se por lui non.
"Dame," fait il, "g'ai bon renon.
N'avez nul si hardi parent
Que ge n'aie plus hardement
Et plus valor et plus pröece.
Ge sui chevalier sanz perece,
Le meillor trestot par ma mein!
Dame, vos le verroiz demain,
Se mes ennemis trover puis.[8]
Demain vorrai, que qu'il ennuit,
Qui m'ont desfié par envie,
Ja nus n'en portera la vie,
Ge les metrai à tel meschief
Qu'à chascun copperai le chief;
Tuit seront mort, que qu'il ennuit."
Ainsi le laissierent la nuit.
Et l'endemain à l'enjornant
Li chevaliers leva avant,
Si fist ses armes aporter
Et son cors richement armer,
Quar armes avoit il molt beles,
Trestotes fresches et noveles.[9]
Quant li chevaliers fu armez
Et desus son cheval montez,
Si se porpense qu'il fera,
Comment sa feme engignera
Qu'el le tiegne à bon chevalier.
En un bos molt grant et plenier
Qu'il voit molt pres de sa maison[10]
Le chevalier à esperon
S'en vait tot droit en la forest
Que onques n'i fist nul arrest.
Quant en mi le bois fu entrez,
Desoz un arbre est arrestez,
Son cheval aresne et ataiche.
Son escu à un arbre ataige,
A un chaine dedenz le bos.
Or escoutez que fist li sos!
Adonc a l'espee sachiee,
Qui estoit bien clere et forbie;
Mien escīent, plus de .C. cox,

The line of knights from whence she'd sprung,
60 Proud, valiant knights who'd never hung
Around the house from dawn to dark.
The husband knew that these remarks
Were aimed at him to put him down.
64 "Lady," he said, "I have renown.
I have more prowess than a dozen
Of your grandfathers. There's not a cousin
Or knight of any clan or class
68 Whose valor I do not surpass.
And I'm not lazy, take it from me.
Tomorrow morning you will see.
If I can find my foes tomorrow,
72 Who envy me and want to borrow
Trouble from me, I'll prove myself.
Not one will get off with his health.
These enemies who scorn and scoff
76 Will not scoff long with their heads off.
At dusk tomorrow they'll be dead."
For the time being, that's all he said.
The knight arose at dawn next day
80 And rang a bell for his valet,
Who brought his buckler, sword, and lance
And armed his lord with elegance.
(The arms and armor all were splendid,
84 Not being dirtied, scratched, or dented.)
When he was geared and rigged for battle
And had been hoisted to the saddle,
He wondered what he should do next
88 To give his wife a good pretext
For thinking him a noble knight.
He saw a forest to his right
A quarter mile from his front door.
92 Without delay he headed for
The forest at a gallop. There
He had to gasp a bit for air.
He rode on further through the wood
96 To where a giant oak tree stood
And cast its shade upon a field.
He tied his horse, unhooked his shield,
And hung it from the lowest bough.
100 Listen to what the fool did now.
He drew his sword, shiny and bright,
And beat the shield with all his might,
Battering like a maniac,

S'en part de l'escu à escox	104	Making it clatter at every whack,
Que tot l'a tranchié et malmis.		Till he had multilated it.
Puis avoit son fort espié pris,		He took his sturdy lance and hit
Sel brisa en .IIII. tronçons.		The branch. The lance splintered in thirds.
Enprés est montez es arçons	108	His work was finished, so he spurred
De la sele de son cheval,		His horse around the woods some more
Poignant s'en vait par mi un val		Before arriving home. He bore
Tot droitement à sa maison.		A third of his lance and but a fourth
De sa lance prent un tronçon,	112	Of the shield that he had carried forth.
Et de l'escu n'ot c'un quartier		He reined his horse. His wife came out
Qu'il avoit porté tot entier;		To ask what this was all about
Le cheval par la resne tint.		And hold his stirrup strap in place,
Et sa feme contre lui vint,	116	But the knight hit her in the face
Au descendre li tint l'estrier.		With the full weight of his big foot.
Li chevaliers la boute au pié.		"Stand back!" he cried, "Hands off the boot!
Qui ert molt forz de grant maniere:		Let it be known it isn't right
"Traiez vos t[ost]," fait il, "arriere;[11]	120	For you to touch so great a knight
Quar ce sachiez, n'est mie droiz		As I am—not with my renown,
Qu'à si bon chevalier touchoiz		For no such knight from Adam down
Com ge sui, ne si alosé;		Adorns the family tree you've vaunted.
Il n'a si preuz ne si osé	124	I'm not defeated, weak, or daunted.
En tot vostre lignaige au meins;		I am the flower of chivalry!"
Ne sui mie matez ne veins,		
Ainz ai los de chevalerie."		
La dame fu tote esbahie,	128	The lady didn't disagree.
Quant el vit l'escu despecié,		In consternation she beheld
Et frait le fust de son espié;		The shattered lance and broken shield,
Selonc ce qu'il li a fait croire,		Not knowing what to think or say
Ne set que dire ne que faire,[12]	132	About the evidence on display,
Que paor a qu'il ne la bate,[13]		Afraid he'd beat her to the ground,
Quar li chevaliers la menace		Because he threatened her and frowned.
Que vers lui n'aut ne que le touche.		She dared not touch, but stood somewhat
La dame tint close sa bouche;	136	Out of his reach. Her mouth stayed shut.
Onques puis mot ne respondi.		What shall I say? He used this game
Que vos diroie? Ainsi servi		To vilify her family name
Le chevalier de tel folie		And put her in her place, that is
Et tenoit la dame pour ville,	140	To set her value under his.
Et despisoit tot son lignaige,		
Dont el nel tenoit pas à saige.		
Un jor refu du bois venuz		Another time the knight came back
Li chevaliers, et ses escuz	144	With another shield all hewed and hacked
Refu tröez et despeciez,		And full of holes. His chain-mail shirt,
Mais il n'est navrez ne plaiez		However, was by no means hurt.
Ne ses heaumes n'a point de mal,		Neither was he—from head to foot
Ainz est tot sain du chief à val,	148	He wasn't bruised, he wasn't cut,

l n'est pas las ne recreüz.[14]
)e la dame n'est pas creüz
. ceste foiz li chevaliers,
Qui dit qu'il a morz ses guerriers
:t ses enemis confonduz
:t à force pris et penduz.
Bien est la dame aparceüe[15]
Que coarz est et par nature,
Que par sa borde la desoit;
:t dit que s'il vait autre foiz
:l bois, qu'ele ira aprés lui
:t si sara molt bien à qui
.i chevaliers se combatra
:t coment il se contendra.
Ainsinc la dame est porpenssee,
:t, quant ce vint la matinee,
.i chevaliers se fist armer
:t dit que il ira tuer
.III. chevaliers qui le menacent
:t qui grant ennui li porchacent;
Gaitant le vont, dont il se plaint.
.a dame li dit qu'il i maint
)e ses serjanz ou .III. ou .IIII.,
.i porra plus seür combatre.
Dame, ge n'i merrai nului;
Par moi lor movrai tel ennui
Que ja nus n'en estordra vis."
Atant s'est à la voie mis,
Par grant aïr el bois se fiert,
:t la dame unes armes quiert;
Com un chevalier s'est armee,
:t puis sor un cheval montee.
Cele qui n'a point de sejor[16]
S'en vait tost aprés son seignor,
Qui ja ert el bois enbatuz,
:t ses escuz ert ja pendux
A un chaine, et si le feroit,
A s'espee le detranchoit.
Si fait tel noise et tel martire
Qui l'oïst, il pooist bien dire
Ce sont .C. et mile deable;
Ne le tenez vos pas à fable:
Grant noise meine et grant tempeste!
:t la damë un pou s'areste;[17]
:t, quant a la chose veüe,

He wasn't even tired out.
That's when his wife began to doubt
Her husband's claim that he'd unhorsed
152 Defeated, subjugated, forced
To pay homage, put to flight
And hanged two dozen enemy knights
That day. The pretense was revealed
156 To her despite the battered shield.
She told herself if he went back
Into the woods again she'd track
Him down to learn what foes he sought
160 And what he did and how he fought.
These were the plans she settled on.

Early next day at break of dawn
164 Her husband armed and said he still
Had three more enemies to kill
Who kept on threatening and defying,
Causing disturbances and spying—
168 Crimes which the noble knight detested.
The lady tactfully suggested
He take some servants, three or four,
To make the victory more sure.
172 "Lady," he said, "I'll go alone.
I'll kill them so well on my own
That they'll be dead this very day."

176 At that he set out on his way.
As he rode forth with zeal and zest
Into the woods, she rose and dressed
Herself in armor like a knight,
180 Mounted a stallion, held on tight,
Did not delay, did not look back
And followed in her husband's track
Till there he was in the same field
184 And from the same oak tree his shield
Was hanging. He was beating it,
Banging and making it submit
To a cruel martyrdom and rigor.
188 A person standing near might figure
A hundred devils were there yelling
This isn't any joke I'm telling:
He raised a ruckus to the sky.
192 The lady reined her horse nearby.
At first the sight of this display

Esbahie est et esperdu,		Of folly filled her with dismay.
Et, quant ot assez escouté,		But when she'd heard her fill of noise,
Atant a le cheval hurté	196	She shouted with a mighty voice
Vers son mari, si li escrie:		And urged her charger straight ahead:
"Vassal, vassal, est ce folie		"Sir Knight! Sir Knight! What folly led
Que vos mon bois me decoupez?		You to come cutting up my manor?
Malvais sui, se vos m'eschapez,	200	Vain are my knighthood and my honor
Que ne soiez toz detranchiez!		If I don't slay you on this field.
Vostre escu porquoi laidangiez		Why are you picking on that shield?
Qui ne vos avoit riens meffait?		What has it ever done to you?
Molt avez hui meü fol plait.	204	You've bit off more than you can chew.
Mal dahait ore qui vos prise,		Fie on whoever says it's fit
Quant à lui avez guerre prise!"		For you to wage a war on it!"
Quant cil a le mot entendu,		And when he heard the speech she made,
Esbahiz fu et esperdu.	208	He was dumbfounded and dismayed.
La dame n'a pas conneüe,		(His wife he didn't recognize.)
Du poig li chiet l'espee nue,[18]		At once, great tears fell from his eyes
Et trestoz li sans li fo(o)ï.		And his damasked sword fell from his grasp.
"Sire," fait il, "por Dieu merci!	212	"Sir, for God's sake," he managed to gasp,
Se ge vos ai de riens meffait,		"Pity! If I've done any wrong,
Gel vos amenderai sanz plait;		I'll make it up. It won't take long.
A vostre gré molt volentiers		I'll give whatever you want: my pony,
Vos donrai avoir et deniers."	216	Lance—here's my shield, saddle, money."
La dame dit: "Se Diex me gart,		The lady said, "As God's my shield,
Vos parleroiz d'autre Bernart[19]		Before you've parted from this field,
Ainz que vos partoiz de cest leu,		You'll change your tune. Now stop this noise.
Quar ge vos partirai un geu:	220	I'm giving you an even choice.
Comment que vos jostez à moi		Either you joust with me right now
Et ge vos creant et ostroi,[20]		(If so, you have my solemn vow
Se vos cheez, ja n'i faudrez:		If you're unhorsed, you will not fail
Maintenant la teste perdrez	224	To lose your head—it won't avail
Que ja de vos n'aurai pitié.		To beg for pity or remorse),
Ou ge descendrai jus à pié,		Or let me get down from my horse
Si me prenrai à estuper.		And I'll bend over on the grass
Vos me venroiz el cul baisier,	228	And you can come and kiss my ass
Tres el milieu se vos volez.		Right in the middle, if you please.
Prenez ce que mielz amerez		Just take whichever one of these
De ce gieu; ice vos commant."		That suits your inclination. Choose!"
Et cil qui doute molt forment	232	He who was shaking in his shoes,
Et qui plains est de coardie,		Whose cowardliness no shame could oust,
Dit que il ne jostera mie:		Declared his purpose not to joust.
"Sire," fait il, "ge l'ai voé,[21]		"Good Sir," he said, "I've deeply sworn
Ne josterai à home né,	236	An oath to joust with no man born.
Mais descendez, si ne vos griet,		But be so kind as to dismount
Et ge ferai ce qu'il vos siet."		And I'll do what it is your want."

La dame ne volt respit querre,
Tot maintenant mist pié à terre. 240
Sa robe prist à sozlever,
Devant lui prist à estuper:
"Sire, metez ça vostre face!"
Et cil regarde la crevace; 244
Du cul et du con, li resanble
Que trestot li tenist ensanble.
A lui meïsme pense et dit
Que onques si lonc cul ne vit; 248
Dont l'a baisié de lorde pais[22]
A loi de coart hom mauvais
Molt pres du trou iluec endroit;
Bien l'a or mené à son droit. 252
Atant la dame est retornee.
Li chevaliers l'a apelee:
"Beax sire, vo non quar me dites,
Et puis vos en alez toz quites." 256
—"Vassax, mes nons n'ert ja celez!
Onc mais tel non ne fu trovez,
De me[s] parax n'en est il nul:
J'ai non Berangier au lonc cul, 260
Qui à toz les coarz fait honte."[23]
  Atant a afiné son conte,
Si s'en est en maison alee.
A l'einz qu'el pot s'est desarmee,[24] 264
Puis a mandé un chevalier[25]
Que ele amoit et tenoit chier;
Dedenz sa chanbre tot aese
L'enmaine, si l'acole et baise. 268
Atant ez le seignor qui vient
Du bois. Cele qui poi le crient[26]
Ne se daigna por lui movoir;
Son ami fait lez lui seoir. 272
Li chevaliers toz abosmez[27]
S'en est dedenz la chanbre entrez;
Quant vit la dame et son ami,
Sachiez point ne li abeli! 276
"Dame," fait il isnelement,
"Vos me servez vileinement
Qui home amenez çaienz.
Vos le comparrez par mes denz!" 280
—"Taisiez vos en, "fait el, "malvais!
Or gardez que n'en parlez mais,
Quar, se vos m'avïez desdite,

The lady didn't wait around,
But lightly leapt upon the ground,
Stood with her back before his nose,
Lifted her tunic, touched her toes,
And said, "Your face goes her, Sir Knight."
But when her crevice came in sight,
It seemed to him the ass and cunt
Were one long crack from back to front.
He thought it surely must have been
The longest ass he'd ever seen.
And there he placed the kiss of truce,
Which cowards customarily use,
Next to the hole. That's how she served
The knight what richly he deserved.
The lady stood, turned 'round and mounted.
Before she left, her husband shouted,
"Tell me your name, Sir, since you're leaving.
Then go in peace. We'll call it even."
—"Vassal, I'll tell it. I don't mind.
Another such name you will not find:
All other men are beneath my class.
I'm Bérangier of the Long Ass,
Who puts to shame the chickenhearted."
  The wife had finished what she'd started.
Now she returned home through the wood,
Disarmed herself as best she could
And sent for the knight she held above
All others in esteem and love.
She led him into the bed chamber,
Where with an eager kiss he claimed her.
And when the husband reached the house,
She, who did not fear her spouse,
Didn't even deign to stir.
But made her lover sit by her.
And when the knight came in the room,
Afflicted by despair and gloom,
The sight of a lover with his wife
Was not the high point of his life.
"Madam," he said, "it's plain to me
That you have done me injury,
Bringing a man to my abode.
You'll pay for this my girl. You've sowed
And you shall reap." —"Shut up, you bore!"
She said, "And don't say anymore,
Because one more insinuation

Foi que ge doi seint Esperite,	284	Against my name and reputation
Tantost de vos me clameroie		And by the saints I'll file a claim
Por le despit que g'en auroie;		Against you for my injured fame.
Si serez vos cous et jalox,		Go on, you cuckold! Go on, be jealous!"
—"A qui vos clamerïez vous	288	—"You'll file a claim? And who, pray tell us,
De moi, par la vostre proiere?"[28]		Will hear a claim that comes from you?"
—"A qui? A vostre chier compere,		—"Your fellow knight at arms is who,
Qui vos tint ja en son dangier,		Who subjugated you today,
Et c'est mesire Berangier	292	I mean my lord Sir Bérangier
Au lonc cul, qui vos fera honte."		Of the Long Ass, who will disgrace
Quant il oit que cele li conte,		You once again!" The husband's face
Molt en ot grant honte et grant ire.		Turned fiery red with rage and shame.
Onques puis ne l'osa desdire,	296	No more could he abuse her name.
Desconfit se sent et maté;		He felt checkmated. He felt ill.
Et cele fait sa volenté,		And from that day, she did her will:
Qui ne fu sote ne vilaine:		She was no common girl or fool.
A mol pastor chie lox laine.	300	*When the shepherd's weak, the wolf shits wool.*

6.

Du Vilain Asnier
(The Villager and His Two Asses)

Despite a somewhat contemptuous view of the villein in the fabliaux, the lower classes are not treated harshly. The peasant undergoes a dual treatment: if he is shrewd, he will be drawn sympathetically but he may also be repugnant because of his ugliness, brutality, or stupidity (N, p. 129). Some peasants are jovial and intelligent, to wit our farmer in *Brunain*. Others are repulsive because of the filth in which they are living (*De la Crote,* MR, 3:46; De *la Coille noire,* MR, 6:90). The unforgivable sin for a peasant is to try to elevate himself out of his social class; however, "there is plenty of affection, both sympathetic and patronizing, for members of the lower classes who are not socially threatening."[1] Nykrog points out that the peasant's major threat is when he attempts to marry his children into noble families (N, p. 129). *Berangier* stands as a good example of the merciless response to such social pretensions. Strongly opposed to interclass marriage, the fabliaux uphold the status quo. The famous three orders are immutable, established as they were by God himself:

Trois ordres establi de genz
Et fist el siecle demoranz,
Chevaliers, clers, et laborans.
Les chevaliers toz asena
As terres, et as clers dona
Les aumosne et les dimages;
Puis asena les laborages
As laboranz, por laborer. (MR, 3:175)

(Three orders of people He established and had them remain in society: knights, clergy, and peasants. He gave the lands to all the knights, and to the clergy the alms and tithes. Then he gave the peasants the farming work that there was to do.)

Class pretension implies a certain amount of pride, a vice that is condemned severely in the fabliaux: misplaced pride motivates Guerin's animosity against the peasant's son in *Berangier,* and pride is also the vice under attack in this fabliau (v. 50).

In hostile fabliaux, the peasant is often compared to animals. In *Du Prestre et du chevalier,* he is compared (MR, 2:49–50) to a wolf or a leopard, "Qui ne sevent entre gent estre" (Who are unable to abide with people). The author of our fabliau, noticeably less virulent in his portrayal of the peasantry, suggests a more domestic animal for comparison: the donkeys refuse to go forward (vv. 22–25) because, without orders, they are as much out of their element as the ass driver is in the street perfumed with spice. As Cooke notes, the usage of the identical adjective, *costumiers,* to describe the donkeys as well as the peasant (v. 2 and v. 24) is an indication of the "importance of habitual action in this story and suggests that the peasant and his donkeys share some important traits" (*Old French,* p. 49).

Our peasant is, of course, not described with the same bestial attributes given to peasants in some other fabliaux. He has no pretensions of his own; no indication is given that he has desired to break the established law of the three orders. As a matter of fact, no background or characterization is presented about him at all, but we are shown the inevitable consequences when he inadvertently crosses the forbidden border: in short, this tale, as LeClerc noticed very early, is closer to an allegory than a story.[2] Other fabliaux have shown, with a wealth of realistic details, how people who attempt to rise above their conditions, and who act arrogantly about it, are often punished. Ours is only a concretization, by a humorous exemplum, of a very clear lesson for the audience, and the barren action is totally dependent on and illustrative of the message. So, within the thinly sketched class confrontation between the *preudom* (v. 26: a member of the country middle class) and the ass driver, whom he calls, ironically, "preudom" (v. 31), the real *preudom,* by drawing the attention of the passers-by to the fainted ass driver (vv. 30–32), not only assumes that nobody really cares about the mishap that has just occurred, but also pretends that he will revive him not for humanitarian reasons but for the purpose of showing off his superior cleverness and of teaching a lesson to his fellow burghers. He is dealing with the peasant not as an individual but as a member of the lower classes. It is he who delivers the ass driver from his fate but at the same time pokes fun at him and at his likes who step out of their element. In actuality, the bourgeois who readily offers twenty sous for the revival of the peasant comes out as the most humanitarian of all, but only if one considers the fainting of the peasant as a serious accident. In this casual treatment lies the secret of the tale; the happenings are contrived, comical, and overshadowed by the overall meaning: when the peasant is revived, he promises that he will never go near "the avenue of spices" if he can avoid it (vv. 46, 47).

As Cooke points out (*Old French,* pp. 49, 155), the confrontation lies between the individual and society since what is harmful for society is actually remedial for the ass driver. His apparent personal triumph and our delight at seeing someone who is sick being made well again are actually deceptive: the cure for the ass driver and our expectation of his social integration are denied since "the personal triumph is not a social reconciliation but rather a social banishment" (p. 155). Precisely what brings him back to life is what irremediably separates society from him, and the definition of "nature" or "natural" differs from one class to another without hope of a communality. The author has tempered his sarcasm toward the lower classes by letting an important message not only permeate but actually take over his tale: he has successfully treated a serious conflict in a very light manner indeed.

However, true to the exemplum tradition from which fabliaux probably sprang, the tale concludes with a wider application than merely the pride of peasants. After all, we are born of the dirt from which God molded us, and to dirt we shall return. If we suffer from *orgueil,* we forget that basic element of our nature, and we are as out of place in our exalted opinion of ourselves as the dung carrier is in the spice-retailers' quarter.

The jongleur lets us have our laugh at the peasant's expense; then he points his finger at us: "Et por ce vos vueil ge monstrer" (v. 48). The inversion of *vos* and *ge* and the placement of *vos* immediately after *por ce* strongly underline the fact that he is now applying the moral to us, his audience.

Du Vilain Asnier

avint ja à Monpellier[3] [4]
'un vilein estoit costumier
e fiens chargier et amasser
.II. asnes terre fumer.
n jor ot ses asnes chargiez;
aintenant ne s'est atargiez,
l borc entra, ses asnes maine,
evant lui chaçoit à grant paine,
ouvent li estuet dire: "Hez!"
ant a fait que il est entrez
evant la rue as espiciers.
i vallet batent les mortiers;
t quant il les espices sent,
ui li donast .C. mars d'argent
e marchast il avant un pas,
inz chiet pasmez isnelepas
utresi com se il fust morz.
uec fu granz li desconforz
es genz qui dient: "Diex, merci!
ez de cest home qu'est morz ci!"
t ne sevent dire por quoi.
t li asne esturent tuit quoi
n mi la rue volentiers,
uar l'asne n'est pas costumiers
'aler se l'en nel semonoit.[5]
Un preudome qu'iluec estoit,
ui en la rue avoit esté,
ele part vient, s'a demandé
s genz que entor lui veoit:
"Seignor," fait il, "se nul voloit
A faire garir cest preudom,
Gel gariroie por du son."[6]
Maintenant li dit un borgois:
"Garissiez le tot demenois;
XX. sols avrez de mes deniers."
Et cil respont: "Molt volantiers!"
Donc prent la forche qu'il portoit,
A quoi il ses asnes chaçoit:
Du fien a pris une palee,
Si li [a] au nés aportee.[7]
Quant cil sent du fiens la flairor,
Et perdi des herbes l'odor,
Les elz oevre, s'est sus sailliz,

The Villager and His Two Asses

Once there lived in Montpellier
A villager who every day
Gathered dung which he wrapped in packs
4 And bore on two fine asses' backs.
One day, as soon as he had loaded
His asses with manure, he goaded
Them into town and drove them through
8 The narrow streets with much to do.
He shouted, "Git up! Move along,"
So loudly that before too long
They reached the spice retailers' quarter.
12 Apprentices were beating mortars
And when he smelled the fragrant spice,
A world of gold could not entice
The man to take one step ahead.
16 He fell, and lay there looking dead.
The people there then felt a great
Uneasiness at the man's fate
And murmured, "For the love of Pete,
20 Look at that dead man in our street."
Not one could tell another why.
The asses meanwhile were standing by
In the middle of the road, for such
24 Is an ass's nature. It won't budge
Unless it feels its master's goad.
A man who was standing up the road
Had seen the driver have his stroke.
28 He sauntered down the street and spoke
To those who stood around the man.
"Sirs," he said, "If no one can
Or wants to cure this man, I will
32 For what he gives me when he's well."
To this a citizen replied,
"Cure this man, and I'll provide
Twenty sous from my own pocket!"
36 —"Thanks," said the other man, "I'll take it."
At that he took the driver's fork,
Which was used to drive the beasts to work,
And forked some dung the size of a rose
40 And brought it to the stunned man's nose.
As soon as the flavor of manure
Had made the spice smell disappear,
He blinked his eyes and up he sprang.

Et dist que il est toz gariz.
Molt en est liez et joie en a,
Et dit par iluec ne vendra
Jamais, se aillors puet passer.
Et por ce vos vueil ge monstrer
Que cil fait ne sens ne mesure
Qui d'orgueil se desennature:
Ne se doit nus desnaturer.[8]

44 "I'm fit as a fiddle now," he sang.
Happy now and overjoyed,
He made a vow that he'd avoid
Forever the avenue of spices.
48 The moral's clear, and my advice is:
Though you be humble as manure,
Stick to your nature. Pride is sure
To make you sick, but Nature cures.

7.

Des Tresces (The Tresses)

In a penetrating analysis (*Les Fabiaux,* chapter 6) of this fabliau, Joseph Bédier deals a serious blow to the Orientalist theory and concludes that the tale of the lady who, caught red-handed, succeeds in refuting the evidence and in convincing her husband he has dreamed has appeared under multiple forms. Granting that any time an oral tale travels from one country to another it loses some elements while acquiring others, becoming a new tale so to speak, Bédier shows that the few links that the fabliau *Des Tresces* still has with the Orient are too fragile to establish a filiation. Indeed, the cut tresses are a primitive Germanic trait: according to Tacitus, adulterous women were chased from the marital domicile with their heads shaved. There are three Germanic versions of the tale, and another variant is Neifile's Tale from the seventh day in Boccaccio's *Decameron*. In French, there exists, in addition to our fabliau, another version, *De la Dame qui fist entendant son mari qu'il sonjoit* (MR, 5:132), different enough to allow a comparative study which, contrary to Rychner's opinion, will show *Des Tresces* to be superior in motivation and in composition.[1]

In *De la Dame* (*B*), motivations for actions are not as pronounced as in *Des Tresces* (*D*): characters' actions in the first tale are often the results of coincidences, while in the second tale the lady is much more in control of the events. The husband in *B* dreams that he is trying to have intercourse with a she-ass. Thus when faced with the substituted mule's tail he is ready to admit that he has been seeing things. That dream lessens the involvement of the lady, whose ingenuity *D* emphasizes and uses as the vehicle for all actions. The husband's repeated awakenings are also weakly motivated in *B:* he first wakes naturally and finds a naked man asleep in bed with him and his wife. Why does he wake up? Is it morning as is implied in the indication that he was accustomed to wake up first (*B,* vv. 33, 34)? If it is morning, why does he go back to sleep (*B,* 128)? The second awakening is provoked by the friend who, substituting for the lady, crawls into his bed. Yet he had not awakened while his wife and her lover were romping beside him earlier or when the lady was rummaging around the room and under his pillow, trying to find her friend's tresses. The third awakening is caused by that strange nightmare in which the she-ass, unimpressed by his advances, kicks him in the ear. What a difference from *D!* In that version, the lover mistakenly grabs the husband's elbow in the dark, waking him up. Later in the night he is twice awakened by the annoying laments of the friend, acting on the instructions of the lady. Lastly, he awakens at dawn. Clearly, *D* is much more careful in presenting believable situations.

The lover in *B* knows the house well (v. 18) and enters it at night in order to be with his mistress, but we are never told why he takes such a risk and why he is so careless during this dangerous incursion as to allow himself to fall asleep! In spite of the fact that *B*'s husband knows he has caught his wife's lover (vv. 39, 40), he still lets her hold him by the hair while he goes out for light, threatening her with death if she lets him go (v. 71). The events in our fabliau are much more plausible: the lover's night excursion is prompted by a mock-courtly request, itself provoked by the lovers' annoyance at having their rendezvous interrupted by the husband's inopportune return. The lover is not familiar with the house (vv. 83, 84) and accidentally wakes the husband. The husband, thinking he has caught a thief (v. 107), lets his wife, at her suggestion, help hold him only because she claims to be unable to find her way in the dark. Although at this point she is still not compromised, she has to free her lover because she is afraid for his life (vv. 108, 109), knowing that this action will reveal the truth of the whole situation to her husband and place her in a dangerous predicament. Thus the author of *B* has minimized the courage of the lady by having the husband immediately recognize the intruder as her lover, whereas in *D* the incident is presented as the spark that sets off the other actions.

During the argument that follows the lady's liberation of her lover, *B* simply has the wife walk out and rejoin her lover. She bribes a friend to take her place so that her husband will not notice her absence (vv. 136–38). Rychner (*Contribution,* 1:95) praises *B* for such excellent motivation but does not take into account the inconsistencies that follow. Certainly the husband must know she is gone: she walked out in front of him ("A cest mot . . . " v. 122). He would also have had to notice her absence when he returned to bed, for when the lady's friend crawls in bed, he marvels at her effrontery for having come back (v. 161). The husband therefore knows she was gone, and her ploy of replacing herself so he won't find out is either very confusing or only meant to convince her friend to go along with her scheme. The lady in *Des Tresces,* on the other hand, is kicked out of the house by her enraged husband. Seizing this opportunity to be with her lover without fear of interruption (vv. 176, 177) but still faced with the prospect of having to eventually confront her angry husband, she devises a marvelous trick (*engig:* vv. 160, 161). She prevails upon her friend (vv. 163, 164), who resembles her greatly, to take her place by her husband, obviously not knowing that the husband is going to cut her hair, as Rychner would have us believe, but hoping that the husband will exhaust his anger on her friend.[2] The *engig* is cruel but believable.

The lady's friend in *De la Dame* is beaten and has her hair cut off in one incident. In our fabliau, following her lady's instructions, the friend loudly laments and is beaten and raked by the spurs. Because of her continuing laments, this time genuine, the husband, awakened again, brandishes a knife, to the terror of the lady (v. 224) who fears for her life, and cuts her tresses. The breaking of that action into two incidents shows rhythmically the mounting anger of the husband (vv. 197–201): the choppy tempo of lines 222–29, emphasized by the jerky motion of the repetitions (*Maintenant . . . Maintenant; Si . . . Si . . .*), marks well his lunatic furor. The increasingly savage and needlessly cruel behavior of the husband probably will help convince him that his anger was so out of control that he indeed might have committed the foolish act of cutting the tail of his favorite horse. It also predisposes the audience to accept the ultimate punishment of the husband. Clearly, this episode, as well as the others, shows the superiority of *D* over *B* and already presents us with a lady quite skillful in handling her problem.

She is quite a good actress: *faire semblant* (to act as if) seems to be the author's favorite expression to describe her action (vv. 60, 127), and she uses the same expression in instructing her friend on how to act with her husband (v. 170). Her answer to her husband's amazement at finding her back in bed in the morning is disarming in simplicity and candor (vv. 285–88). She carefully and deliberately, part by part, shows her unblemished body to her incredulous husband: each part reinforcing her point and destroying his (vv. 324–31). At the beginning of the confrontation (vv. 286 ff.) the husband is absolutely sure of what he has seen (*pris prouvé,* v. 291), in other words, of the presence of the lover (whom he paradoxically never actually "saw" in the dark, but whose presence he only deduced, by a mental operation, once the light was brought in).[3] To this truth he swears by the Divinity (vv. 292, 293, 299), oaths that the lady will similarly use (vv. 300, 304, 308) all the while already implanting in his mind the likelihood that he has had visions (vv. 310, 311) and regretting the earlier, healthier times when he was more reasonable (v. 307: *Bien ensaigniez*). She is therefore already preparing her final advice to him: to go on a pilgrimage in order to ask God to restore his sight and to return him to normal behavior. She later cleverly mixes her version of his aberration (his "vision" is a sign from God, and His promises of restoration) with his version (Satan: *Malfé,* v. 339; *merveille,* v. 318), by insisting on the term *folie* (vv. 365–69). In a veritable verbal delirium intended to confuse him, she has him too frightened to go against her advice. The scheme works: he crosses himself and believes that he has been enchanted (v. 396), finally persuaded of the danger of his predicament (v. 411).

The same care noticed in the preparation and elaboration of the character of the lady is also evident in the portrayals of the husband and the lover. The description of the valorous knight (vv. 1–15), which Rychner, for some reason, deemed needless and harmful to the tale (*Contribution,* 1:97), is an example of such care. Honeycutt judiciously observes that the complimentary description of the knight is an ironical treatment of his character (CH, pp. 88, 89): we should expect his triumph over wife and lover but are skillfully drawn away from such conclusions by his demented behavior during that ill-fated night where, having completely lost control of his senses and dressed only in his nightshirt, he rides the lady's friend and rakes her with his spurs. The earlier description, in contrast to this aberration, is, according to Rychner (*Contribution,* 1:97), more than "une amplification courtoise, dont il est bien difficile de saisir l'intention" (A courtly amplification whose intention is very difficult to grasp). The use of the spurs, symbolic of the chivalric worth of this man, contrasts shamefully with the glory he is used to winning for himself, wearing them into battle.[4] As to the lover, the praise given him because he distrusts procuresses like Richeut and prefers dealing with more honorable persons (v. 38) is not only, according to Cooke (*Old French,* p. 29), slightly ironic, since he sneaks recklessly into the house to be with her, but is also intended to render a favorable impression "needed for the audience to respond sympathetically when the lover escapes after the husband catches him."

The parodic nature of some scenes, already evident in those two descriptions, is also noticeable in the mock-courtly tone of the beginning of the tale. The romantic rendezvous at the lover's sister's, prompted by the noble desire to avoid any blemish on the lady (v. 38), are euphemistically and sensitively articulated as "à s'amie . . . parler" (v. 40). The "don contraignant" (blank request) test of courage that medieval noble ladies often require of knights is here reversed and requested by the lover who wishes to accomplish the perilous feat of sleeping with the lady in the very presence of her husband (vv. 48, 49).

And what does this fine lad who had "mastered fin'amor" do (v. 55)? He enters her house like a thief (v. 81), "à senestre" (from the left).

The preparation of the author is also evident in the care he shows for the explanatory, realistic details. Few fableors go to that much trouble to make their stories believable. The author invents a sister to the knight and a cousin to the lady to act as accomplices. (After all, the latter is said to look like her.) The author is careful to explain several items: the lover's accidental waking of the husband is due to his unfamiliarity with the house; the fight between the lover and the husband is uninterrupted because the help live far enough away that they can't hear the tumult (vv. 90, 91); the constant going back to sleep by the husband, so necessary to all the substitutions, is accounted for by his exhaustion (vv. 248, 249), and, finally, the lady reassures her friend that she will be reimbursed for her sufferings and that she will retrieve the tresses for her and pin them back to her hair so adroitly that nobody will ever notice the repair (vv. 237–43).

The author of our fabliau was technically talented: to this Rychner agreees, noting that over half of the total rhymes are rich (one third are either *léonines* or *équivoques*), and that only five are faulty.[5] He must have been concerned with the complexity of this tale of multiple substitutions because he felt obliged to intervene often (vv. 64, 67, 266, 397, and so on). He obviously wished to remain in total control of his tale, balancing and contrasting its episodes. He contrasts, albeit cruelly, the two ladies: the one who has been tricked is ridden by the husband, the other, who engineered the deception, by the lover (vv. 202–4). In the three episodes forming this tale, the lady contrives a complex deception against her husband but only confronts him directly in the last episode, when all items for the deception are in place. The fabliau itself should have been entitled "The Substitutions," for at the climaxes of all three episodes the lady provides a replacement for the object under contention: the mule for her lover, her friend for herself, and the mule's tail for her friend's hair. Like a magician, she substitutes everything so that her victim is totally under her power, confused and incapable of discerning between illusion and reality. Like a magician also, the author has made us react sympathetically to a lady who is basically cunning, manipulative, ruthless, and adulterous. Indeed, the whole blame is left to rest on her husband, to whom shame is brought deservedly, "droite achoison" (v. 432).

Des Tresces		The Tresses
Jadis avint c'uns chevaliers,[6]		Once there was a noble knight
Preuz et cortois et beax parliers,		Whose courtly speech, chivalric might
Ert saiges et bien entechiez:		And wisdom made him celebrated.
S'ert si en pröesce affichiez	4	In arms he was so dedicated
C'onques de riens ne se volt faindre		To prowess that success forsook
En place où il pooist ateindre,		Him never in what he undertook.
Et partot si bien le faisoit		People he met on any quest

Et à toz sis erres plaisoit	8	Admired him and were impressed
Tant qu'il fu de si grant renom,		So much that he gained such esteem,
Qu'en ne parloit se de lui non.		People spoke of none but him.
Et s'en li ot sen et pröesce.		While he was wise and valorous,
Il ert de si haute largece,	12	He also was magnanimous
Quant il avoit le heaume osté:		When he had laid aside his shield:
Preuz ert au champ et à l'osté.		A good man on or off the field.
Il ot feme de grant paraige,		His wife, who was of noble birth,
Qui avoit mis tot son coraige	16	Loved more than anyone on earth
A un chevaliers du païs.		A knight who lived some five miles down
N'ert pas de la vile naïs,		The highway, in another town.
Ainz avoit un autre recet		Her lover visited rarely though,
Pres de .VI. liues ou de .VII.;	20	Lest people see him come and go.
Il n'i osoit venir souvent		Whisperings of their affair
Qu'en ne s'alast apercevant.		Had reached him, so he didn't dare
Bien ot parler de son affaire		Confide with anyone in town.
Ne il n'en ose noise faire	24	He said it soiled a knight's renown
A nului qui soit de sa vile,		And that his love would be demeaned
Et di que chevaliers s'aville		To trust Richeut, the go-between.
Et de ses amors ne li chaut,		He didn't want to court disaster.
Qui se fie et croit en Richaut:[7]	28	Besides, he had a clever sister
Por ce n'en volt faire mesaige.		Who helped his cause by being chosen
Mais une suer qu'il ot molt sage		In marriage to the lady's cousin.
Fait tant c'un vallet l'ot à feme;		The sister and the cousin dwelt
Cousin estoit à cele dame	32	In that same town. The young man felt
Qui en la vile ot son estaige,		Their house a proper place to meet,
Et cil baa à l'aventaige		Safe, convenient, and discreet,
De son couvent, se il puet estre,		Free from all scandal whatsoever,
Que ja nus ne saiche lor estre	36	To come and go and talk together.
Qui puist tesmoigner ne savoir,		
Que [molt] mielz valt sanz blasme avoir		
Chiés sa seror venir, aler,		
Et à s'amie iluec parler.	40	
Un jor ot mandee s'amie		He summoned his lady there one day,
Chiés sa suer; ne demora mie		But when she came, she couldn't stay,
Que il oïrent tex noveles		Because the lady hadn't been
Qui ne li furent gaires beles,	44	There long before bad news came in:
Quar l'en dit que li sires vient.		Her husband would be coming home
La dame voit qu'il l'en covient		The lady knew the time had come
Aler, si se commande à Dé.		To leave. They said good-bye and kissed.
Tantost li a cil demandé	48	But first he had a small request,
Un don, mais ne sait quel i fu,		Though what it was, he wouldn't tell,
Cele ne l'en fist onc refu,[8]		And since she loved him very well,
La dame qui molt l'avoit chier.		She promised him that she'd comply.
Lors dit qu'il se voloit couchier	52	And now he said he wished to lie

O son seignor et ovuec lui:
"Ja ne remaindra por nului,"
Fist cil qui fin amor mestroie.[9]
Et la dame le li ostroie,
Quar tant ne se set entremetre,
Qu'el i puisse autre conseil metre.
Lors s'en est à l'ostel venue,
Et fait senblant de la venue
Son seigneur et que bel l'en soit,
Mais à autre chose penssoit
Li cuers, qui molt estoit plains d'ire.
Ne vueil des autres choses dire,
Mais assez mengierent et burent,
Et se couchierent quant il durent.
Mais d'une chose me remembre,
Que li sires ot lez sa chanbre
Fait [faire] une petite estable
Qui ert à son cheval metable,
Qui estoit à son chevauchier.
Il avoit son cheval molt chier,
Quar .XL. livres valoit,
Mais des autres ne li chaloit
S'il fussent bien ou malement,
Fors d'une mule seulement.
Et quant ce vint endroit prinsome,
Qui tuit cou[c]hié erent si home,
Que reposer la gent covint,
Li amis à la dame vint
Par devers la chambre à senestre,
Et entre par une fenestre;
Et vint leanz, mais ne set mie
De quel part se gisoit s'amie.
Belement oreille et escoute,
Lor taste et prent par mi le coute
Le seignor qui ne dormoit pas,
Et li sires eneslepas,
Si le ra saisi par le poing.
En une autre maison bien loig[10]
Se gisoient li escuier:
Molt pooist li sires huschier
Ainz que d'ax eüst mule aïe!
Lors i [a] fait une envaïe
A celui que par le poing tient;
Et cil qui bien se recontient,
Se deffent de sa force tote:

With her in bed, beside her lord.
"Nothing can keep me out," he swore,
Ruled by his courtly love ideals.
56 To his demands she had to yield,
For there was nothing else to say
Except to let him have his way.
She hurried home and prepared the house
60 For the arrival of her spouse,
Pretending pleasure at his coming
While all the while her heart was drumming
From anger rather than from bliss.
64 I won't speak any more of this
Except to say they drank and ate
And went to sleep before too late.
But one fact shouldn't be neglected:
68 There was a stable which connected
To where the couple went to sleep.
Her lord had had it built to keep
The horse he rode the oftenest
72 And loved the most, for he assessed
Its value right at forty pounds.
His other beasts and hawks and hounds,
Except one mule, he could have spared,
76 Lost, sick, or dead, and never cared.
Now when the chimes struck nine o'clock
And all the people there were locked
In sleep, for people need their rest,
80 The lover came upon his quest
To find the lady where she slept.
Beneath the windowsill he crept
And clambered in, but had no way
84 Of knowing where the lady lay.
He paused and listened; then he latched
Onto the elbow which attached
To the husband, who was not asleep.
88 The lover had no time to leap.
The husband seized him by the fist.
Far off, in another house than this,
The husband's men were sleeping soundly.
92 However long, however loudly
He called, they wouldn't come that night.
He threw himself with all his might
Upon the man whose fist he caught.
96 The lover held his own and fought
With hand and foot as best he could.

Li uns tire, li autres boute,
Tant qu'il se sont bien esprouvé.
Lors se tint cil por fol prouvé
Qui la folie ot commenciee.
A l'uis de la mareschauciee
Se sont ambedui aresté.
Pres d'iluec out lonc tens esté[11]
Une cuve trestote enverse,
Et li sires dedenz enverse
Celui qu'il tient por robeor.
Molt ot la dame grant poor
De son ami plus que de lui,
Que li sires tint bien celui,
Et tant l'a batu comme toile.
Lors a dit: "Alumez chandoile!"
A la damë, et que tost queure.[12]
—"Beax sire, se Diex me sequeure,
Onques ne soi aler de nuiz:
Trop me seroit ja granz enuiz
A trouver l'uis de la cuisine!
Mais or me faites la saisine
Du larron, gel tenrai molt bien."
—"Ne vorroie por nule rien,
Si m'aïst Diex, qu'il eschapast:
Jamais ne prenra un repast[13]
Quant il eschapera de ci."
—"Sire," fait ele," ja merci[14]
N'en aiez quant il est repris."
Lors l'a la dame au cheveus pris,
Et fait semblant que bien le tiegne,
Mais li sires, comment qu'il preigne,
Por du feu se met à la voie.
[Et] maintenant la dame envoie[15]
Son ami à grant aleüre,
Pui saut et deslie la mure;
Si l'a par les oreilles prise,
Et por estre mielz entreprise,
Li boute en la cuve la teste.
Et li sires gaire n'arreste,
Ainz prent du fu et prent s'espee,
Et dit que ja avra coupee
La teste cil que pris avoit.
Mais quant la mule tenir voit
A la dame, si s'esbahist,
Et dist: "Dame, se Diex m'aïst,

One of them pushed. The other pulled
Till both of them were tired out.
100 What a fool he'd been, the lover thought,
To get himself in such a fix.
They rested from their knocks and kicks
Inside the stable, where there stood
104 Up end a tub made out of wood.
The husband tilted it and stuck
Under it the man he took
To be an ordinary thief.
108 The lady ached from fear and grief,
Not for her lord's—for her lover's sake,
Seeing her husband hold and shake
The tub and beat the man like flax.
112 "Go for a candle! Get an ax,
And make it quick," he told his wife,
But she replied, "Not on your life.
Why God forbid I go back there
116 As dark as it is! I wouldn't dare
I'd never find the kitchen door.
Give him to me, Lord. I'll make sure
This thief stays put. You'll never see
120 This rascal get away from me.
He can't get out of here. He's mine."
—"When he gets out, he won't go dine,"
The husband said, "not in this life."
124 —"Yes, sir, that's right," replied his wife,
"Don't pity that intruder there."
She grasped her lover by the hair
And seemed to hold it hard and tight.
128 Like it or like it not, the knight
Had to go groping through the house.
The lady let her lover loose
Before her lord got through the hall.
132 The mule she guided from its stall
And grabbed it fiercely by the ears,
And just to make the scene appear
More credible, she shoved its head
136 Under the tub. Her husband sped
With fire and sword through the kitchen door.
"I'll have my captive's head!" he swore.
"His neck won't hold when I have struck it!"
140 But when he saw the mule and bucket
And wife holding on, he was dumbfounded.
"I swear to God," he cried, "Confound it,

Bien estoie musarz et fox
Quant ge crui onques vostre lox.
Assez ai plus que vos mespris!
Quant ge vostre lecheor pris,
Gel deüsse tenir de pres!
Or vos covient aler aprés.
Bien sai qu'il vos en est à pou,
Mais par la foi que doi saint Pou,
Ne gerroiz mais lez mon costé."
Lors l'a mise hors de l'osté.
Ainsi cil sa feme en envoie;
Et cele trespasse la voie,
Si s'en entre chiés son cousin
Que el avoit pres à voisin,
Li vallez qui ot pris (l)à feme[16]
La suer son ami, et la dame
A leanz son ami trouvé,
Un tel engig avoit trové[17]
Jamés n'orroiz parler de tel!
Quar el s'en voit à un ostel
Où une borgoise menoit,
Qui en beauté la resanbloit.
Fait la lever, tant la pria,
Que la dame li ostroia
A faire quanqu'ele vorroit:
"Alez donc," fait ele, "orendroit
En ma chanbre sanz demorer,
Et faites senblant de plorer
Androit le chavez mon seignor.
Ne pöez moi faire graignor
Servise qui cestui vausist."
Cele s'en vait et puis s'assist
Dedenz la chambre endroit la couche.
La dame o son ami se couche
Qui longuement i fist son vueil.[18]
Et cele commence son duel,
Et se claime lasse, chaitive,
Et dit que "ja longues ne vive,
Ne je ne past ceste semaine
Qui à tel honte me demaine."
Le sires s'i torne et retorne
Et fait pesante chiere et morne,
Mais il ne set tant retorner
Que à dormir puisse assener.
Lors est levez par maltalent,

I was a fool and a sucker, too,
144 Ever to take advice from you!
My fill of you is what I've had.
I'm worse than you, though. I was mad
To leave your lover when I had him.
148 You'd better follow him now, Madam.
It shouldn't give you cause for weeping,
But by St. Paul, you won't be sleeping
With me beside you anymore."
152 At that he opened wide the door,
And out into the dark and cold
He thrust his wife. The lady strolled
To where her cousin and his spouse,
156 Her lover's sister, had their house
And met her love. By this time she
Had figured out a strategy
Whose cleverness was more than human.
160 She went to the house of a bourgeois woman,
A woman who could almost match her
In beauty, elegance, and stature,
And woke and rousted her from bed
164 And pleaded till the woman said
She'd help her in this time of need.
"Then go at once," she said, "God speed.
And do not stop until you've come
168 Into my house and to my room
To where my husband lies asleep.
Fall upon your knees and weep
As loud as you are able to.
172 No greater service you can do
Than this which you have promised me."
The woman went immediately
And knelt beside the husband's cover.
176 (The lady lay beside her lover,
Who spent the night doing all she wanted.)
The other woman loud lamented
Her wretched fate, Oh God, how wrong
180 She was! She never would prolong
Her life beyond this night, when trust,
Love, faith, and honor all were lost.
The lady's husband tossed and turned,
184 Groaned and ground his teeth and burned,
But though he tossed and counted sheep,
He couldn't toss himself to sleep.
Out of the bed the husband surged.

Onques mais n'ot si grant talent	188	Never had he greater urge
De feme laidir et debatre		To beat a woman than to beat
Com il avoit de cele batre.		The one who knelt before his feet.
Demanois ses esperons chauce,		On each bare foot he strapped a spur,
Mais n'i chauça soler ne chauce,	192	And nothing else, confronting her
Ne ne vest riens fors sa chemise.		Naked but for the shirt he wore.
Lors vient à cele, si l'a mise		He came and seized her hair and bore
Contre terre par les cheveus.		Her body down upon the ground.
El chief li a ses doiz envox,	196	About her head his fingers wound.
Lors tire et fiert et boute et saiche,		He yanked and jerked and pushed and pulled
Qu'à paine ses mains en arrache,		Until his hands could hardly hold.
Et fiert des esperons granz cox,		A hundred lines of blood he drew
Qu'il en fait en plus de .C. leus	200	Across her flanks and belly too,
Le sanc saillir par mi la cengle.		Striking and raking with his spurs.
Molt pot ore la dame atendre		(The care she got from him was worse
De son ami graignor soulaz[19]		Than what the lady was receiving
Que cele qui prise est as laz.	204	From her lover on that evening.)
Ainsi la damoisele bat		He beat, and kept on beating her,
Le chevalier et se debat		And the more he beat, and angrier
Et de parole la laidist;		He got, and heaped her with abuse.
Et quant s'ire li refroidist,	208	And when his anger was diffused,
Si s'en vait couchier en son lit.		He got back into bed again.
Mais molt i ot poi de delit,		But little joy it gave him then:
Qu'el commence grant duel à faire:		Again the weeping had begun.
Molt se repent de cest affaire,	212	Much she repented what she'd done.
Et si fait chiere mate et morne,		The woman wailed and sniffled and gulped,
Quar il l'avoit batue à orne.		For he had beaten her to a pulp.
Ce ne torne à geu n'[ë] à ris.		Why should she laugh? This whole affair
Por ce que el avoit empris.	216	Hadn't been much fun for her.
Si crie plus haut que ne sielt,		She cried out louder than her part
Quar de ses plaies molt se dielt.		Required because she really hurt.
Mais li sires pas ne s'en rit,		And neither was the knight amused
Ainz est corrouciez et marriz	220	By her whose outcry so abused
De cele qui ainsi l'assaut.		His ears. He was enraged instead.
Maintenant de son lit s'en salt		He jumped like a wild man from his bed,
Com celui qui estoit espris.		Dripping sweat from grief and anger,
Maintenant a son coutel pris,	224	Then leaped before her with his dagger
Si est sailliz en mi la rue,		And cut her tresses off. The shock
Son cors tot d'angoisse tressue,		Was so severe for her it struck
Si li a coupee les treces		Her dumb, and she could weep no more.
Dont el a au cuer grant destrece,	228	Her heart was weary to the core
Si que ses plors entroublia.		And almost burst from so much weeping.
Tant a ploré qu'afebloia		At last the husband left her, keeping
Le cuer que par poi ne li part.		The tresses cut from off her head.
Li chevaliers d'iluec s'en part	232	

Qui les treces o soi enporte.
Et cele qui se desconforte
Vient à la dame, si li conte
Si com oï avez el conte,
Mais la dame jure et afiche
Qu'à toz jors mais la fera riche.
Ne ja douter ne li estuet
Des tresces, se trouver les puet,
Que si bien ne li mete el chief
Que ja n'en savra le meschief
N'ome ne feme qui la voie.
La dame s'est mise à la voie,
Q'onques nului n'i encontra:
Tant fist que en la chambre entra,
Si trouva son seignor dormant
Qui travailliez estoit forment
Et du corroz et du veillier.
La dame nel volt esveillier,[20]
Mais söef lez le lit s'assist,
Quar des treces bien li souvint
Que la dame ot eü tranchiees,
Qui bien seront encor vengiees,
Se la dame en vient au desus.
Lors les queroit et sus et jus.
Bien s'est du cerchier entremise;
Lors a sa mein au chavez mise,
Les treces trueve, ses en trait:[21]
Ne vos avroie droit retrait
La grant joie que la dame ot!
D'iluec s'en vet sanz dire mot,
Et [s'en] vient à la chanbre aval,
Si a coupé à un cheval
La queue, au meillor de l'estable.
Or oiez un proverbe estable
Qui en mainz leus, ce m'est vis, cort,
Que: *tel ne pesche qui encort.*[22]
Ainsi la dame a escorté,
Le cheval, si l'a aporté
La queue au chevez son seignor:
Onques mais n'ot jöe graignor[23]
Qui à ceste s'apareillast!
Söef, que cil ne s'esveillast,
Si coiement s'est contenue
Et couchiee trestoute nue,
Qu'à soi ne trest ne pié ne main.

The woman dragged herself, half dead,
To meet the lady, and reported
236 What happened, just as you have heard it.
The lady promised her and swore
She'd make her rich forevermore.
As for her tresses, if she could get
240 Them back, the woman needn't fret:
She'd fix them to her head so well
No man or woman could ever tell
That they had suffered any violence.
244 The lady left and walked in silence
Unnoticed through the morning gloom
Until she came into her room,
And there she saw her husband sleeping,
248 Worn out and overworked from keeping
Awake and angry, cutting hair.
To waken him she did not dare,
But sat in silence by the bed,
252 Wondering where he could have hid
The tresses stolen from her friend,
Which, by the saints, would be avenged
If she could get the best of him.
256 From end to end she searched the room,
Looking for their hiding place,
Then reached inside the pillowcase
And groped and pulled the tresses out.
260 Her sorrows you have heard about,
But this was happiness she found.
She left the room without a sound,
Went through the stable door and cut
264 The horse's tail off at the root,
The horse on which her husband doted.
Now hear a proverb often quoted
And known to almost everyone:
268 "The sin is gone with penance done."
And so the horse endured the knife.
The greatest joy of all her life
Was at that moment when she put
272 The horse's tail which she had cut
Into her husband's pillowcase.
With everything arranged in place,
Quietly, softly, lest he wake,
276 She slipped into the bed all naked
And slept until the morning light.

ssi fu jusqu'à lendemain,
:t dormirent grant matinee.
Quant vit que prime fu sonee, 280
.i sires s'estoit resveilliez,
Mais de la dame est merveilliez
Qu'il vit gesir lez son costé:
Et qui vos a ci amené," 284
'ait cil, "et qui vos coucha ci?
–"Sire, la vostre grant merci,
Mais] où devroit donc couchïer,
e lez vos non vostre moillier?" 288
–"Comment, "fait il," donc ne vos membre,
Que ge hersoir en ceste chambre
'ris prouvé vostre lecheor?
'ar celui qui li peche[o]r 292
'rient de cuer parfondement,
'rop avez fait grant hardement
Quant vos estes çaienz entree!
)effendue vos ert l'entree 296
toz les jours que j'ai à vivre.
Je me tenroiz pas si por ivre,
Quant vos cuidiez, se Diex me salt."[24]
–"Beax sire, se Diex me consalt," 300
'ait ele, "mielz poïssiez dire!
)e ce me puis bien escondire
'onques ne fis autrui servise,
'ar toz les sainz de seint[e] yglise, 304
Je qui vos tornast à hontaige:
'rop par avez dit grant outraige,
Qui si solez estre ensaigniez!
Reclamez Dieu, si vos seigniez! 308
ie crieng que en vos se soit mis
)u fantosmes ou enemis
Qui ainsi vos ait desvoié."
–"Or m'avez vos bien avoié," 312
'ait il, "se vos voloie croire,
'olez me vos faire mescroire
:e que ge tieg à mes .II. mains?
vostre char pert il al mains 316
Qu'as esperons vos fis merveille,
)e nule riens n'ai tel merveille
:om de ce que vos estes vive."
–"Ja Dieu ne place que ge vive," 320
'ait cele qui par guile pleure,
S'onques hersoir de nes une eure

The bells at six awoke the knight
Who sat up in his bed and stared
To see the lady lying there
Again beside him in his bed.
"Who brought you back?" the husband said,
"Who tucked you in with me?" —"But sir,
What place could there be properer
To lie in peace the whole night through
For your own wife than next to you?"
—"What!" he cried, "Don't you remember
Last night? —What happened in this chamber!
I caught your lover in the act
Right in this bed, to be exact.
By God, who hears the sinner's prayer,
What fit of folly, what despair
Brought you crawling back to me?
From this day on the doors will be
Barred against you while I live.
I'm not the drunken lout you give
Me credit for, I thank the Lord."
—"As God's my help," the wife implored,
"You should speak better. I deny
And can refute that ever I
Served any other man than you
Or brought you shame. I swear that's true
By all the saints and sacraments.
You always used to make good sense,
But this is madness—every word!
Cross yourself! Call on the Lord!
Some evil spirit, ghost, or ghoul
Or devil has possessed your soul
And has misled you in the night."
—"You'd lead me by the nose all right
If I believed your words. Why you
Would have me misbelieve what's true
And evident in my two hands.
Your skin should show how matters stand.
I certainly raked it with a will.
In fact I'm shocked to see you still
Alive. It's almost past believing."
—"God forbid I keep on living,"
Cried she who wept from make-believe,
"If for one hour I received
A beating from you—not a smack."
At that she threw her covers back

Me donastes cop ne colee."
Tantost a la robe levee,
Si l[i] mostre costez et hanches,
Et les braz et les cuisses blanches.
Et le vis qu'el n'ot pas fardé.
Par tot a li sires gardé,
Mais n'i voit nes une bubete:
Bien guile la dame et abete
Son seignor qui tant s'en espert:
"Dame," fait il, "itant se pert
Qui feme bat s'il ne la tue;
Ge vos avoie tant batue,
Que ge de fi savoir cuidoie
Que jamais n'alissoiz par voie:
Certes se vos bone fussiez,
Jamais par voie n'alissiez!
Or vos ont malfé respassee,
Mais n'iert pas si tost trespassee
La grant honte que vos avroiz;
Ja si garder ne vos savroiz
De vos treces qu'avez perdues:
.II. anz les avroiz atendues,
Ainz que soient en lor bon point!"
—"Sire, "fait el, "un tot seul point
N'i a de ce que vos me dites[s]:
Grant tort avez qui me mesdites,
Onques hersoir por nul corroz
Ne fu de mon chief cheveus roz,
Se Dieu[s] me giet de cest[e] place!"
Maintenant le coissin deslace,
Si a les tresces avant traites
Qu'il i duidoit avoir fors tra[i]tes:
"Sire," fait la dame, "veez;
Ge cuit qu'il fu jor deveez
Quant du destre braz vos seignastes,
Ou mauvaisement vos seignastes
Hersoir au couchier, ce m'est vis,
Vos avez si trouble le vis
Et les elz que ne veez goute.
Espoir il vos avint par goute,
Ou par avertin, se Dé vient,[25]
Ou ce est fantosme qui vient
As genz por ax faire muser,
Et por ax folement user,
Et por faire foler la gent.

And showed her thighs and her white waist
324 And breasts and legs and flanks, and face
Without a dab of make-up on.
The husband looked her up and down,
But couldn't even find a bruise.
328 He was confounded and confused
And baffled. "Lady," he protested,
"I see a husband's time is wasted
Who beats and doesn't kill his wife.
332 I beat you to an inch of your life.
In honest faith I thought for sure
You wouldn't walk straight anymore.
If you were decent, if you were good,
336 Arise and walk you never could.
Devils healed you, didn't they?
You won't so easily find a way
To heal your shame: You've lost your tresses.
340 Two years—that's what my lowest guess is—
You'll wait before they grow back in."
—"My lord," she said, "this is a sin
To slander me. I cannot eke
344 A grain of sense from what you speak.
If but one hair of my head was severed
For any anger whatsoever,
May God expel me from this place."
348 Her net of ribbons she unlaced
And let the tresses, which he thought
He'd shorn away, come tumbling out.
"Look here, my lord," the lady said,
352 "Last night I saw you get in bed
The wrong foot first and cross yourself
From right to left. I fear your health
Has gotten worse. It's no surprise
356 You're having trouble with your eyes.
Or else the vertigo or gout
Has put reality in doubt,
Or else it is the evil one,
360 Who clouds men's minds. When he has done,
And made great fools of clever men,
To nothing everything turns again.
When all the world is led astray,
364 His works will break and pass away—
For the love of God, sir, when you spoke,
Were you sincere? Is this a joke?"
The husband gasped and shook his head

Au chief du tot devient nïent;
Quant il a fait foler le siecle,
Tot quanqu'il a fait si despiece.
Beax sire, dites moi por Dieu
Me dites vos tout ce par geu?"
Son seignor de ce se merveille,
Et si s'esbahist et merveille,
Lors lieve sa mein, si se saigne;[26]
Mais la dame pas ne s'en saigne
De riens que la nuit fet eüst,
Mais encor pas ne se teüst
Qui li donast tote Prouvence;
Monstrer en cuide la provence,
Quar il cuide qu'el ait apostes[27]
Les tresces qu'il avroit repostes.
Maintenant le coissin sozlieve,
Mais a poi li cuers ne li crieve
Quant il a trovee la queue:
"Or voit il tot à male voe,"
Fait il, "se Damedieu n'en pense;
J'ai hui fait une tel despensse
Qui m'a cousté .L. livres.
Bien ai esté desvez et yvres
Quant j'ai escorté mon cheval."
Lors li veïssiez contreval
Les lermes couler sor la face,
Mais [il] ne set mais que il face,
Tant est dolenz et abosmez
Que il cuide estre enfantosmez.
Et si est il, n'en doutez mie!
Lors apele la dame: "Aïe!
Sainte Marie! Mon seignor,
Si se demaine à deshenor!"
Li sires li respont ainsi:
"Dame," fait il, "dolenz en sui."
Si li a dit isnelepas:
"Dame," fait il, "ne prenez pas
A mon forfet ne à mes diz;
Ge vos en cri par Dieu merciz!"
Et la dame li respondi:
"Beau doz sire, devant Diex ci,
Je vos pardoig molt bonement:
Diex gart vostre cors de torment
Et d'ennemi et de fantosme!
Sire, vöez vos à Vendosme,

368 And gaped and crossed himself for dread.
His wife, however, didn't swear
Or cross herself.—she didn't dare!
But not the wealth of Aquitaine
372 Could keep him quiet even then,
Because of the evidence he thought
He had: the tresses he had cut.
He reached inside the pillowcase
376 And almost fell upon his face,
When out he pulled the horse's tail.
Now he saw all, in false detail.
"Oh God!" he cried, "What did I do?
380 In one fell swoop last night I threw
Fifty pounds straight down the drain.
I must have been berserk, insane
Or drunk to cut my horse's tail."
384 You should have seen the teardrops trail
In rivers down his cheeks and chin.
He was so shaken with chagrin,
He had no notion what to do.
388 He thought he was bewitched (That's true!
Bewitched is what he really was).
"Mary, most holy, pray for us,"
She wept; "I watch my lord go wander
392 Far from his wits and from his honor."
"Lady," he said, "Behold a wretch!
Don't hold me liable, I beseech,
For folly that you hear and see.
396 Lady, for God's sake, pity me!"
The lady answered, "Good my lord,
Before high God, I give my word,
I freely pardon your offenses.
400 God keep your body and your senses
From evil spirits and the devil.
Go to Vendôme, sir, so the evil
That clouds your mind may go away.
404 Do not forget. Do not delay.
Do not let business interfere.
Go to the Church of the Holy Tear,
Gaze upon the Tear and pray,
408 And God will wash your scales away."
"Lady," he said, "your word is true.
Tomorrow morning that's what I'll do,
Because I dearly long to see!"
412 Nor did the lord forget. When he

Que li oeil vos sont ennubli.
Ne le metez mie en oubli,
Ne requerez respit ne terme,
Mais alez à la seinte Lerme: 416
Bien sai, quant vos l'avroiz veüe,
Que Diex vos rendra la veü[e]."
Dist il: "Dame, vos dites voir;
Ge vorrai le matin movoir, 420
Quar du veoir ai grant envie."
Et au matin pas ne s'oublie;
Le chevaliers chose ne dist,
Se la dame le contredist, 424
Qu'il ne cuidast ce fust mençoinge
Ou qu'il l'eüst trouvé en songe.
Par cest fableau pöez savoir[28]
Que cil ne fait mie savoir 428
Qui de nuiz met sa feme hors:
S'el fait folie de son cors.
Quant el est hors de sa maison,
Lors a ele droite achoison 432
Qu'ele face son mari honte.
Ici vueil definer mon conte.

Came back to her, he never breathed
A word, which, if she disagreed,
He didn't hasten to deny
And swear it was a dream, or lie.

This story shows it isn't right
To put a wife outside at night
If she does folly with her flesh.
It only gives her means afresh
To load on shame and more distresses.
Thus ends my fabliau, *The Tresses.*

8.

De la Borgoise d'Orliens (The Wife of Orléans)

The Anglo-Norman *Du Chevalier et sa dame et un clerc* (MR, 2:215), in which the protagonists are all noble, in which the clerk pines almost to death for love, and in which the lady betrays the husband she loves to save the clerk's life, is a so-called courtly version of this tale but one that Nykrog considers to be an inept attempt at blending a romance with a fabliau (N, pp. 66–68). In addition to this "fabliau," Bédier cites a Provençal poem by Ramon Vidal and a German poem, all variations on the theme of the husband beaten and content, to show how a theme can be molded to fit the tastes of different classes of people (*Les Fabliaux,* pp. 449, 450).[1] Our tale (*A*) has also two variants: the Berne 354 (*B*), which contains several mistakes and is somewhat poorer in construction and articulation, and the Hamilton 256 (*C*), which contains some good parts but at times is repetitive and laboriously precise. *C* expands the beating of the husband by twenty-six lines and the farewell scene between wife and lover by twelve lines: neither expansion adds or improves on the tale in any measurable way. Indeed, *C* would gain in being as succinct as *A: C*'s husband talks too much, harming the overall effectiveness of some scenes (see Rychner, *Contribution,* 2:84, vv. 76–88, 96–99, and pp. 94, 96, vv. 280–86). On the other hand, *C* (vv. 100–108) describes more carefully the suspicion of the lady, explaining that the pseudo-lover's surprising silence at her greeting drove her to double-check his identity: *A* could have profited from such a skillful motivation. On the whole, however, *A* is a more representative choice from among the variant versions because of its conciseness, restraint, and emphasis on the action: Paul Theiner calls it a "fine example of a tightly organized, well-constructed fabliau narrative" (CH, p. 127).

Our author shows signs of having been a learned man: his mentions of the university city of Orléans and his apparently sympathetic treatment of students (albeit somewhat ironic) might hint at a university background. He is able to use sarcasm skillfully, as evidenced by the mob's invective against the clerk, which expresses the familiar burgher resentment and scorn toward university people ("sire clercgaut, / Vous serez ja desciplinez!" vv. 184, 185). He is at times gently ironic, delivering some lines tongue-in-cheek. Lacy notes the irony of calling this story an "aventure assez cortoise" (v. 2, note the sly use of the reductive *assez*), which would be unlikely to escape the medieval audience (CH, p. 110); neither would the author's marveling at the lady's qualities of "preude" and "sage" at the end of the tale (vv. 242, 243), especially when contrasted to her husband's parting admonitions to take care of things, "si com preude fame doit fere" (v. 55). His condemnatory observation on the disloyalty of women (vv. 85–87) could conceivably be taken seriously, but Cooke, understandably, opposes such a view because "it would be difficult to do so after hearing this comment in which husband and wife are compared to ass driver and ass" (*Old French,* p. 71).[2] The lines immediately preceding this unflattering comparison must also have been delivered in a sanctimonious tone, for the author is deriding the husband just eight lines later when he cooly remarks that the lover in bed with his wife is much more at ease than the husband, locked in the loft (vv. 112, 113). Likewise, the courtly atmosphere surrounding the sexual union (vv. 122, 123) is destroyed when love is said to have driven the lady to give the clerk a sum of money for services rendered, begging him to come back whenever he is free (vv. 210–13).

He is also a good parodist. The "epic" assault on the loft under the leadership of the wife is a model of parody (vv. 141–99). All the elements of the epic fight are there: the preliminary orders, the harangue by the chief urging his troops to fight courageously (vv. 172, 173) to avenge the insult leveled at the household (v. 174), the preparation for battle, the enumeration of the combatants, the inspection of the troops (v. 143), the handing over of the symbol by the chief (v. 179), the description of the battle (vv. 186–90) and of the marvelous blows, the courage of the fighters (vv. 180, 181), the presence of the "epic" nephews (this time two of them, v. 195), the ignominious defeat of the enemy (vv. 198–200), and the postvictory feast (v. 203) for the combatants who now feel like noble kings (v. 204). All that is lacking is the motif of the council that the leader traditionally holds with his trusted entourage. This motif is, however, reserved for the lady and her lover: "Si tient à son ami concile" (v. 208). The author then establishes carefully the contrast between the boisterous, feasting, and drinking heroes (vv. 201–4), victorious over the evil enemy, and the softness of the moment when the lover enjoys the fine cakes and wines and his lady's "council" (vv. 205–9).

The author even parodies his own craft: if anyone could count the blows delivered to the husband during the battle, he says, he would consider him a superior storyteller (vv. 180–81). Only a poet sure of his talent could afford to poke fun at his own art. There are indeed some delightful lines to give evidence of his talent, such as the description (v. 67) of the twilight at the rendezvous, "Quar la nuit fu au jor meslee" (For the night was mixed with the day), explaining already the difficulty of identifying people, or the anticipation of the lady who, at the moment, anxiously but furtively sneaks through the garden (vv. 69, 70) to open the gate for the one she thought was her lover but, unfortunately, as the author dramatically declares (v. 72): "esperance la deçoit" (Hope deceived her).

Nykrog (CH, p. 70) explains that within the representations of the triangular relationship between husband, wife, and lover, a woman–lover relationship is more apt to be sublime; a lover–husband one, tragic, violent, and even bloody; but the woman–husband relationship, comical. In our fabliau, the lover and husband never actually meet and no violent confrontation occurs as does in *Des Tresces*. (The beating of the Borgoise's husband can in no way be considered tragic or cruel in the manner of *Conebert* or the *Sacristains* fabliaux.) As Nykrog has noted (N, p. 69), the entire action revolves around the confrontation between husband and wife: " . . . le conte comique insiste sur les relations entre le mari et la femme, l'amant étant souvent réduit à l'état d'ombre ou de 'ressort' pur" (the comic tale emphasizes the relations between man and wife, the lover being often reduced to a shadow or to a "spring"). The clerk/lover plays this limited role in the six fabliaux in which he has an affair with a townswoman: he is much more active in dealing with peasant women, or women of an unspecified class, in which cases he uses his superior intelligence to achieve his goals (Wailes, CH, p. 52).

In our fabliau, his participation in the action is minimal: while he has been portrayed, along with his three friends, as a life-loving fellow who particularly delights in the pleasures of the table, the reasons for his being singled out as particularly attractive to the lady are not stated (aside from his courtliness and lack of arrogance, vv. 19, 20). Once this choice is made, the lady directs all events: she informs the clerk that he should be at the garden door (v. 63); there she grabs hold of him, kisses and hugs him (vv. 110, 111), and leads him to the bedroom where she places him in bed, under the covers (vv. 119–21). She does not even bother to inform him of her plan of action but merely tells him to wait in bed, promising to bring him back some food (v. 133): she is assured that he will do as she says since she knows of his love for food (vv. 13, 14). For his docility, she will reward him as promised (v. 205). His only spoken part in this tale is his obedient, acquiescent answer: "Dame, à vostre commandement" (v. 135, † 99). In view of the fact that the interest in the tale resides in the other relationship, the author, as Cooke notes judiciously, "gives the best preparation for the lover: none at all" (*Old French,* p. 122). At the end of the tale, he is simply said to have gone back to his country (v. 248).

At first sight, the treatment of the husband seems unduly harsh since he has done no apparent harm to anybody in the tale. However, in nine out of fourteen tales where the lover is a clerk or silhouette, the merchant husband comes out bested by his opponent: "Quand sa femme le trompe," says Nykrog (N, p. 125), "ce n'est pas nécessairement à cause de ses défauts personnels . . . s'il s'adonne à l'importation d'objects de luxe, il jouit de la pleine faveur de nos conteurs; si par contre il travaille de ses mains ou s'il est usurier, il s'élève à peine au dessus des paysans."[3] We are warned immediately that our bourgeois is immoderately rich, that he is a usurer, tightfisted, and possessive (vv. 5–9). He falsely claims to go far away for business reasons, hypocritically stating his faith in his wife's ability to take care of things, and, without her asking, informing her that the date of his return is undecided (vv. 52, 53). A trap is never considered a very noble device, no matter how legitimate one's cause may be. These negative elements probably account for the fact that in addition to his deserved beating, he is thrown on the dung heap (v. 199). Furthermore, there is a certain sadistic delight on the part of the author in forcing the husband to answer twice to the embarrassing inquiries over what has happened: the first time, to his inquisitive traveling companions, he abruptly declares that he does not wish to talk about his mishap; the second time, to his "concerned" wife who is comforting him physically but baiting him verbally (v. 235), he fabricates a curt explanation. In addition, he has to listen anguishingly to his nephews' eulogistic account of how they valiantly defended his wife's honor and reputation (vv. 239–41).

Bédier believed that the wife elicits no sympathy in this tale (*Les Fabliaux,* p. 299), but it is obvious that the author is on her side in view of his concluding comments in the tale. She is as liberal and generous as her husband is stingy and possessive: she feeds her household graciously (vv. 136–42). That household, we gather, has not experienced such lucky occasions too often with the husband present: thus she rewards them appropriately with a royal feast after their valorous performance. We can imagine the distress of the avaricious husband when he hears his wife, who had just penetrated his disguise, promise a monetary reward for his obedience (vv. 91, 92). The generous granting of ten *mars* to the lover must have seemed like a personal vengeance against the stinting nature of her husband. Indeed, the exhilaration of her victory over her husband and over what he represents is evidenced not only by her fit of liberality but also by the envigorating moment when, feeling absolute freedom, she asks her lover to come back as soon and as often as he can, now that she has the situation well in hand. Her cleverness in response to her husband's trap also elicits our sympathy. Not only is she clever in her deceit of her husband, but she is also quite attentive to the little details: she is careful to account to her household for the fact that she has let the suitor inside in order to teach him a lesson, especially in the presence of the niece (v. 148), who, she now must realize, was also aware of her plans for a romantic rendezvous and whom she must now convince of her loyalty. In all, "we certainly do not condemn her for that but rather admire her cleverness in pulling off such duplicity" (Cooke, *Old French,* p. 140).

It is Paul Theiner (CH, pp. 120–21, 127–31) who draws most attention to the dramatic nature of the tale, to its artistic worth, and to the overwhelming importance of the action. According to him, the uncertain localization of the action (we actually do not know whether the couple lives in Orléans, Amiens, or some third town)[4] is to set this tale "into the ongoing sequence of fabliaux" (CH, p. 122); it is an authenticating device, so to speak, alerting us that we are about to hear a comic tale, a fabliau. Theiner emphasizes the dramatic nature of the tale in which the action must dominate all the other elements: the characters will be conventionalized, the setting kept to a bare minimum ("heraldic," to use a modern dramatic term).[5] The setting is "never at any time larger than a space that could be covered by a spotlight, . . . the theatrical metaphor is strikingly apt. . . . whatever is not in the spotlight is for the time being out of all existence, just like a character who has left the stage" (CH, p. 128). Paul Theiner also points out the lack of precise time relationships: events in the fabliau are linked with weak connectives (vv. 198–209). Consequently the comic tale, in its austerity, has cut all connections with time and space in order to let the action fulfill itself in its full humor. In view of that independence and our release from realities of space and time (and therefore of moral judgment), we can laugh without restraint and accept the final outcome of the story where everything is under control, and since the lover does not exactly ride off into the sunset at the end, we at least know that the marriage remains intact and that, if the husband is "cocu" (cuckold) and "battu" (beaten), he is also "content."

De la Borgoise d'Orliens

The Wife of Orléans

Or vous dirai d'une borgoise[6]		A courtly romance I will tell
Une aventure assez cortoise.		Of a bourgeois' wife who used to dwell
Nee et norrie fu d'Orliens,		In the ancient town of Orléans.
Et ses sires fu nez d'Amiens,	4	Her husband was from Amiens,
Riches manaz à desmesure.		A rich landowner who had made
De marcheandise et d'usure		Money at usury and trade.
Savoit toz les tors et les poins,		He knew the ruses, tricks, and shifts
Et ce que il tenoit aus poins,	8	For getting gold, and once his fists
Estoit bien fermement tenu.		Closed on a thing, they held it tight.
En la vile furent venu		There came to town one summer's night
.IIII. noviaus clers escoliers;[7]		A company of four young scholars

Lor sas portent comme coliers.
Li clerc estoient gros et gras,
Quar molt manjoient bien sanz gas.
En la vile erent molt proisié
Où il estoient herbregié.
Un en i ot de grant ponois,[8]
Qui molt hantoit chiés un borgois;
S'el tenoit on molt à cortois;
N'ert plains d'orgueil ne de bufois,
Et à la dame vraiement
Plesoit molt son acointement;
Et tant vint et tant i ala,
Que li borgois se porpenssa,
Fust par samblant ou par parole,[9]
Que il le metroit à escole,[10]
S'il en pooit en leu venir
Que à ce le peüst tenir.
Leenz ot une seue niece,
Qu'il ot norrie molt grant piece;
Priveement à soi l'apele,
Se li promet une cotele,
Mes qu'el soit de cele oevre espie,
Et que la verité l'en die.
Et l'escolier a tant proié
La borgoise par amistié
Que sa volenté li otroie;
Et la meschine toute voie
Fu en escout tant qu'ele oï
Comme il orent lor plet basti.
Au borgois en vient maintenant
Et li conte le couvenant;
Et li couvenanz tels estoit
Que la dame le manderoit
Quant ses sires seroit errez:
Lors venist aus .II. huis serrez
Du vergier qu'el li enseigna,
Et el seroit contre lui là,
Quant il seroit bien anuitié.
Li borgois l'ot, molt fu haitié,
A sa fame maintenant vient:
"Dame," fet il, "il me covient
Aler en ma marcheandie;
Gardez l'ostel, ma chiere amie,
Si com preude fame doit fere;
Je ne sai rien de mon repere."

12 With bookbags hanging from their collars.
These boys were handsome, smart, and portly.
They were big eaters too, and courtly.
The people of the town all said
16 They were fine fellows, nicely bred.
The plumpest of the four was granted
To be a little bit romantic,
Not proud, but quiet as a mouse.
20 He frequented the husband's house.
The lady of the house delighted
In his acquaintance and invited
The boy to come and visit her
24 So often that the usurer
Determined that by some deception
He'd teach this scholar boy a lesson.

28

For a long time he had had the care
Of his young niece, who was living there.
He secretly called her aside
32 And promised her that if she spied
Upon the lady and her guest
He'd pay her with a pretty dress.
Meanwhile the scholar strove and pleaded
36 For friendship till the wife conceded:
She'd give him what he hungered for.
The niece was listening at the door.
She listened well enough to catch
40 The plot the wife and scholar hatched.
Back to her uncle the young girl ran
To tell him all about their plan.
The plan was, when the husband's work
44 Called him away, she'd call the clerk.
He'd come to the orchard gate and knock,
And she'd be waiting to unlock
And let him in when evening fell.
48 These tidings pleased the merchant well.
He called his wife and told her, "My
Affairs have summoned me and I
Must hurry immediately from here.
52 Take good care of the house my dear.
I don't know how long I'll be gone.
Be a good wife and carry on."
His wife replied, "I will, my Lord."
56 The husband gave his drivers word

—"Sire," fet ele, "volentiers."
Cil atorna les charretiers
Et dist qu'il s'iroit herbregier,[11]
Por ses jornees avancier,
Jusqu'à .III. liues de la vile.
La dame ne sot pas la guile,
Si fist au clerc l'uevre savoir.
Cil, qui les cuida decevoir,
Fist sa gent aler herbregier,
Et il vint à l'uis du vergier,
Quar la nuit fu au jor meslee;[12]
Et la dame tout à celee
Vint encontre, l'uis li ouvri,
Entre ses braz le recueilli,
Qu'el cuide que son ami soit;
Mes esperance la deçoit.
"Bien soiez vous," dist el, "venuz!"[13]
Cil s'est de haut parler tenuz,
Se li rent ses saluz en bas.
Par le vergier s'en vont le pas,
Mes il tint molt la chiere encline,
Et la borgoise un pou s'acline,
Par souz le chaperon l'esgarde,
De trahison se done garde,
Si connut bien et aperçoit
C'est son mari qui la deçoit.
Quant el le prist à aperçoivre,
Si repensse de lui deçoivre:
Fame a trestout passé Argu;[14]
Par lor engin sont deceü
Li sage des le tens Abel.
"Sire," fet ele, "molt m'est bel
Que tenir vous puis et avoir;
Je vous donrai de mon avoir,
Dont vous porrez vos gages trere,
Se vous celez bien cest afere.
Or alons ça tout belement,
Je vous metrai priveement
En un solier dont j'ai la clef.
Iluec m'atendrez tout souef,
Tant que noz genz auront mengié;
Et quant trestuit seront couchié,
Je vous menrai souz ma cortine:
Ja nus ne saura la couvine."
—"Dame," fet il, "bien avez dit."

That they would start the journey right
By leaving now. They'd spend the night
At a small inn three miles from there.
60 The wife did not suspect the snare,
At once she sent the clerk the news.
Meanwhile the rich man worked his ruse,
For when his drivers were in bed,
64 Back to the meeting place he sped.
That evening, as he lay in wait,
The lady stole to the orchard gate,
Opened it, and welcomed in
68 And held the man who should have been
Her lover, for she still believed
In what she hoped. She was deceived.
He who deceived her whispered low.
72 She hardly heard his quick, "Hello."
"I'm glad you're here," the lady said.
Along the orchard path she led
The way. He turned his face aside.
76 The lady peered around and spied
Beneath his hat where she detected
Something entirely unsuspected.
She hastily concluded that
80 Her husband hid beneath the hat
And set her mind to outmaneuver
This man who claimed to be her lover.
(Women have known how to deceive
84 Men ever since the time of Eve.
Not even Argus could guard women.)
With whispered words she welcomed him in:
"It's good to have you by my side.
88 Be kind to me. I will provide
Some of my funds for you to pay
Your little debts if you will say
Nothing about this. Come, my love,
92 I'll hide you safely up above
In a small room I have the key to.
Be patient here and I will meet you
After my people have been fed.
96 When all of them have gone to bed,
I'll lead you to my bed downstairs.
Then nobody will know you're there."
—"Lady," he said, "that's very good."
100 Lord, how little he understood
Of what his lady thought about.

Diex! comme il savoit or petit
De ce qu'ele pensse et porpensse!
Li asniers un[e] chose pensse,
Et li asnes pensse tout el.
Tost aura il mauvés ostel.
Quar quant la dame enfermé l'ot
El solier dont issir ne pot,
A l'uis del vergier retorna,
Son ami prist qu'ele trova,
Si l'embrace et acole et baise.
Molt est, je cuit, à meillor aise
Li secons que le premerain.
La dame lessa le vilain
Longuement ou solier jouchier.
Tost ont trespassé le vergier
Tant qu'en la chambre sont venu,
Où li drap furent portendu.
La dame son ami amaine,
Jusqu'en la chambre le demaine,[15]
Si l'a souz le couvertoir mis;
Et cil s'est tantost entremis
Du geu que Amors li commande,
Qu'il ne prisast une alemande[16]
Toz les autres, se cil n'i fust,
Ne cele gré ne l'en seüst.
Longuement se sont envoisié;
Quant ont acolé et baisié,
"Amis," fet ele, "or remaindrez
Un petit et si m'atendrez;
Quar je m'en irai là dedenz
Por fere mengier cele gent,
Et nous souperons, vous et moi,
Encore anuit tout à recoi."
—"Dame, à vostre commandement."
Cele s'en part molt belement,
Vint en la sale à sa mesnie,
A son pooir la fet haitie.[17]
Quant li mengiers fu atornez,
Menjüent et boivent assez.
Et, quant orent mengié trestuit,
Ainz qu'il fussent desrengié tuit,
La dame apele sa mesnie,
Si parole comme enseignie.
.II. neveus au seignor i ot,
Et un garz qui eve aportoit,[18]

(A driver, though he plans his route,
Won't get there if the mule won't move.)
104 The husband's lot will not improve,
For when the merchant's wife had stuck
Him in the attic, she turned the lock
And ran from the house to the orchard gate.
108 The clerk was there, though she was late.
She hugged and kissed and let him pet her.
This second comer had it better
Than he who reached the orchard first.
112 She let the one who had it worse
Stay in the upstairs room and stew
And brought the other safely through
The orchard to the hall which led
116 To the guest-bedroom door. The spread
Was folded back. They both got in.
She urged her scholar to begin
The game of love. He played so well
120 He wouldn't have given a hazel shell
For any other game, and neither
Would she, for they played well together.
They had good fun while the time sped.
124 They cuddled and kissed. At last she said,
"My friend, I have to go. Please stay
A little while. Don't go away.
Now I must go and be the lady
128 And see that the evening meal is ready.
We'll have our own meal by and by
Later tonight, just you and I."
The scholar nodded in assent.
132 She left him quietly and went
To the eating hall and did her best
To treat her husband's crowd like guests.
The lady put on quite a spread.
136 The people guzzled wine and fed
Themselves until they almost burst.
They finished and had not dispersed
When the lady asked for them to pay
140 Attention to what she had to say.
Her lord's two nephews were at the table,
A handyman who kept the stable,
A water boy, a cook, two grooms,
144 And three young girls who cleaned the rooms,
Not to mention the lady's niece.
"Ladies and gentlemen, God give you peace,"

Et chamberieres i ot .III.;
Si i fu la niece au borgois, 148
.II. pautoniers et un ribaut.
"Seignor," fet el, "se Diex vous saut,
Entendez ore ma reson:
Vous avez en ceste meson 152
Veü ceenz un clerc venir,
Qui ne me lest en pes garir;
Requise m'a d'amors lonc tens;
Je l'en ai fet .XXX. desfens; 156
Quant je vi que je n'i garroie,
Je li promis que je feroie
Tout son plesir et tout son gré
Quant mon seignor seroit erré. 160
Or est errez, Diex le conduie![19]
Et cil, qui chascun jor m'anuie,
Ai molt bien couvenant tenu.
Or est à son terme venu:[20] 164
Là sus m'atent en ce perrin.[21]
Je vous donrai du meillor vin
Qui soit ceenz une galoie,
Par couvant que vengie en soie: 168
En ce solier à lui alez,
Et de bastons bien le batez,
Encontre terre et en estant;
Des orbes cops li donez tant 172
Que jamés jor ni li en chaille
De prier fame qui rien vaille."

Quant la mesnie l'uevre entent,
Tuit saillent sus, nus n'i atent, 176
L'un prent baston, l'autre tiné,
L'autre pestel gros et mollé;
La borgoise la clef lor baille.
Qui toz les cops meïst en taille, 180
A bon conteor le tenisse!
"Ne soufrez pas que il en isse;
Ainz l'acueilliez el solier haut."
—"Par Dieu," font il, "sire clercgaut, 184
Vous serez ja desciplinez!
Li uns l'a à terre aclinez,
Et par la gorge le saisi;
Par le chaperon l'estraint si 188
Que il ne puet nul mot soner;
Puis l'en acueillent à doner;
De batre ne sont mie eschars.

The lady said, "Listen to me;
Lately you may have chanced to see
Hanging around this house a clerk
Who will not let me do my work.
He's begged for love in prose and rhymes.
I told him *no* a hundred times
Then learned I'd get no rest unless
My tactics changed, so I said *yes*.
I'd give him what he was begging for
As soon as my lord was out the door.
My husband's gone. God be his guide.
And now this clerk, this thorn in my side,
Has kept his part of the deal all right.
He thinks he's come to spend the night.
He's in the attic, waiting for me.
To each of you I guarantee
The finest wines in my husband's cellar
If you will fix this saucy fellow.
Arise, my people! Up to the attic!
Give him an answer that's emphatic.
Beat him up and beat him down,
Black and blue from toe to crown.
This is the last time in his life
He'll woo a self-respecting wife."

As soon as the people there had heard,
Up they jumped with one accord.
One took a log, another a stick,
A third a pestle big and thick.
She gave the key. They rushed the stair.
"Don't let him get away from there!
Grab him before he's out the door."
(Some other teller could tell the score
Of all the blows that fell—I couldn't.)
"By God," they shouted, "Mr. Student,
We'll make you smart!" The elder brother
Wrestled him to the floor. The other
Laid hold of his uncle's overcoat
And yanked it over his face and throat
So that he couldn't utter a sound.
Then they really began to pound.
They were not bashful with the sticks.

S'il en eüst doné. .M. mars,	192	He couldn't have gotten better licks
N'eüst miex son hauberc roulé.		If he had paid ten sous apiece.
Par maintes foiz se sont mollé,		Both of the nephews and the niece
Por bien ferir, ses .II. nevous,		Sweated to give him many a blow
Primes desus et puis desous;	196	First above and then below.
Merci crier ne li vaut rien.		It did no good to weep or shout.
Hors le traient comme un mort chien,		Like a dead dog they dragged him out,
Si l'ont sor un fumier flati,		Dumped him on a pile of manure
En la meson sont reverti;	200	And clumped back through the kitchen door,
De bons vins orent à foison,		They set themselves to drinking dry
Toz des meillors de la meson,		The best of the husband's wine supply:
Et des blans et des auvernois,		Red burgundies, bordeaux, champagne.
Autant com se il fussent rois.	204	They drank like lords of Charlemagne.
Et la dame ot gastiaus et vin		The lady took good wine and cakes
Et blanche toaille de lin		And a large candle of fine wax
Et grosse chandoile de cire,		And linen cloths with lace cutwork
Si tient à son ami concile	208	And held good council with her clerk
Toute la nuit dusques au jor.		All night until the night was spent.
Au departir si fist Amor		True love decreed that when he went
Que vaillant .X. mars li dona,		She give him gifts of marks and sous.
Et de revenir li pria	212	She begged for other rendezvous
Toutes les foiz que il porroit.		Whenever he could get there to her.
Et cil qui el fumier gisoit		At last the man in the manure
Si se remua comme il pot,		Moved his muscles to begin
Et vait là où son harnois ot.	216	The three-mile crawl back to the inn.
Quant ses genz si batu le virent,		His drivers, when they saw him bruised
Duel orent grant, si s'esbahirent;		Showed much concern. They weren't amused,
Enquis li ont comment ce vait.		But kindly asked him how he was.
"Malement," ce dist, "il me vait;	220	"Bad," he said. "Now no more fuss.
A mon ostel m'en reportez		Just take me home." He wasn't kidding.
Et plus rien ne me demandez."		They saddled up and did his bidding.
Tout maintenant l'ont levé sus,		But after all, it did him good,
Onques n'i atendirent plus.	224	And put him out of his bad mood
Mes ce l'a molt reconforté		To know his wife was free from stain.
Et mis hors de mauvés penssé,		He snapped his fingers at his pain.
Qu'il sent sa fame à si loial;[22]		If he survived the day, his wife
Un oef ne prise tout son mal	228	Would have his confidence all his life.
Et pensse, s'il en puet garir,		
Molt la voudra toz jors chierir.		
A son ostel est revenu,		He got home. When his wife perceived
Et, quant la dame l'a veü,	232	His bruises, she was deeply grieved.
De bones herbes li fist baing,		She poured an herb bath, put him in it
Tout le gari de son mehaing.		And eased his hurt in half a minute.
Demande lui com li avint.		She asked him what on earth had happened.
"Dame," fet il" il me covint	236	"Lady," he said, "I have been destined

Par un destroit peril passer,		To pass through perilous straits alone
Où l'en me fist des os quasser."		Whereby I've broken every bone."
Cil de la meson li conterent		His nephews told about the work
Du clercgaut comme il l'atornerent,	240	They had accomplished on the clerk
Comment la dame lor livra.		And how she led him to his lair.
Par mon chief, el s'en delivra[23]		By gosh, she handled this affair
Com preude fame et comme sage:		Discreetly and responsibly!
Onques puis en tout son eage	244	Never more would the husband be
Ne la blasma ne ne mescrut,		Suspicious, critical, or spying!
N'onques cele ne se recrut		And never would she fail at lying
De son ami amer toz dis,		With him she loved until the day
Tant qu'il ala à son païs.	248	He went to his own hometown to stay.

9.

De Guillaume au faucon (William of the Falcon)

This fabliau illustrates difficulties of identity: the characters have severe difficulties in expressing their personal feelings and in articulating concepts. Verbal communication between two individuals is not effective, and the tale itself is in danger of never reaching a conclusion, being saved from its impasse by a timely metamorphosis into a fabliau.

Throughout the tale, Guillaume's difficulties in expressing his feelings seem to stem from an identity crisis: from a timid and awkward adolescent, he is finally transferred to manhood by masterful handling on the lady's part. Not yet a knight (v. 11), the *vallez* has trouble acting in the manner imposed by his courtly surroundings. When the excitement of being taken to the tourney turns even the most cowardly bachelors into valiant men, Guillaume, terrified, prefers to stay home with the ladies (vv. 130–34).[1] The author's favorite phrase for describing the young man is *en effroi* (vv. 20, 131, 353), a terror that paralyzes verbal, cognitive, and physical activities and that finds expression in his feverish delirium and animated dreaming during the period of his sickness (vv. 348–73). His interior monologue (vv. 139–60) is a languishing complaint on his inability to express himself clearly ("Tu li diras . . . Que diras tu . . . ?" v. 153) a recognition of his basic lack of confidence in the choice of a proper method of action and of the disparity existing between intention and implementation. Unable even to start his declaration of love (v. 158), he nearly backs out (v. 160). After this hesitation, he is spurred to action by an irresistible outside force (Love), not by an intellectual resolution. Indeed, language plays little role here, and his ultimate decision to act, tersely contrasting with the wild, incoherent babblings that have just led to no results, is now, in the second part of the monologue, rendered by a well-balanced line ("Amors m'eschaufe, Amors m'esprent," v. 164), signifying the equilibrium achieved momentarily between language and action.

That healthy equilibrium is of only short duration, however. In spite of very favorable circumstances amid the charming scene of the *puceles* sewing in the background (interestingly, they are sewing a knight's emblem, v. 179) and amid the atmosphere of joy, laughter, and softness (vv. 177, 186, 189, 190, 201), Guillaume, awed by the lady's beauty, just stands there, silent, letting his thoughts once again paralyze him (v. 184). The lady welcomes him warmly (vv. 189, 190), encourages him by calling him "beax amis chiers" (v. 194, † 192), but fails to make Guillaume bolder: he smiles (v. 201) and sighs (v. 192). His inability to verbalize his emotion is evidenced by these sighs: Guillaume, indeed, sighs a lot (vv. 192, 204, 252, 253, 362, 554). This attempt at paralinguistic communication is not successful because the lady fails to react to it (vv. 195–97, 205–6). The author's implicit message is that language and reality must go hand in hand, each mutually supporting the other, and Guillaume's sighing is not worth decoding because he lacks the basic internal *vertu* (v. 154) that would give him a proper mode of expression. Gratification cannot be expected with such poverty of assertion. When Guillaume finally manages to articulate his love for her, he must weather a furious barrage of outraged invectives. The reason for the furor is her realization that Guillaume, by presenting an apparently hypothetical situation and requesting her advice (vv. 205–28), has not been forthright with her. Not having displayed the boldness expected in such love declarations (see v. 222 and the lady's answer in vv. 242–46) and having tricked the lady by making her commit herself without full knowledge of the parties involved (vv. 235–37), Guillaume must endure the lady's anger, aroused primarily because she has been deceived ("Onques mais gabee ne fui . . . ," v. 284, † 284–85).

Guillaume's sudden burst of courage in his plaintive declaration is misleading: what courage he has mustered stems not from his inner self but, again, from elsewhere, namely from the lady's unaware, hypothetical answer. Her reply to Guillaume's request of *jugement* coincidentally matches verbally his earlier interior monologue in which, as we have stated, the words found no inner strength, no virtue to complement them. The desired connection is accidentally made by the lady: she uses the same motif of *folie* (vv. 231, 236) and of timorous withdrawals (v. 239, compare with v. 162) contrasted with the desirability of boldness (vv. 242, 245, 249; compare with v. 165) and the same advisability of open declaration that Guillaume had debated within himself (a veritable festival of declarative verbs, see vv. 232, 233, 241, 249, 250 as compared with vv. 148, 150, 153, 155, 157, 159). Hearing the very same words that he has already used while pondering his misery, Guillaume gathers enough fortitude to declare, painfully, his love for her. That surprising display of courage on Guillaume's part baffles the lady momentarily. With the help of complex chaotic sentences, the author emphasizes that the lady is in shock and temporarily irrational in view of her great anger (vv. 275–80). When she regains her composure, despite strong language, numerous exclamative phrases, and imperative verbs that give her reply a furious and terrifying tone, she is unable to communicate to Guillaume the urgency of abandoning such expectations of gratification or, if that be impossible, of vacating the premises altogether. Guillaume falls ill and is obstinate in his feelings toward her. Three times the lady visits him with the hope of persuading him to relinquish his foolish position: the first time no communication occurs and she merely observes his delirium; on the second visit, she pokes him twice to bring him back to this world (v. 401) in order to reason with him on the impropriety of his request (vv. 416–21) and on the foolishness of his refusal to eat. In spite of her threat to reveal his disloyalty to her husband, Guillaume remains adamant in his desire to die, an obstinacy that necessitates a third visit, this time in the presence of her husband. The communication between Guillaume and the lady is effected in such a manner that the husband remains in total ignorance of the message actually transmitted: her persistent questions ("Mengerez-vos?" v. 553, †551; also vv. 525, 540, †523, 538), capable of being decoded only by Guillaume, ring like sinister threats but fail to achieve the desired goal.

Having displayed impressive courage and firmness even in the face of danger, Guillaume earns the pity of the lady who misleads her husband into believing that the reason for Guillaume's illness and the object of his desires is his master's falcon (the identification of the lady with the falcon had already been prepared for very early when the author compared her beauty to that of a molted hawk, v. 70). Having realized the power of words in that they can signify literally as well as symbolically and having seen that her husband conveniently (and crudely, by the feet, v. 604: "par les giez") hands over to

Guillaume his prized possession, the lady follows that ambiguity to its utmost by offering herself to her pretendant. From a near tragedy we move into the realm of game-playing, word games to be exact, where equations are easily and magically made. Actions are devoid of moral significance just as words are freed from the reality they signify. In the exhilaration of this discovery, the lady finds further examples of that astonishing truth: if the falcon signifies a bird for one person and the lady for another, then two bezants are worth one gold piece just as two signifiers are actually one word (vv. 608–10).

Furthermore, the quarrel of that epoch between the realists and the nominalists is here pushed to an Ionescoan conclusion[2]: if personality and language are irremediably interchangeable (as was postulated by Guillaume's interior monologue), then reality itself is highly manipulable and personalities as well are interchangeable, for words lack solid ties with reality and are subject to aberrant interpretations. Thus the firm, noble, virtuous lady suddenly becomes the replica of Guillaume (just as the Martins became the Smiths in Ionesco's masterpiece): she sighs (v. 588), and, spurred by Love (v. 589), she undergoes the identical pains of cold, heat, and loss of color that Guillaume had suffered earlier (vv. 591–92, compare with vv. 164, 350, 373).

The delicate interpretation should not surprise us: the author warned us very early of his subtlety (*par soutill guise,* in a subtle manner, v. 66). Underlined throughout the tale is his treatment of the *fol/sage* theme (vv. 34, 112–13, 147–49, 231, 236, 364). Just as Guillaume used the device of the judgment to elicit a response from the lady, the author uses the "jeu parti" or the "débat" formats, where the audience is asked to judge the merit of erotic casuistry in order to treat the following disturbing question: under what circumstances is adultery ever admissible?[3] The author slips free of the impasse by seeming to declare that adultery is reprehensible in reality but admissible in fiction: the thought of adultery infuriated the lady earlier, but once it is transformed into the conventional symbol of the falcon and once its malleable, playful nature is discovered, adultery becomes the innocent and natural outcome of the literary game. At the end, however, nothing has been solved. We find ourselves, like the husband, *ne fol ne saige* (neither wise or foolish) (v. 597), since we do not realize that we have been tricked by a piece of verbal wizardry: the serious tale has lapsed into a fabliau and the author is able to deliver a tongue-in-cheek moral in which he claims to have produced a new twist to such stories by not condemning adultery (v. 616) and to have answered the question posed at the beginning (vv. 209–28), when actually the only praiseworthy element he finds in the tale is the lover's obstinacy (vv. 623–25).[4]

The tale, in its serious tone, was heading straight for an impasse: courtly casuistry demanded a clever answer to that perturbing problem, but morality, good sense, and wisdom are intransigently negative on the question of adultery. The author started by presenting us with a tale akin to the tearful comedies of the eighteenth century, with their eternal dilemma of an impossible love, but already he was including plenty of elements familiar to fabliaux audiences: the preparation for the love affair, the departure of the husband, his return. The tale loses its serious quality once it becomes evident that the problem is unsolvable: Guillaume truly cannot help himself and is dying while the lady, also genuinely, attempts desperately to remedy the situation. All characters, even the husband, who is labeled a "frans hom" (v. 499, † 497), are sympathetic, yet someone has to be hurt. The most dramatic scene is the one in which all three characters are present (vv.

491–599). The moment is exciting not only because of the event itself, but als because it holds in suspense the outcome and the nature of the tale: a quick reasonable, or tragic resolution here and the tale would not have been a fabliau Suddenly, the tale shifts to a fabliau: the husband, frustrated by his exclusion fror the apparent communication, goes into a rage, threatens to beat his wife right on th spot (vv. 548–49), and apparently makes a move to do so (v. 550: *ostez,* "stop!"), i he is not informed about what is going on. As soon as his wife mentions tha Guillaume has come to see her in her room, the husband is transformed into th stereotyped jealous and brutal husband of the fabliaux. The author must have realize that the only way of bringing his narrative to a conclusion was to give it the fablia ending.

If laughter is a definitional requirement of the fabliau (and it is), our present tale i a fabliau that almost wasn't. If the narrative stratagem of having the husband himsel authorize the adultery had not been available, *Guillaume au faucon* would assured have been a *lai.* As Bédier judiciously notes (*Les Fabliaux,* pp. 364, 365), th separation between the two sides of the medieval literary coin, the fabliau and Renar on one side and the Round Table on the other, is indeed thin. Our fabliau stands a an admirable connector.

De Guillaume au faucon

Qui d'aventure velt traiter,[5]
Il n'en doit nule entrelaisser
Qui bonne soit à raconter:
Or en vorrai d'une paller.
Jadis estoit un damoiseax
Qui mol estoit cointes et beax;
Li vallez ot à nom Guillaumes.
Cerchier peüst on .XX. realmes
Ainz c'on peüst trover si gent,
Et s'estoit molt de haute gent.
Il n'estoit mie chevaliers;
Vallez estoit. .VII. anz entiers
Avoit un chastelain servi;
Encor ne li avoit meri[6]
Li service qu'il li faisoit:
Por avoir armes le servoit.
Li vallez n'avoit nul talent
D'avoir armes hastivement;
Si vos dirai raison por quoi:
Amors l'avoit mis an effroi.
La feme au chastelain amoit,

William of the Falcon

Whoever wishes to repeat
A good adventure should delete
Nothing that's worth the leaving in.
4 With that in mind I shall begin.
Once long ago there lived a youth,
A handsome, bright young man in truth,
Named William. Even if you tried
8 A hundred countries, far and wide,
You'd find no better man than he.
Though of the aristocracy,
His knighthood he had not attained,
12 But he had served a chatelain
For seven years now as a squire,
Receiving nothing for his hire
Because he worked to win his arms.
16 The time it took did not alarm
The young man though, and here's the reason:
Love held him locked within a prison:
He loved his master's wife, and thus
20 Was satisfied with where he was.
He loved her so distractedly,

Et li estres molt li plaisoit,
Quar il l'amoit de tel maniere
Qu'il ne s'en pooit traire arriere. 24
Si n'en savoit cele nïent
Qu'il l'amast si destroitement.
S'ele seüst que il l'amast,
La dame molt bien se gardast 28
Que lui parlast en nule guise.
De c'est feme trop mal aprise
Ne vos en mentirai noient:
Quant feme set certainement 32
Que home est de s'amor espris,
Se il devoit arragier vis,[7]
Ne vorroit ele à lui parler;
Plus volentiers iroit jöer 36
A un vill pautonier failli,
Qu'el ne feroit à son ami.
S'ele l'aime de nule rien,
Si m'aïst Diex, ne fait pas bien 40
La dame qui ainsi esploite,
De Diex soit ele maleoite,
Quar ele fait molt grant pechié.
Quant el a l'ome entrelacié 44
Ou mal dont en eschape à peine.
Ne doit pas estre si vileine
Que ne li face aucun secors,
Puis qu'il ne puet penser aillors. 48
Reperier vueil à ma raison.

Guillaumes a s'entencïon
Et s'amor en la dame mise.
Mis l'a Amors en sa justise, 52
Soffrir li estuet grant martire.

De la dame vos voldrai dire
Un petitet de sa beauté.
La florete qui naist el pré, 56
Rose de mai ne flor de lis,
N'est tant bele, ce m'est avis,
Com la beauté la dame estoit.
Qui tot le monde cercheroit, 60
Ne porroit on trover plus bele,
Ne el realme de Castele,[8]
Où les plus belles dames sont
Qui soient en trestot le mont. 64
Si vos dirai ci la devise
De sa beauté par soutill guise:

He had no way of getting free.
But she had no idea at all
How much she held his heart in thrall.
If she had seen into his heart,
She would have kept herself apart
Without exchanging any words.
I will not lie to you, my lords:
Women in this are much to blame.
When any woman knows the game
Of Love is hers, the lover had,
Then she will let love drive him mad,
And never have a word to say
To him, for she would rather play
With some vile tramp, not worth a curse,
Than with a friend who's truly hers.
But if the lady even cares
A little, if she never spares
A word for him, she does not well.
May God condemn her soul to Hell
For the great sin that she commits.
When she has caught him in the nets
From which he cannot struggle loose,
It's surly of her to refuse
To be the one to help him out,
Since she is all he thinks about.
Now to my tale. Enough discourse.

William put all his strength and force
In loving her. Love had control
And jurisdiction of his soul.
Great martyrdom he must endure.

And now I'd like to speak of her:
She was exceeding beautiful.
The wild flowers blooming on the hill,
The lily flower, the rose of May—
She was more beautiful than they.
If you had searched the whole world round,
No fairer lady could you have found
In all the lands from East to West—
Not even where women are loveliest,
The noble kingdom of Castile.
By subtle art I shall reveal
The riches of her loveliness.
Arrayed in jewels and perfect dress,

Que la dame estoit plus tres cointe,
Plus tres acesmee et plus jointe,[9]
Quant el est paree et vestue,
Que n'est faucons qui ist de mue,
Ne espervier, ne papegaut.
D'une porpre estoit son bliaut,
Et ses menteaus d'or estelee,
Et si n'estoit mie pelee
La penne qui d'ermine fu.
D'un sebelin noir et chenu
Fu li menteax au col coulez,
Qui n'estoit trop granz ne trop lez,
Et, se ge onques fis devise
De beauté que Dex eüst mise
En cors de feme ne en face,
Or me plaist il que mes cuers face[10]
Oü ja n'en mentirai de mot
Quant desliee fu, si ot
Les cheveus tex qui les veïst,
Qu'avis li fust, s'estre poïst,
Que il fussent tuit de fin or,
Tant estoient luisant et sor.[11]
Le front avoit poli et plain,
Si com il fust fait à la mein,
Sorciz brunez et large entr'ueil;
En la teste furent li oeil
Clair et riant, vair et fendu;
Le nes ot droit et estendu,
Et mielz avenoit sor son vis
Le vermeil sor le blanc assis,
Que le synople sor l'argent;[12]
Tant par seoit avenanment
Entre le menton et l'oreille;
Et de sa bouche estoit vermeille
Que ele sanbloit passerose,
Tant par estoit vermeille et close;
Et si avoit tant beau menton,
N'en puis deviser la façon;
Neïs la gorge contreval
Sanbloit de glace ou de cristal,
Tant par estoit cler et luisant,
Et desus le piz de devant
Li poignoient .II. mameletes
Auteles comme .II. pommetes.
Que vos iroie ge disant?

What joy the lady was to look on!
68 More lovely than the molted falcon,
Royal parrot or sparrow hawk!
Her dress was purple, and her cloak
Was stitched and starred with shining gold.
72 The ermine lining wasn't old
Or worn and frayed, but fresh and thick.
The cloak was hemmed about the neck
In white and gray with sable hide,
76 Neither too narrow nor too wide.
If ever yet I have portrayed
The form God gave to wife or maid,
Now may my heart receive the grace
80 To sketch her lovely form and face
Without their being falsified,
For when her hair was left untied,
It shone so bright that anyone
84 Who saw would swear that it was spun
From purest gold. Her forehead shone
Like finely cut and polished stone,
Her eyebrows brown and widely spread,
88 Her eyes were laughing in her head,
Deep and clear, gray-green and bright.
The *fleurs de lis* on field of white
Are not so aptly set in place
92 As every feature of her face
To make the work of art complete.
Her nose was slender, straight, and neat.
Her mouth was small and round and closed,
96 Vermillion as the passerose;
Her chin was fresh as can be thought;
Smooth as crystal was her throat.
Her breasts were round as little apples,
100 Firm and small with little nipples.
There's nothing more for me to say:
To lead men's hearts and minds astray
God made her perfect—no! much more—
104 Never her like was seen before.
Never was lady lovelier.
Nature gave all in making her,
And when there was no more to give,
108 Nature impoverished had to live.
About her beauty no more I'll say.

Por enbler cuers et sens de gent 112
Fist Diex en lui passemerveille,
Ainz mais nus ne vit sa pareille.
Nature qui faite l'avoit,
Qui tote s'entente i metoit, 116
I ot misë et tot son sens,
Tant qu'el en fu povre lonc tens.
De sa beauté ne vueil plus dire.
Un jor estoit alez li sire 120
Li chastelains por tornoier,
Son pris et son los essaucier.
En un loigtieng païs ala,
Molt longuement i demora, 124
Quar molt ert riches et poissanz.
Chevaliers mena et serjanz
A grant foison ensanble o lui.
En sa route n'avoit celui 128
Qui ne fust chevaliers esliz;
Li plus coarz estoit hardiz.
Guillaumes ert en grant effroi;
Ne volt pas aler au tornoi, 132
Ençois amoit mielz le sejor.
A l'ostel fu; li diex d'amors
Si l'a sorpris ne sait que faire,
Et si n'en set à quel chief traire 136
Du mal qui ainsi le destraint.
A soi meïsme se complaint,
"Hé! las", dit il, "maleürez!
De si male heure ge fui nez! 140
En tel leu ai mise m'amor
Ja ne porrai veoir le jor
Que ge soie à ma volenté!
Trop longuement ai voir cleé 144
Mon cueur vers lui, ce m'est avis;
Se ge por lui toz jors languis,
Qu'el ne le saige, c'est folie.
Il es bien droiz que ge li die; 148
Bien sai grant folie feroie,
Se ge par tens ne li disoie.
Ainsi porroie ge amer
Totes les femes d'outre mer . . . 152
Tu li diras . . . Que diras tu?
Tu n'auras ja tant de vertu
Que tu ne l'oseroies dire
Que por lui fusses en martire. 156
Ge li dirai bien par mon chief,

The lady's husband went one day
A long way off upon a journey
To gain more honor at a tourney
Far away in another land.
Since he was mighty, rich, and grand,
He took along a great parade
Of knights and serving men, and stayed
For many months. No knight that went
With him was less than excellent.
The greatest coward in his party
Was unreservedly brave and hearty.
William was scared. He didn't want
To go to any tournament.
He much preferred to stay around
The house. The god of love had wound
Him up so tight, he didn't know
What to do or how to throw
The evil off that held him tied.
Now to himself he moaned and sighed,
"Oh God! How wretched and forlorn
I am. Alas that I was born!
I've lifted all my love to where
I haven't even got a prayer
Of ever getting love repaid.
I think I shouldn't have delayed
So long in telling her I love her.
If all my life I pine and suffer
Without her knowledge, I'm a fool.
I know: I'll tell her how I feel.
(I've had sufficient time to court
Every lady in every port.)
You'll tell her . . . well?—You'll tell her what?
You must be brave—which you are not—
To let her know how you endure
Anguish and martyrdom for her.
—I'll speak to her, you mustn't doubt.—
The hard part though is starting out.
I'll speak my love aloud and clearly.

Mais le comenc[em]ent m'est grief.
Tant li dirai que ge l'aim bien,
Ja n'i doie ge faire rien."[13] 160
Guillaumes dit: "Ne sai que faire;[14]
Bien m'en cuidoie arriere traire
Quant ce vint au commencement.
Amors m'eschaufe, Amors m'esprent." 164
Guillaumes s'est lors enhardiz;
Molt volentiers, non à enviz,
Si est en la sale venuz.
Coiement, sanz faire granz huz, 168
Il boute l'uis, en la chanbre entre,
. . . .
Aventure li adona
Que la dame seule trouva. 172
Les puceles totes ensanble
Erent alees, ce me sanble,
En une chanbre d'autre part.
Ne sai lïoncel ou liepart 176
Cousoient en un drap de soie;
Entr'eles menoient grant joie;
Ce ert l'ensaigne au chevalier.
Guillaumes ne se volt targier. 180
La dame seoit sor un lit,
Plus bele dame onques ne vit
Nus hom qui de mere soit nez.
Guillaumes fu toz trespenssez 184
Où voit son leu, molt li est tart,
La dame fait un doz regart[15]
Guillaumes et puis la salue.
Ele ne fu mie esperdue, 188
Un molt beax ris li a gité;
Tot en riant l'a salué,
"Guillaumes," dit el, "or avant."
Cil li respont en soupirant, 192
"Dame," fait il, "Molt volentiers."
—"Seez vos ci, beax amis chiers."
La dame point ne se gardoit
Du coraige que cil avoit, 196
Quant son chier ami l'apela;
S'el le seüst, n'en pallast ja.
Guillaumes s'est el lit assis
Joste la dame o le cler vis 200
Rit et parole et joe à li,
Et la dame tot autresi.

Oh, what's the use! I shouldn't really!
I really don't know what to do!
When all this started, then I knew
I could retreat when the time came,
But love has set me all aflame."
William summoned up his nerve
And didn't hesitate or swerve,
But straight to the lady's room he rushed,
And when he reached the door, he pushed
It open wide without a sound
And came into the room and found,
By chance, the lady there alone.
Her maids in waiting had all gone
Into another room to stitch
A lion or leopard (I don't know which)
Upon silk cloth. They laughed and played
And had good fun. Their work displayed
The coat of arms of the lady's knight.
William didn't want to wait.

The lady sat upon her bed.
Never had man of woman bred
Beheld a lovelier form alive.
William was worried. When would arrive
His golden opportunity?
William looked long and longingly
Upon her; then he said, "Hello."
The lady wasn't nervous, though.
"William, she answered, "come inside."
She sweetly laughed. But William sighed
And answered, "Yes, ma'am, willingly."
—"My dear friend, come and sit by me."
But little did she apprehend
How much her greeting, "My dear friend,"
Had set the young man's heart aflutter.
Nothing could have made her utter
Such words of friendship had she known.
Her face was beautiful. It shone
As William sat there on her bed.
They laughed and joked, and much they said
On many subjects far and wide
William took a breath and sighed:

De mainte chose vont pallant,
Guillaumes fait un soupir grant.
"Dame," fait il, "or m'entendez,
En bonne foi quar me donez
Conseil de ce que vos diroie."
—"Dites," fait ele, "ge l'otroie."
—"Se clers ou chevaliers amoit,
Borgois, vallez, qui que il soit,
Ou escuiers meïsme ensanble,
Dites moi que il vos en senble,
S'il amoit dame ou damoisele,
Reïne, contesse ou pucele,
De quele guise qu'ele soit,
De haut liu ou de bas endroit;
Il aura bien .VII. anz amee,
Itant aura s'amor celee,
Ne ne li ose encore dire
Que por lui soit en tel martire,
Et tres bien dire li porroit
Se tant de hardement avoit[16]
Assez aisement et loisir
De son coraige descovrir.
Or me dites vostre pensee;
Puisqu'il a tant s'amor celee,
Itant vorroie ge savoir
S'il a fait folie ou savoir."
—"Guillaumes," dit ele, "endroit moi
Dirai molt bien si com ge croi.
Ge ne l'en tieg mie por saige
Que ne li a dit son coraige,
Puisque il puet parler à lui.
Elë eüst de lui merci,[17]
Et, s'ele amer ne le voloit,
Certes grant folie feroit
Se por lui entroit puis en peine.
Mais, des qu'Amors si le demeine
Qu'il ne s'en puet arriere traire,
Itant li löerai [g]e à faire[18]
Que li die seürement:
Amors demande hardement.
Un jugement droit vos en faz:
Cil que Amors a pris au laz,
Ne doit pas estre acoardi;
Seürs doit estrë et hardi.
Se ge ere d'amor esprise,

"Lady, I beg of you, pay heed
204 To what I ask of you. I need
Your counsel. Tell me what you'd say. . . ."
—"Of course I'll give it. Ask away."
—"If clerk, or knight of high degree,
208 Or someone from the bourgeoisie
Should fall in love—or even a squire—
With lowly woman, or with higher,
With duchess, dame or demoiselle,
212 Fine lady or young mademoiselle
Of any station or degree,
What would your opinion be
If he has loved her seven years
216 And kept it hidden and he fears
Still to tell her anything—
What martyrdom he's suffering—
And yet he still could tell his love
220 If only he were brave enough
And the occasion would appear
To open up his heart to her,
And what I really wish I knew
224 Is what you think he ought to do
And whether he does right or wrong
To keep his love from her so long."
The lady answered, "Listen William,
228 Here's my advice. Here's what I'd tell him.
I don't believe he's very smart
Not to tell her from his heart
How much he loves her, since he can.
232 She'd have to pity the poor man.
It would be very foolish of her
Not to accept the love he's offered
And one day wish to God she had.
236 But since Love rules and drives him mad
And willy-nilly pulls him along,
Then he should speak. He must be strong
And tell his love. That's what I'd urge.
240 He loves her, yes, but love takes courage.
This principle must be observed:
The god of love cannot be served
By cowards. Lovers must be brave,
244 Since they are bound to be Love's slave.
By Paul, if I were in his place,
I'd tell the lady face to face,
And she would have to hear me, too.

Foi que ge doi à saint Denise	248	And that's what this man ought to do,
Diroie li comme hardie.		And let her love him if she will."
Itant li lo ge que li die;		
S'ele le velt amer, si l'aint."		
Guillaumes a jeté un plaint;	252	William looked a little ill
En soupirant li respondi:		And moaned and sighed and then began:
"Dame," fait il, "veez le ci		"Lady," he said, "behold the man,
Cil qui a trate ce dolor		The one who long, without relief,
Tant longuement por vostre amor.	256	For love of you has suffered grief.
Dame, ne vos osoie dire		Lady, I didn't dare to tell
Ne la dolor ne le martire		The martyrdom and bitter hell
Que g'ai tant longuement sofferte;		I've had to bear these seven years,
A grant paine l'ai descoverte.	260	And telling it, I'm filled with fears.
Ma douce Dame, à vos me rent,		Lady, I give myself to you.
Tot à vostre commandement		Do with me what you want to do.
Sui mis en la vostre menoie.		I am your serving man and slave.
Dame, garissiez moi la plaie	264	Sweet lady, heal this wound I have
Que g'ai dedenz le cors si grant.		Inside my body, deep and raw.
Il n'est voir nul homme vivant		There isn't anyone at all
Qui me peüst santé doner.		Who can restore me to my health,
D'itant me puis ge bien vanter[19]	268	But you. I boast of this myself.
Ge sui tot vostre et fui et iere;		All yours I am, was, will remain.
En plus doulereuse maniere		In greater agony or pain
Ne pot onques vivre nus hom.		No man has ever had to live.
Dame, ge vos requier par don[20]	272	Lady, I'm asking you to give
Que me faciez de vostre amor,		Your love to me, the love whose lack
Par qoi ge sui en tel error."		Has put my body on the rack."
La Dame entent bien que il dit,		And now the lady fully grasped
Mais tot ce prise molt petit.	276	What it was that William asked,
Elle li respondi itant		But not a coin or crust of bread
Ne pris un seul denier vaillant		Would she have given for what he said.
Ce qu'el oï Guillaume dire.		The lady looked at him and spoke.
Ele li commença à dire,	280	"William," she asked, "is this a joke?
"Guillaumes," dist ele, "est ce gas?		I wouldn't love you for the world.
Ge ne vos ameroie pas,		Go play your jokes on some poor girl.
Vos gaberoiz encor autrui.		No one has ever dared to play
Onques mais gabee ne fui,	284	Such jokes on me before today.
Par mon chief, com vos m'avez ore!		But one thing's sure. By God I vow
Se vos me pallïoiz encore		If you should speak as you spoke now
De ce que vos m'avez ci dit,		To me again, I'll have you shamed.
Ne remandroit, se Diex m'aïst,	288	I didn't know your love was aimed
Que ge ne vos feïsse honte.		At me. What are you asking for?
Ge ne sai riens que amors monte,		You've got your nerve. Go! There's the door!
Ne de ce que vos demandez.		Get out of here, get off this place.
B[e]ax sire, quar vos en alez!	292	Don't you ever show your face

Fuiez de ci, alez là fors!
Gardez que mais li vostre cors
Ne viegne mais là où ge soie!
Molt en aura certes grant joie 296
Mes sires quant il le saura!
Certes, tantost com il vendra,
Li dirai ge ceste parole
Dont vos m'avez mis à escole. 300
Molt me sanblez musarz et fox;
Maldahez ait parmi le cox,[21]
Sire, qui ci vos amena!
Beax amis, traez vos en là!" 304
Et quant Guillaumes ce oï,
Sachiez que molt fut esbahi;
De ce qu'il ot dit se repent.
Onques ne respondi noient, 308
Tant fu dolenz et esbahiz.
"He! las," fait il, "ge sui trahiz!"

De ceste chose me sovient
Que li mesaiges trop tost vient[22] 312
Qui la male novele aporte.
Amors li commande et enorte
Qu'encore voist paller à lui;
Ne la doit pas laisser ainsi, 316
"Dame," dit il, "ce poise moi
Que ge n'ai de vos autre otroi;
Mais vos faites molt grant pechié,
Quant vos m'avez pris et lié, 320
Et plus mal faire me baez;
Ocïez moi se vos volez.
De vostre amor vos ai requise;
Un don vos pri, par tel devise 324
Que jamais jor ne mengerai
Jusqu'à cel eure que j'aurai
Le don eü de vostre amor
Dont ge sui en itel error." 328
Dist la dame: "Par saint Omer,
Molt vos covient à jeüner
Que se devant lors ne mengiez
Que vos aiez mes amistiez. 332
Ce n'ert, si com j'ai enpensé,
S'erent soiez li noveau blé."

Guillaumes fors de la cha[m]bre ist;
Onques point de congié ne prist. 336
Un lit a fait appareillier,

Anywhere within my sight.
Your little offer will delight
My husband when he finds it out.
When he comes home, you needn't doubt,
I'll tell my husband word for word
The whole, long sermon I've endured.
I think you are an imbecile.
Whoever was responsible
For bringing you here should be drowned.
Get out, young man! Don't stick around!"
When William realized what she said,
He was amazed and half struck dead.
Much he repented having come.
He stood there, stupified and dumb,
Downhearted, mortified, dismayed.
"Alas," he thought, "I am betrayed."

Messengers, who always lose
Their welcome when they bring bad news,
Are what young William reminds me of.
And still he was compelled by love,
Still felt the need to speak to her
And not leave matters as they were.
"Lady," he said, "I'm sorely grieved
That this is all I have received
From you. But lady, you have sinned.
You have me trapped and tied and pinned
And treat me worse. You want my death—
Kill me and get it over with.
Listen, I asked you for your love.
I beg a gift, and I will prove
My need for it. I will not eat
Until the day that you see fit."
The lady answered, "By the mass,
You're really going to have to fast
To get my love. You will not eat
Before the sowing of the wheat."

Then William rose and went away
Without good-bye, without good day,
Arranged his bed and went to bed,

Lors si i est alez couchier.		But little rest did William get.
Quant il se fu couchié el lit,		He stayed in bed three days complete
Si se reposa molt petit.	340	And nothing did he drink or eat,
Trois jors toz pleins en son li[t] jut,		And on the fourth he still was there,
Onques ne menga ne ne but;		And still the lady didn't spare
Pres fu du quart en tel maniere.		A look at him when she went past.
Molt fu la dame vers lui fiere	344	But William did know how to fast.
Qu'ele nel daigna regarder.		He wouldn't even eat a crust.
Bien sot Guillaumes geüner		The sickness in him would not rest.
Qu'il ne menja de nule chose.		It nagged and worried him night and day.
Son mal qu'il a point ne repose;	348	He lost his color, pined away.
Tant le destraint et nuit et jor		No wonder he was losing weight:
Tote a perdue la color.		Three days, he never slept or ate!
S'il amegrist n'est pas merveille,		William lay in bed and shook,
Riens ne menjue et toz jors veille.	352	And when he rolled his eye to look,
Guillaumes est en grant effroi		The lovely lady, full of charms—
Quant li hueil li tornent un poi;		He thought he felt her in his arms,
La dame, qui tant par est gente,		Lying there with him and granting
Ce li est vis que il la sente	356	Everything that he was wanting.
Entre ses braz dedenz son lit,		And while this lasted, it was bliss
Et qu'il en fait tot son delit.		To hold her, trading kiss for kiss.
Tant com ce dure est molt a ese,		And when at last the vision waned,
Quar il l'acole et si la baise;	360	He trembled, sighed, reached out his hand,
Et, quant cel avisïon faut,		But air is all that he embraced.
Donques soupire et si tressalt		Foolishness is what fools chase!
Estent ses braz, n'en treuve mie;		He searched for her throughout the bed.
Fols est qui chace la folie.	364	She wasn't there. He beat his head,
Par tot son lit la dame quiert;		His face and chest, and tore his hair.
Quant ne la trueve, si se fiert		Love held him tied. Love was the snare.
Sor la poitrine et en la face.		Love held him hurt in chains of steel.
Amors le tient, Amors le lace,	368	He wanted her to be there still.
Amors le tient en grant torment.		The vision should have stayed forever,
Il vosist que plus longuement		But nothing else but chills and fever
Li durast cel avisïsons,		The god of loving would allow.
Le dieu d'amors le r'a semons	372	
De froit avoir et de tranbler.		
Du chastelain vorrai parler		I'll speak about the husband now,
Qui revient du tornoiement;		Riding from the tournament
Ensanble o lui ot molt gran[t] gent.	376	With many men at arms. He sent
Atant ez vos un escuier		A messenger to his chateau
A la dame venu noncier		To find his wife and let her know
Que se[s] sires vient du tornoi.		The day her lord was coming home.
.XV. prisons enmaine o soi,	380	Fifteen prisoners came with him,
Chevaliers riches et puissanz;		All of them rich and wealthy knights,
Li autres gaainz est molt granz.		And many other spoils besides.

La dame entendi la novele;		The message of this messenger
Molt par li fu joieuse et bele,	384	Was joyous, welcome news to her.
Molt par en est joianz et liee.		Delighted, she made sure that all
Tost fu la sale apareilliee.		Was ready in the banquet hall
Et mengier fist faire molt gent;		To wine and dine the many guests.
Molt fist bel apareillement	388	Everything must look the best
La dame encontre son seignor.		For the arrival of her lord.
Guillaumes fu en grant freor;		As for William, he was scared.
Et la dame se porpensa		The lady thought she ought to tell
Que à Guillaume le dira	392	William that her lord was well
Que ses ires vient du tornoi;		And coming from the tournament,
Demander li vorra por quoi		And ask him what on earth he meant
Il est si fox qu'il ne menjue.		Not touching any of his food.
Droit à son lit en est venue;	396	She came beside his bed and stood.
Grant piece fu devant son lit;		A good long while she waited there,
Onques Guillaumes ne la vit.		But William didn't notice her.
Donc l'a apelé par son non;		"William," she called at last, "Hello!"
Il ne li dit ne o ne non,	400	He didn't answer *yes* or *no*.
Quar toz en autre siecle estoit.		His mind was somewhere in a cloud.
Elle l'a bouté de son doit,		This time she called his name quite loud
Et si le husche un poi plus haut.		And with her finger poked his head.
Et quant il l'entent, toz tressaut,[23]	404	When William heard, he jerked in bed.
Quant il la sent, toz en tressue,		And when he felt, he broke out sweating.
Quant il la voit, si la salue:		He saw her, and he shouted greeting:
"Dame, bien soiez vos venue		"Lady, welcome! Thank God you're here!
Comme ma senté et m'ajue;[24]	408	You've come to bring me health and cheer.
Dame," fait il, "po Dieu vos pri		Please for the sake of God almighty,
Que vos aiez de moi merci."		Lady, I beg you, show some pity."
Itant la dame respondi:		She answered, "By the faith I owe you,
. . . .	412	William, no pity will I show you,
"Guillaumes, foi que ge vos doi,		Not the kind you're asking for.
Vous n'aurez ja merci par moi		Is this the way you thank my lord
En tel maniere com vos dites.		For all the kindness he has done?
Rendu avez males merites	416	Wooing his wife when he is gone?
A mon seignor de son servise,		You love him too. Is that the way
Quant vos sa feme avez requise.		You love? You'll never see the day
Amez le vos de tel amor?		You manage me or make me love you.
Ja ne porroiz veoir le jor	420	William, it's very foolish of you
Que vos m'aiez en vo baillie.		To keep from eating night and day.
Mais vos faites molt grant folie,		You know, you'll kill yourself that way.
Guillaumes, que vos ne mengiez.		Your soul will perish if you do,
Quant vos ainsi vos ocïez,	424	For I will never give to you
La vostre ame sera perie,		The gift you keep on asking for.
Quar ge ne vos donroie mie		Get up! Get out of bed! My lord
Le don que vos me demandez.		Is riding homeward from the tourney.

Faites le bien, si vos levez,	428	I cannot tell how long the journey,
Que mes sires vient du tornoi.		But when he comes and finds you there,
Par cele foi que ge vos doi		Lying in bed, by God, I swear,
Ge ne gart l'eure que il viegne.		He'll learn from me what the reason is.
Se Diex," fait ele, "me sostiegne,	432	You'll never get away with this."
Il saura por quoi vos gisez,		—"It won't be any use," he said,
Si que ja n'en eschaperez."		"To slice my arms and legs and head,
—"Dame," dist il, "ce n'a mestier,		Because I'll never eat, I swear.
Por trestoz les menbres trenchier,	436	Lady, around my neck I wear
Que ne mengeroie jamés.		A heavy weight that will not fall.
J'ai sor le col un si grant fes		I can't defend myself at all
Nel puis jus metre ne descendre.		Against you, though I fast and die.
Vers vos ne me puis ge deffendre;	440	Tell what you want, I won't deny."
Por jeüner ne por morir.		At that the lady turned and went
Dame, dites vostre plaisir."		With no love promised and none meant.
Atant la Dame s'est partie		She came to where the dining hall
De Guillaume sanz estre amie;	444	Was decorated wall to wall.
En la sale en est retornee,		The tables all were set in place
Qui fu richement atornee,		With tablecloths of white cut lace
Et les tables basses assises,		And loaded with good things to eat:
Et les blanches napes sus mises,	448	Bread and wine and skewered meat.
Et anprés les mes aportez,		
Pain et vin, et hastes tornez.		
Lors sont venu li chevalier,		At last the knights came riding in,
Et sont tuit assis au mengier,	452	And now the feasting could begin,
Et plus tres bien furent servi		More men were served and eating well
C'on ne porroit raconter ci.		Than this short narrative could tell.
Le sire et la dame menja;		Lady and lord together ate.
Parmi la sale regarda	456	The husband looked up from his plate
Se Guillaume veīst venir		To see if William would be there
A son mengier por lui servir.		To stand and serve behind his chair,
A molt grant merveille le tint		But he was nowhere to be seen.
Que Guillaumes à lui ne vint.	460	He wondered where he could have been
"Dame," dit il, "en bone foi		And turned to her and said, "My dear,
Me sauriez [vos] dire por quoi		I cannot see young William here.
Guillaumes n'est à moi venuz?"		I pray you, can you tell me why?"
—"Il est trop cointes devenuz,"	464	—"Lately William's been too shy,"
Dit la dame, "gel vos dirai;		The lady said, "But I'll explain
De mot ne vos en mentirai.		What's going on. The simple, plain
Il est malades d'un tel mal		And honest truth is this: he's ill.
Dont ja n'aura medecinal,	468	And there will never be a pill
Si com ge cuit, en nule guise."		To cure the sickness William has."
—"Dame," fait il, "par saint Denyse,		Her husband answered, "By the mass,
Moi poise qu'il a se bien non."		I'm sorry he's not feeling good."
Mais, s'il seüst bien l'aquoison	472	But if the lord had understood

Por quoi Guillaumes se geüst,		The reason he was feeling bad,
Ja du lit ne se remeüst.		William would have died in bed.
Il ne le set encore pas,		(So far, he doesn't understand.
Il i a un molt fort trespas	476	But death and danger are at hand.
Ge cuit à toz tens le saura,[25]		He'll find out soon. If William still
Que la dame li contera		Refuses food, I'm sure she'll tell
La parole, s'il ne menjue,		What sickness keeps him in his bed,
Por quoi la teste aura perdue.	480	And William will have to lose his head.)
Lors ont monté li chevalier;		The knights got up from empty plates.
La dame ne volt plus targier.		The lady didn't want to wait.
Son seignor prist par le mantel,		She took her husband by the sleeve:
Et dit: "Sire, molt me merveil	484	"My Lord, I'm shocked. I can't believe
Que Guillaume n'alez veoir.		You've not seen William yet. You ought
Vos devrïez tres bien savoir		To visit him and find out what
Quel mal ce est qui le destraint;		His ailment is and why he's ailing.
Encore cuit ce qu'il se faint."	488	Day by day the boy is failing."
Lors i sont maintenant alé;		They went together to the room
Guillaume ont trouvé trespensé.		And found him pensive, full of gloom,
Li sires et la dame vient		But unaffected by the fear
Devant Guillaume, qui ne crient	492	Of death, which surely must be near.
La mort qu'il a à trespasser,		He'd had enough of pain and grief
Qu'il ne velt mais plus andurer		And hoped his dying would be brief.
Ne tel martire, ne tel paine;		The lord knelt down beside the bed
Bien velt la mort li soit prochaine.	496	At William's feet and bowed his head,
Li sires s'est ageloigniez		And like an honest man and good,
Devant Guillaume vers les piez;		Reasoned with him as best he could.
De ce fist il comme frans hom;		"William, my dear young friend," he said,
Doucement le mist à raison:	500	"What sickness keeps you locked in bed?
"Guillaumes, dites, beax amis,		Tell me what's wrong. I'll help you gladly."
Quex maus vos a ainsi sorpris;		—"My lord," he said, "I'm doing badly.
Dites moi comment il vos est."		The sickness runs from head to toes.
—"Sire," fait il, "malement m'est.	504	In sudden fits it comes and goes.
Une molt grant dolor me tient;		Every limb is racked with pain.
Une goute, qui va et vient,		I don't think I'll get up again."
Me tient es membres et el chief;		—"Well, won't you eat or take some water?"
Ge ne cuit que jamais en lief."	508	—"No food or drink. It doesn't matter.
—"Porrīez vos menger ne boivre?"		Nothing God made could suit my diet."
—"Ge nel porroie pas reçoivre		The lady couldn't have kept quiet
Nule riens c'onques Diex feīst."		If she had choked on every word:
La dame plus ne se tenist,	512	"By God, we're wasting time, my lord!
Qui la deüst vive escorchier:		William may speak the way he wishes,
"Sire, par Dieu, ce n'a mestier;		But *I* know what the truth of this is—
Guillaumes dit sa volenté,		What the cause is, where it lingers.
Mais ge sai bien de verité	516	This sickness isn't in his finger!
Quex maus le tient et où endroit.		This sickness makes the victim sweat,

Ce n'est mie du mal du doit,
Ainz est un maus qui fait suer
Ceus qui l'ont et souvent tranbler." 520
Pui dist à Guillaume la dame:
"Sire, se Diex ait part en m'ame,
Guillaumes se vos ne mengiez,
Or est li termes aproschiez 524
Que vos ne mengerez jamais."
—"Dame," dit il, "ge n'en puis mais;
Vostre plaisir pöez bien dire.
Ma dame estes et il mes sire, 528
Mais ne porroie pas mengier
Por toz les menbres à tranchier."
—"Sire," dit ele, "or esgardez
Com Guillaumes est fox provez. 532
Tantost com au tournoi alastes,
Guillaumes, qui ci gist malades,
Vint en ma chambre devant moi."
—"Il i vint, dame? Et il por quoi? 536
Que fu ce qu'il vos demanda,
Quant dedenz vostre cha[m]bre entra?"
—"Sire, ce vos dirai ge bien. . .
Guillaumes, mengeroiz vos rien? 540
Ge dirai ja à mon seignor
La grant honte et la deshenor."
Dist Guillaumes: "Nenil, par foi;
Jamais ne mengerai, ce croi." 544
Lors dist li sires à la dame:
"Vos me tenez por fol, par m'ame.
Et por musart et por noient,
Quant ge ne vos fier maintenant 548
D'un baston parmi les costez."
—"Avoi, Sire," dit ele, "ostez,
Ainz le vos dirai par mon chief.
Guillaumes," dist el, "ge me lief. 552
Mengerez vos? Ge dirai ja."
Guillaumes donques soupira,
Et respondi piteusement,
Com cil qui grant angoisse sent: 556
"Ge ne mengeroie à nul fuer,
Se le mal qui me tient au cuer
Ne m'est primes assoagiez."
Lors en ot la dame pitié, 560
Et à son seignor respondi:
"Sire, Guillaumes que vez ci

Tremble in his bed and fret."
She looked at William in the eye:
"So help me God, I will not lie.
William, unless you break your fast,
The hour has come around at last
When all you eating days are over."
But William only answered, "Never.
You have the power. You give the word.
You are my lady, he my lord,
But though you sliced my hands and feet,
Even then I would not eat."
The lady cried, "Now hear the truth,
My lord, about this foolish youth!
When you rode to the tournament,
William, who's lying sick here, went
Into my room to visit me."
—"What? Lady! Into your room, did he?
What on earth did he do that for?
Why did he cross your chamber door?"
—"I'll tell you sir. He came and stood—
William, will you have some food?
My husband's going to hear the shame
And gross dishonor to his name."
—"No! shouted William, "By Saint Pete,
Never! I will never eat!"
The lord said, "Lady, you will make
A fool of me if I don't take
This heavy stick I have in hand
And beat you till you cannot stand
And bruise your sides and back and head!"
"Wait, my lord. Hold on!" she said,
"I'm going to tell you everything—
William! are you listening?
Now will you eat? I'm telling him."
But William didn't move a limb.
He heaved a sigh most pitiful:
"Never will I eat until
This nagging heartache is assuaged."

At last the lady's anger changed
To pity, and "My lord," she said,
"This William, whom you see in bed,

i me requist vostre faucon,		Asked me for your—falcon, sir,
t ge ne l'en voil faire don,	564	And I refused, you may be sure,
i voz dirai par quel maniere		Because I'm very much aware
Qu'en voz oiseax n'ai ge que faire."		Your birds, my lord, are your affair."
)ist li Sires: "Ne m'est pas bel.		The lord said, "This was badly done.
'amasse mielz tuit li oisel,	568	I'd rather all the birds I won—
'aucon, ostoir et espervier		Falcon, peregrine, and hawk—
ussent mort que un jor entier		Were dead than William on his back
n eüst Guillaumes geü."		And hungry even for a day."
ien a la dame deçeü	572	The wife deceived her lord that way.
Sire," dit el, "or li donez,		"Then give it to him," she replied,
uisque faire si le volez;		"If that will keep you satisfied.
nel perdra mie par moi.		I'm not the one to tell him no.
uillaumes, foi que ge vos doi,	576	William, by the faith I owe,
Quant mes sire le vos ostroie,		My lord and husband has agreed,
Iolt grant vilenie feroie		And it would be an evil deed
e vos par moi le perdīez."		If I continued to refuse."
uillaumes fu joianz et liez,	580	William, when he heard this news,
Quant il oī ceste raison,		Almost burst from joy and pleasure
'lus que ne puet dire nus hom.		His happiness could know no measure.
'ost s'apareille et tost se lieve;		Soon he was up and soon was dressed,
i maus qu'il a point ne li grieve;	584	His sickness gone, no more distressed.
Quant il fu chauciez et vestuz,		He put his socks and his shoes on
)roit en la sale en est venuz.		And straight to the lady's room was gone.
Quant la dame le vit venir,		And when the lady saw him come,
)es elz a gité un soupir;	588	She breathed a sigh and gazed on him.
mors li a gité un dart;		Love had pierced her to the heart,
le en doit bien avoir sa part.		And now she had to have her part.
'roidir li fait et eschauffer;		Love chilled and burned her with the fever.
ovent li fait color muer.	592	Love made her pale and blush and shiver.
)it li sires à Guillemet:		"William, young man," the master said,
Il a en vos molt fol vallet		"You must have really lost your head
Qu'à mon faucon vos estes pris;		To crave my hawk so desperately.
'en ai esté molt tres pensis:	596	Letting her go is hard for me.
e n'en sai nul, ne fol ne saige,		There's no one else, not mad or sane,
'rince, ne conte de parage		No prince or count or noble thane
Que gel donasse en tel maniere		With prayers or service who could hope
'or servise ne por proiere."	600	To make me give my falcon up."
ors a dit à un damoisel:		The knight gave orders to his men
Alez moi querre mon oisel."		To bring the falcon to him then.
il li aporta arroment.		They brought it quickly, and the lord
i sires par les giez le prent;	604	Took the jess and gave the bird
i l'a à Guillaume doné,		To William, who accepted it
t cil l'en a molt mercïé.		With thanks and pleasure, as was fit.
Dist la Dame: "Or avez faucon;		The wife said, "Now you have your falcon.

.II. besanz valent un mangon."	608	Two half crowns are a crown, I reckon."
Ce fu bien dit, .II. moz à un,		And she was right: one thing—two words.
Que il en auroit .II. por un,		One word would get him two rewards,
Et cil si ot ainz l'endemain		For by next morning, he had more:
Le faucon dont il ot tel faim,	612	The falcon which he hungered for,
Et de la dame son deduit		And from the lady, joy more sweet
Qu'il ama mielz que autre fruit.		Than pear or plum is good to eat.
Par la raison de cest flabel		This fabliau is one more proof
Monstré ai essanple novel	616	That I am giving of a truth
As vallez et as damoiseax,		For all young men who ever went
Qui d'Amors mainent les cenbeax,		Tilting in Love's tournament:
Que, quant auront lor cuer doné		When they have given up their heart
As dames de tres grant beauté,	620	To a lovely lady, they must start
Que il la doit tot arroment		Immediately, and they must dare
Requerre molt hardīement.		To press their love with pleas and prayer,
S'ele l'escondit au premier,		And if at first she answers *no,*
Ne la doit mie entrelaissier;	624	He must press on and not let go.
Tost amolit vers la proiere,		No matter who he is, if often
Mais que il soit qui la requiere;		And stubbornly he prays, she'll soften:
Et tot ausi Guillaumes fist		For that's how William wooed the lady,
Qui cuer et cors et tot i mist,	628	With all his heart and soul and body
Et por ce si bien en joī		And took great joy as his reward
Com vos avez oī ici.		For all his pains, as you have heard.
Et Diex en doint ausi joīr,		And may God give great joy today
Sanz demorer et sanz faillir,	632	Without postponement or delay
A toz iceus qui par amors		To those who, serving love, must bear
Sueffrent et paines et dolors:		Sorrow, anguish, and despair,
Si ferai [je], se ne lor faut[26]		And I will also, when the lover
Bon cuer. Ici li contes faut.	636	Keeps courage. Now this tale is over.

10.

De la Saineresse (The Lady-Leech)

In *De Guillaume au faucon,* the lady discovered the power of the word, how its nterpretation can fluctuate between the concrete and the symbolic almost at will, how its ack of absolute meaning can correspond to a lack of individual personality, and even how, inconnected to morality and to reality, it can justify a reprehensible act. In *De la Saineresse,* he lady discovers the power of the sustained metaphor which brings about justice and ymmetry in the deserved punishment of the husband who bragged loudly that no woman ould ever deceive him (vv. 2, 3).

In view of that boast alone, by virtue of the rule that any excessive trait of character is to e punished, we should expect the husband to suffer some mishap. The author has stated ery early, in the second line, that it was foolish to do so, but when the husband, piggishly nd crudely, invites the *saineresse* to come sit close to him, *lez moi ici* (v. 25, † 23), we expect omething more than the traditional cuckolding.[1] He has made a claim of intellectual uperiority over what he thinks (so we infer) to be inferior creatures, and that claim must e repudiated (*fera mençongier,* v. 7). We have, thus, a two-part fabliau: the familiar leception of the husband cuckolded under his very nose is followed by the allegorizing of he event by the wife who challenges him to grasp something that is perfectly and iumorously clear to the audience.[2] As Roy J. Pearcy notes, the humor lies in the fact that he dupe is told what happened "in an almost brutally direct and detailed fashion, and yet . . totally fails to comprehend it" (CH, p. 180). It is with great enjoyment that we hear im recommending that his wife pay the lover well since he was so generous with his ervices (v. 57), generous indeed in view of their repeated intercourse (.III. *fois foutue,* v. 14, † 42). It is equally rewarding to hear the dupe, who claimed to be so wise, marvel at the xcellence of the ointment described by the lady (v. 99).

The lady could have been satisfied with merely cuckolding her husband since all she had o do was to prove her husband wrong (vv. 5–9). Her delightful double entendres already int that her revenge is going to be more than physical: she claims to be in need of the aineresse's services (v. 34), telling her husband not to worry (v. 35) about the marvelous" pain in her loins (v. 37). She tells her husband not to trouble himself with the ayments to the bloodletteress because they have both agreed on acceptable wages (vv. 58, 1). Her masterful allegory of erotic-medical language begins soberly by explaining her lushed state. As she regains her breath, she seems to get carried away with excitement, ising intensifyers (*Tant, molt, tel,* and so on) over fifteen times in the short passage, and rushing dangerously close to an unmetaphorical explanation of the ointment's origin *forel, pel,* vv. 94, 95). The realization that she may have gone too far probably accounts or her abrupt ending of the allegory with a succinct conclusion (v. 96).[3] The Old French anguage has allowed her to relate the entire scene without one subject pronoun to identify he sex of the doctor. The author himself seems to have been caught in the ironic

presentation when, as a parting comment (v. 115), he gives the suffering, overactive, an
bruised lady the epithet of *qui ot mal es rains* (who had pain in the loins).

Economy of expression is a most desirable quality in such a short fabliau and a good indicator of an author's talent. After having succinctly and sufficiently portrayed the braggart, oafish husband and the hardy, vigorous wife, he sketches with rapid brush strokes the arrival of the lover. Unlike the traditionally insipid lover of most fabliaux, thi guileful rogue (v. 50) bursts upon the scene with his colorful (v. 17) and effeminate (v. 15 garb, designedly in a neglected state (v. 16), and stands in the middle of the room and salutes the *borgois* (v. 21). His outfit must have been of his own invention: obviously summoned by the lady who is intent on making a liar of her husband (vv. 28, 29), his gaudy, loud appearance and risqué remark that he came here for her pleasure momentarily take her by surprise (*esbahie,* v. 31). His effeminate demeanor and feminin disguise stand in contrast to the virile disposition of his services: with ferretlike swiftnes (*de maintenant,* v. 41; *esrant,* v. 42) he performs the duties for which he has been called then quickly abandons the scene by saluting the husband and leaving the lady flushed an breathless.

The two highpoints of the fabliau, the cuckolding of the husband and the allegorizing c the event by the lady, are thus identically marked by a crescendo rhythm, mounting to frenetic pace. When things calm down, the author blames more the husband's foolishnes in claiming superiority over women (v. 108): she tested him, and won (v. 104), but sh also felt the need to tell him of her enjoyable victory (v. 106). We agree with him and wit Pearcy, who praises that verbal composition as "an extensive allegory rivaling that at th conclusion of *Le Roman de la Rose*" (CH, p. 179).

De la Saineresse		The Lady-Leech
D'un borgois vous acont la vie[4]		The life of a businessman I'll tell
Qui se vanta de grant folie		Who one day boasted like a fool
Que fame nel porroit bouler.		No woman could deceive him, but
Sa fame en a oï parler;	4	Too bad for him—his wife found out.
Si en parla priveement,		The more she pondered it, the more
Et en jura un serement		She was annoyed. At last she swore
Qu'ele le fera mençongier,		However much the man might spy,
Ja tant ne s'i saura gueter	8	She'd prove his foolish boast a lie.
Un jor erent en lor meson		One day the boaster and his spouse
La gentil dame et le preudon;		Were sitting quietly in their house
En un banc sistrent lez à lez.		Upon a bench. A rogue came knocking,
N'i furent gueres demorez,	12	A noble rogue and quite good looking,
Ez vos un pautonier à l'uis		Except that he resembled more
Molt cointe et noble, et sambloit plus[5]		A woman than a man. He wore
Fame que homme la moitié,		A linen dress, loosely fit,
Vestu d'un chainsse deliié,	16	And saffron wimple. He brought a kit
D'une guimple bien safrenee,		Of tubes and bleeding cups, and sailed
Et vint menant molt grant posnee;[6]		Inside as bold as brass and hailed

Ventouses porte à ventouser,
Et vait le borgois saluer
En mi l'aire de sa meson:
"Diex soit o vous, sire preudon,
Et vous et vostre compaignie."
—"Diex vous gart," dist cil, "bele amie;
Venez seoir lez moi ici."
—"Sire," dist il, "vostre merci,
Je ne sui mie trop lassee.
Dame, vous m'avez ci mandee
Et m'avez ci fete venir.
Or me dites vostre plesir."
Cele ne fu pas esbahie:
'Vous dites voir, ma douce amie,
Montez là sus en cel solier;[7]
Il m'estuet de vostre mestier.
Ne vous poist," dist ele au borgois,
'Quar nous revendrons demanois;
J'ai goute es rains molt merveillouse,
Et, por ce que sui si goutouse,
M'estuet il fere un poi sainier."
Lors monte aprés le pautonier;
Les huis clostrent de maintenant.
Le pautonier le prent esrant;
En un lit l'avoit estendue
Tant que il l'a .III. fois foutue.
Quant il orent assez joué,
Foutu, besié et acolé,
Si se descendent del perrin
Contreval les degrez. En fin
Vindrent esrant en la meson.
Cil ne fut pas fol ni bricon,
Ainz le salua demanois,
'Sire, adieu," dist il au borgois.
—"Diex vous saut," dist il, "bele amie.
Dame, se Diex vous beneïe,
Paiez cele fame molt bien,
Ne retenez de son droit rien
De ce que vous sert en manaie."[8]
—"Sire, que vous chaut de ma paie,"
Dist la borgoise à son seignor,
'Je vous oi parler de folor,
Quar nous .II. bien en couvendra,"
Cil s'en va, plus n'i demora,
La poche aus ventouses a prise.

The businessman and said, "Hello, sir.
20 May heaven's grace be ever closer
To you and everybody here."
—"God bless you, too, my lovely dear,"
The husband said, "Come sit by me."
24 —"No thank you, sir!" he said. "You see,
I don't feel tired, not at all.
Here I am, Madam, at your call.
You summoned me here, didn't you?
28 What are you wanting me to do?"
The wife was not abashed by this.
"That's right," she said, "my dear young miss.
Please come upstairs with me an instant.
32 I need professional assistance."
She told the businessman, "Don't worry.
We'll be right down again. We'll hurry.
I've got the gout. My kidneys, sir,
36 Get goutier and goutier.
When I've been bled, they'll feel much better."
Lady and rogue went up together.
She shut the door and turned the lock.
40 The rogue grabbed hold of her and rocked
Her body backwards, stretched her flat
And screwed her three times. After that,
When they'd had all the fun they wished,
44 Screwed, embraced, and hugged and kissed,
They rose and went downstairs again.
The rascal was no fool, for when
They got downstairs, he turned to say
48 A word to the husband: "Sir, good day."
—"My dear," he answered, "God protect you.
And you, my lady, I expect you
To pay this girl a goodly sum
52 Since she's been good enough to come
And give you freely of her service."
—"What's that to you, sir? Don't perturb us
With money talk," the lady said.
56 "You talk as though you've lost your head.
We two can settle this affair."
The rascal left them then and there
And took his bleeding instruments.
60 The lady sat upon the bench,
Red in the face and out of breath.
"Madam, you look worn to death.
That treatment must have been too long."

La borgoise se r'est assise	64	—"Thanks, sir. Whew! You aren't far wrong.
Lez son seignor bien aboufee.		I strained as hard as a woman could.
"Dame, molt estes afouee,		A hundred strokes. It did no good.
Et si avez trop demoré."		I couldn't bleed. She thumped me till
—"Sire, merci, por amor Dé,	68	My flesh was soft as dough, and still
Ja ai je esté trop traveillie;		I didn't bleed a single drop.
Si ne pooie estre sainie,		Three times she took me, and atop
Et m'a plus de .C. cops ferue,		My loins she placed two heavy tools
Tant que je sui toute molue;	72	And struck me blows so long and cruel
N'onques tant cop n'i sot ferir		I felt the pangs of martyrdom,
C'onques sans en peüst issir.		But not a drop of blood would come.
Par .III. rebinees me prist,[9]		Such hard and frequent blows she struck,
Et à chascune fois m'assist	76	I would have died had not good luck
Sor mes rains .II. de ses peçons,[10]		Brought comfort with a soothing salve.
Et me feroit uns cops si lons		Whoever had this salve would have
Toute me sui fet martirier,		Relief and every anguish eased.
Et si ne poi onques sainier.	80	When all the hammering had ceased,
Granz cops me feroit et sovent;		This easeful ointment she applied
Morte fusse, mon escïent,		Upon my wounds both deep and wide
S'un trop bon oingnement ne fust.		Until it cured me of my ache.
Qui de tel oingnement eüst,	84	This medicine was good to take.
Ja ne fust mes de mal grevee.		Such doctoring could be endured!
Et, quant m'ot tant demartelee,		And yet, don't get me wrong, my lord:
Si m'a aprés ointes mes plaies		This ointment issued from a dropper
Qui molt par erent granz et laies,	88	Down through a pinhole in a stopper
Tant que je fui toute guerie.		That was grotesque and dark and rude.
Tel oingnement ne haz je mie,		But glory be, the salve felt good!"
Et il ne fet pas à haïr,[11]		—"My dear," the businessman replied,
Et si ne vous en quier mentir,	92	"I fear you must have almost died.
L'oingnement issoit d'un tuiel,		That must have been effective ointment."
Et si descendoit d'un forel[12]		
D'une pel molt noire et hideuse,		
Mes molt par estoit savoreuse."	96	
Dist li borgois: "Ma bele amie,		
A poi ne fustes mal baillie.[13]		
Bon oingnement avez eü."		
Cil ne s'est pas aperceü	100	She told her medical appointment
De la borde qu'ele conta,		As one long joke he didn't get.
Et cele nule honte n'a		She gloried in her sinning, yet
De la lecherie essaucier;[14]		No shame she suffered from her jest.
Por tant le veut bien essaier:	104	Though she had put him to the test,
Ja n'en fust paié à garant,		She did not feel the game was won
Se ne li contast maintenant.		Till she had told him all she'd done.
Por ce tieng je celui à fol		That's why I say that any man's
Qui jure son chief et son col	108	A fool who swears by head and hands,

Que fame nel porroit bouler		"No woman makes a fool of me.
Et que bien s'en sauroit garder.		I keep close watch. It couldn't be."
Mes il n'est pas en cest païs		This country doesn't have, however,
Cil qui tant soit de sens espris	112	A man so wise, a man so clever,
Qui mie se peüst guetier		Despite his prying, spying, snooping,
Que fame nel puist engingnier,		Who can avoid a woman's duping,
Quant cele, qui ot mal es rains,[15]		Since such a husband did not doubt
Boula son seignor premerains.	116	The woman with the kidney gout.

Notes

Introduction

1. Joseph Bédier, *Les Fabliaux,* p. 30.
2. Per Nykrog, *Les Fabliaux: Etude d'histoire littéraire et de stylistique médiévale,* p. 15.
3. Knud Togeby, "The Nature of the Fabliaux," p. 9.
4. Thomas D. Cooke, *The Old French and Chaucerian Fabliaux: A Study of Their Comic Climax,* pp. 162–69.
5. Clem C. Williams, Jr., "The Genre and Art of the Old French Fabliaux: A Preface to the Study of Chaucer's Tales of the Fabliau type."
6. Mary Jane Schenck, "The Morphology of the Fabliau." The ten functions she analyzes are: Arrival, Departure, Interrogation, Communication, Deception, Complicity, Misdeed, Recognition, Retaliation, and Resolution. Schenck emphasizes the importance of the Deception and Misdeed functions in "Functions and Roles in the Fabliau."
7. Bédier's hypothetical calculations have put their number at over two thousand. See also Charles H. Livingston, *Le Jongleur Gautier le Leu: Etude sur les Fabliaux,* p. 112.
8. For a good summary of this question, see Nykrog, *Les Fabliaux,* pp. xx–xxxvii.
9. Charles Muscatine, "The Social Background of the Old French Fabliaux."
10. Edmond Faral, "Le Fabliau latin au moyen âge." See also Peter Dronke, "The Rise of the Medieval Fabliau: Latin and Vernacular Evidence."
11. Grace Frank, *Medieval French Drama,* 3d ed., pp. 213–14.
12. Edmond Faral, ed., *Courtois d'Arras,* pp. iii–iv.
13. JO, pp. xiii–xviii. See Nykrog, *Les Fabliaux,* pp. 242–62. See also T. B. W. Reid, ed., *Twelve Fabliaux: From MS. F. FR 19152 of the Bibliothèque Nationale,* p. x.
14. Robert Harrison, *Gallic Salt,* p. 5. The fabliaux have long been considered folkloric material. To wit, their inclusion in Stith Thompson's *Motif-Index of Folk-Literature,* 2d ed.
15. On the subject of parody of courtly and epic genres, Jean Subrenat in "Notes sur la tonalité des fabliaux. A propos du fabliau: *Du Fèvre de Creeil,*" and Roy J. Pearcy in "Chansons de Geste and Fabliaux: *La Gageure* and *Berenger au long cul,*" support Nykrog's thesis. L.-F. Flutre, in "Le Fabliau, genre courtois?," cautions against too much of an exclusive and systematized usage of this theory.
16. Harrison, *Gallic Salt,* pp. 9, 10.
17. Jean Rychner, *Contribution à l'étude des fabliaux: Variantes, remaniements, dégradations,* p 58 (Hereafter referred to as *Contribution*).
18. See Roy J. Pearcy, "Relations between the D and A Versions of *Berengier au long cul*"; the conclusion to Roy J. Pearcy's "Structural Models for the Fabliaux and the *Summoner's Tale* Analogues"; and Raymond Eichmann, "The Search for Originals in the Fabliaux and the Validity of Textual Dependency."
19. Krystyna Kasprzyk, "Pour la sociologie du fabliau: Convention, tactique et engagement," restates well the problems of attributing fabliaux to a specific social class. Interestingly, *Le Fol Vilain* and *Le Sot Chevalier* (Livingston, *Le Jongleur Gautier le Leu,* p. 85) are both from Gautier Le Leu and show no substantial differences in "style" either. Attributing a different audience to these tales on the bases of characters or style (J. Rychner, *Contribution*) is, therefore, very problematic.
20. See Raymond Eichmann, "The Question of Variants and the Fabliaux."
21. Thomas D. Cooke, "Formulaic Diction and the Artistry of *Le Chevalier qui recovra l'amor de sa dame.*"
22. Benjamin Honeycutt, "An Example of Comic Cliché in the Old French Fabliaux." See also Raymond Eichmann, "The Artistry of Economy in the Fabliaux."
23. Paul Theiner, "Fabliau Settings."
24. For Norris J. Lacy, "Types of Esthetic Distance in the Fabliaux," "This economy is effective in the creation of esthetic distance" (p. 111) that avoids drawing the audience into the story, thereby enabling it to laugh without restriction. See also Cooke, *Old French,* pp. 24–39.
25. These are Nykrog's figures. See *Les Fabliaux,* p. 28.
26. Cooke, *Old French,* p. 154.
27. See Henry C. Lea, *The History of Sacerdotal Celibacy in the Christian Church,* especially pp. 42–58, 87–88, 91–300; Earl Evelyn Sperry, *An Outline of the History of Clerical Celibacy in Western Europe to the Council of Trent;* and P. Delhaye "Celibacy, History of."
28. Sperry, *History of Clerical Celibacy,* pp. 47–48.
29. For example, *Le Segretain Moine* and its several variants (MR, 5:115; 5:215; 6:117) *Estormi* (MR, 1:198).
30. For example, *Du Prestre Crucefié* (MR

1:194); *Connebert* (MR, 5:160).

31. For example, *Aloul* (MR, 1:255), *Du Prestre qui fu mis au lardier* (MR, 2:24).

32. Charles Ray Beach, *Treatment of Ecclesiastics in the French Fabliaux of the Middle Ages*. Marie-Thérèse Lorcin, in "Quand les Princes n'épousaient pas les bergères · ou mésalliance et classes d'âge dans les fabliaux," believes that the fabliaux favor the "young" over the "old," the aspiring ones over those who are already settled in society. Thus, the fabliaux' dislike of priests is due not so much to a current evidence of anticlericism but to the fact that the priest, endowed with a benefice, is a representative of the class of people settled in society, just like the merchant, the blacksmith, and so on. For more information about the deserved miseries inflicted on lecherous priests, see Bédier, *Les Fabliaux*, pp. 335–40.

33. Glending Olson would probably disagree with such a seriousness of intent: the fabliau "is meant to entertain rather than to teach, to offer relaxation and refreshment rather than spiritual understanding." See "The Medieval Theory of Literature for Refreshment and Its Use in the Fabliau Tradition."

34. Ferdinand Brunetière, "Les Fabliaux du moyen âge et l'origine des contes."

35. See Thomas D. Cooke, "Pornography, the Comic Spirit, and the Fabliaux," for a discussion of how the final result of many fabliaux is to disappoint pornographic expectations.

36. In *Des Trois Dames qui trouverent l'anel* (MR, 1:168), *Du Chevalier qui fist sa fame confesse* (MR, 1:178), *Des Braies au cordelier* (MR, 3:275), *Des Tresces* (MR, 4:67), and many others.

37. Thomas Aquinas, *The Summa Theologica of St. Thomas Aquinas. Pt. III (Supplement)*, 19:301. For a study of the portrayal of woman's roles in the Middles Ages, see Joan Ferrante, *Woman as Image in Medieval Literature*, and Raymond Eichmann, "The Anti-Feminism of the Fabliaux."

38. In addition to the articles in CH, see Lacy's "The Fabliaux and Comic Logic" and Willem Noomen, "Structures narratives et force comique: Les fabliaux."

39. Cooke, *Old French*, p. 93.

40. Edmond Faral, *Les Jongleurs en France au moyen âge*.

41. Larry D. Benson and Theodore M. Andersson, eds., *The Literary Context of Chaucer's Fabliaux*, p. 205.

1. Du Bouchier d'Abevile (The Butcher of Abbeville)

Throughout the notes to the stories, vv. refers to the Old French text and a † symbol to our translation.

1. During the seduction scene, the maid ironically tells David, "a holy hermit you are not" (v. 218).

2. Thomas D. Cooke, *The Old French and Chaucerian Fabliaux: A Study of Their Comic Climax*, pp. 119, 120.

3. *The Art of Courtly Love*, trans. John Jay Parry, p. 36.

4. The Old French text is from the manuscript B.N. fr. 837 (*A*), fol. 158 vo. to 161 ro. Montaiglon and Raynaud do not follow that manuscript with integrity, borrowing without acknowledging, sometimes a word, sometimes six verses at a time, from another manuscript, the B.N., fr. 2168 (*H*). At times, the loan is accountable and improves the fabliau. In that case, we have kept the addition and placed the borrowed verses in brackets. At other times, we chose to translate from one of the other manuscripts, for reasons explained in the notes. The five manuscripts in which this fabliau is found are, using Nykrog's siglum system: *A, C, H, O, T* (R, p. 9). A line-by-line translation of the fabliau is found in Larry D. Benson and T. M. Andersson's *The Literary Context of Chaucer's Fabliaux*, pp. 282–311, as an analogue of the Shipman's Tale. In addition, John Orr, *Eustache d'Amiens: Le Boucher d'Abeville* (London and Edinburgh, 1947), edited it with a modern French translation.

5. V. 17. MS *A: le bouchier*. Other such case errors have been corrected (v. 166: *le fais;* v. 390: *le prestre*). It should also be noted that in the Picard dialect the feminine direct object pronoun is *le* (vv. 40, 446). See also *Du Prestre ki abevete*, note 6.

6. V. 25. *Espars* means "dispersed." Literally: "after the market was dispersed," in other words, "after the closing of the market."

7. V. 33. MR borrows from *H* the line "Pensa c'ui mais avant n'ira" (He thought he wouldn't go any further today), which Rychner also prefers. We see no reason to change the text of *A*.

8. Vv. 41—43. Literally: "Is there, in this town, something for sale where one could spend what is one's own in order to refresh oneself?"

9. Vv. 55, 56, also v. 62. Note the ironic involvement of the Divinity in the salutations and in the butcher's request. It probably will shock the butcher that what would ordinarily be good strategy, to remind a priest of his religious duty, has no success with *this* priest. The priest will answer in a gruff and unbecomingly sarcastic tone: "God lodge you then!" († 63).

10. V. 67. MR chooses "ceenz nuit ne girra" from *H*. Again, we see no reason to change the reading of *A*.

11. Vv. 81, 82. Note the clever usage of the rhyming couplet, *ramposne* (insolence) *aumosne* (charity). The second part of the couplet is stressed by the rhyme, rebuking severely the priest's insolent and inhospitable attitude. His scorn for *vilains* (common folk) is of course not the only reason for refusing hospitality: Eustache informs us later on (vv. 184–87) that he was very jealously guarding his concubine.

12. † 83–86. Of the MSS, only *H* and *O* have the butcher mention wine, which is a first clue to the butcher's craftiness after his unsuccessful attempt at convincing the priest with references to God. He already knows, thanks to the poor woman with whom he has talked, that the priest has had some barrels of wine brought in from Nogentel, and he is tactfully reminding the priest of the fact. The other MSS are more general and might be translated:

My money's good. Just let me stay
The night. I won't be cheap. I'll pay
For any services and food.
You'll have my lasting gratitude.

13. † 85–86. *A* and *C* have the butcher offer money first, then gratitude, whereas we have followed *H, T,* and *O*. Once again, it is more consistent with his craftiness that only after his offer of gratitude elicits no response does the butcher offer money. However, it could also be argued that the butcher should be innocent of craftiness until that side of his character is aroused by the priest's harsh inhospitality.

14. V. 92. The oath "Par saint Piere!" is more than a line filler. Helsinger points out the irony in that invocation of the celestial gatekeeper while the priest refuses to open the door to the butcher (CH, p. 99).

15. V. 103. Eustache draws attention to the allegorical nature of his tale. Instead of *mouton,* he uses "tropé d'oeilles" (a flock of lambs). *Ouailles,* in modern French, is of course also used to represent the "flock" under the care of a minister. Therefore, our attention is again drawn to the priest's severe dereliction of his duties since his "oeilles" are in dilapidated surroundings. The reader will also note the clever exclamation "Por Dieu" and the warning that a "merveilles" (miracle) is about to happen, again drawing us to the spiritual side of the interpretation of the story.

16. V. 116. *foraine rue,* "a back street."

17. V. 118 († 117). *H, O,* and *C* call the priest *fiers* (proud). *A* and *T* call him *fel* (crude). Certainly *pride* is the more important characteristic: pride will be his basic reason for refusing hospitality to the *vilain* (commoner) butcher. It is his pride that is most deeply hurt at the end of the poem when the butcher has gotten the best of him. However, since the climax of the poem reveals him to be *crude* also, we have used both characteristics to introduce him: "the crude and haughty priest."

18. Vv. 121–34. († 118–34). There is a serious narrative problem here in that the priest does not seem to recognize the butcher the second time. It was almost dark at the first encounter, and by now it should be completely dark, but there is still the problem of the voice. From a psychological point of view, we can say that the priest is so deficient in personal warmth and so greedy that for him it is the property that makes the man. A "man with a sheep" is of an altogether different species from a man without. But this kind of interpretation, though it might be acceptable for a literary critic, does not explain how an audience would have found the priest's mistake believable. We suspect that the *jongleur* altered his voice at this point, giving the butcher a more high-toned accent to impress the priest.

Also, † 133, 134. See *H:*

"il est grans si a char asses
Cascuns en aura bien son ses."

These lines are missing in *A* but make a persuasive climax to the butcher's speech. The addition of *H* in our translation helps account for the priest's change in attitude: having allayed the priest's suspicion by declaring that he is tired of carrying the sheep, the butcher appeals to his gluttony (v. 132). *Mengié* (v. 132), as all feminine past participles in Picard, is trisyllabic. See Guy Raynaud de Lage, *Introduction à l'ancien français* (Paris: SEDES, 1966), p. 91.

19. Vv. 137, 138. These lines are difficult reading. We don't know who the subject of "Dist" is, the priest or an impersonal *on*. *H* avoids the ambiguity by using a filler verse, "Ensi com moi en est avis" (as it seems to me). The two lines could be translated: "As it seems to me, he is said to prefer one dead sheep to four living." As Helsinger points out (CH, p. 99), this is a blatant mocking of Christ's parable (Matthew 18:13).

20. V. 160 († 161). Rychner accepts *H*'s "lectio difficilior bauch" (beam), rather than *banc* (bench) of the other MSS. But *H* does not seem to have known what the word meant, since he has it beside (*la dencoste*) the characters rather than above. In order to have the line make sense, Rychner uses lines from *C,* substituting *bauch* for *banc* in *C,* where there is no mention of the position of the bench (or beam). This seems fairly reasonable, if complicated. One cannot blame the jongleurs of *C, T, O,* and *A* for getting rid of a word their audiences

probably would not understand. *Beam,* however, is not a rare word in English, and the effect is a little more dramatic when the skin is hung from the ceiling rather than flung on a bench; so we have kept *beam.*

However, for those who prefer a synonym for bench:

He killed the sheep. Upon a seat
He threw the skin. He dressed the meat
And hung it up before their eyes.

21. Vv. 170, 171. "Have the rest of the sheep put to boil in a pot for the household." Rychner correctly states that "avoec" must be a copyist's mistake and must be read as *à ués* (which *O* used): "for the benefit of, for."

22. V. 179. "I'll leave it up to you."

23. †200. This line comes from *H,* v. 200: "Par lui avons esté bien aaise" (Since we have profited by him). It reemphasizes the greedy and gluttonous nature of the priest.

24. V. 203. "biau samblant": *Bel accueil,* "warm welcome." See *Le Roman de la Rose.* The verses 186 to 205 of our fabliau do indeed have a courtly flavor. This passage has several variants among the MSS, which can be summed up with the differences between *H* and *R* and *A:*

H/R

The priest makes a show
of holding the lady dear.

The lady herself has the
butcher's bed made up.

The sheets are white and
washed.
The priest names the
guest, "Sir David."

The priest reminds the
maid that they have already
benefited from the butcher.

A

More is made of the
excellence of the supper.

Some indefinite person
(*on*) has it made up.

The sheets are white and
linen.

Except for making the sheets linen as well as white and washed, we have followed the *H* and *R* version here, because it is richer in detail. The mention of wine and meat is the only detail in *A* that is lacking in *H* and *R*. It would be gratifying for the jongleur to tell us at this point that after having been informed of the wine by the poor woman, and after having hinted for it unsuccessfully at the pastor's door, the butcher finally gets to enjoy it; but since the butcher does *not* hint for wine in *A,* the only MS where wine is mentioned at the supper, we do not feel obliged to follow *A* in this detail.

Ms. *T.* 192. † 190–91: "Sanblant li fait qu'il l'ait molt chier," the show of cherishing his mistress that the priest puts on, a detail that is mentioned in all MSS except *A,* adds an important touch to the relationship between the two. She is obviously unloved, since his love is only something for show. His relationship with her is not much different from his relationship with God: he uses his office of priest to snub the layman who begs for lodging; he uses his role of lover to impress the man with the sheep.

The lady's impassioned prisoner-in-a-cage speech († 476–86) will be a little more believable with this line as a prelude, and though we will not be apt to like her any better for it, we will pity her more.

25. Between vv. 208 and 209, there is the following couplet in *H:*

Diex com cist home sont vilain
Laissié me empais, ostés vo main!

(God! How vile these men are! Hey!
Leave me alone! Take your hand away!)

The first line is delightful. It further develops the spirited character of the maid. The second line, asking David to keep his hands off, can be uttered with a variety of tones: angry, mocking (perhaps with slapping of the hand), or shocked. An identical command will be made by the lady (v. 268). The repetition takes nothing away from the scenes in question. On the contrary, it characterizes David's seduction techniques: he is a smooth talker with active hands. Such a repetition is frequent in the fabliaux, and as a typical oral composition device (*construction similaire*) it can often be used to engender laughter. Notice the similarities of motifs in the two seduction scenes: the "hands off" command, the expressed fear that David will tattle, a quick summary of the sexual act in euphemistic terms (vv. 228 and 294, 295). In both scenes, as well as in the scene where he tricks the priest into buying his own sheepskin, David mentions the pleasure he has felt from their hospitality in identical courtly terms—"biau samblant" (vv. 203, 251, 305). The ironical and biting nature of this sarcasm iterated to all three members of the household has the effect of lingering in each individual's mind and of coming to consciousness during the final scene of confrontation. It is unfortunate that *A* does not have this couplet.

26. Vv. 247, 248. Only in *A* does the lady ask where the butcher came from and what he has in mind. In the others, she only wonders. We hold with *A* here, because it is in any woman's character to wonder what a strange man is doing in her bedroom, but it is characteristic of this particular woman's arrogance to ask him where he came from and what he is thinking of—questions designed to put him in his place more than to obtain information.

27. V. 285 († 283). In all the MSS except *C,* the butcher offers the lady money, which might be translated: "Besides the money that I'll pay." At first glance, the other four variants seem better, because in them it is only upon the offer of money that the lady begins to give in, and the lady's greed, as principal motivation, is emphasized. But further examination bears out Rychner's claim that these variants weaken the interest in the story (R, p. 16). For one thing, the offer of money leaves some unanswered questions: why didn't the lady demand the money right away? Did the butcher pay her (in which case the completeness of his triumph is somewhat mitigated), or are we supposed to think that it is clever of him to walk off without paying? In any case, the value of the skin, which is central to the conflict at the latter half of the tale, is unnecessarily diminished by the fact that the skin alone was insufficient to buy the lady's virtue. Besides, the evidence of the lady's greed is not altogether lost in *C.* Although the offer of money is not what begins to break down her resistance, at least the reminder of it does.

28. †293–94. This couplet is only in *T* and *C,* not in *H, A, O,* or in MR, but it is in R. It adds nothing to the action, but it provides strong authorial comment, emphasizing that the lady gets the worst of the deal, trading a whole body for a mere skin. This putting of her *self* into subjugation in exchange for material wealth parallels her relationship with the priest and the degradation that she endures because of her financial dependence on him, a degradation of which she later shows herself to be sadly aware († 493–98).

The couplet, though an intrusion, does not mitigate the perfunctoriness of the lovemaking, because it comes before, rather than between, the butcher's taking his refreshment and his having taken it.

Rychner states that these lines are more likely to have been in the original and dropped, rather than added later (R, p. 13), but he does not explain why he thinks so.

29. Vv. 300, 301 († 300). Only *H* mentions the fact that the butcher did not hesitate, a fact worth mentioning, because it reminds us that from a spiritual point of view he should have hesitated to interrupt the mass, and the priest should have hesitated to be interrupted (see Helsinger, CH, p. 102). With regard to the *Jube Domine,* Helsinger remarks that it is a prayer for a blessing, "to which the butcher's offer is a markedly ironic response" (CH, p. 102).

30. Vv. 342, 343. Rychner attributes these two lines to the lady without explanation. We feel they belong to the maid who constantly addresses her mistress in the *vous*-form. The lady always uses the *tu*-form when speaking to her servant. The two lines would thus mean: (The maid is speaking), "In faith, even if you are resentful / You should try to speak politely" (*bien*).

31. V. 361. MR differs from Rychner in its punctuation of this line. MR gives the second half of the line, "toute voie" (*anyway* or *in any case*), to the lady; Rychner to the maid. We prefer MR's because the lady's midline introduction is more dramatic. Besides, in *A* the scribe definitely placed some sort of a punctuation mark after "s'est ele moie."

32. Vv. 380, 381. For formulas "à la rime," in which names of places are used, and their capacity for humor, see Benjamin L. Honneycutt, "An Example of Comic Cliché in the Old French Fabliaux."

33. V. 407 († 406). Only *O* uses the vulgar word *culomee,* which I have translated *laid.* All the others use *engan[n]ee, seduced:*

> Having listened to what she said,
> The priest concluded that the maid
> Had bought the sheepskin from the butcher
> Between the sheets when he seduced her.

Why MR, which generally follows *A,* chose *O* here is not certain. However, the grosser description of the real situation is preferable in response to the maid's sanctimoniousness.

34. Vv. 425, 426 († 422, 423). *H, T,* and *C* have an extra couplet, which MR includes for some reason, though it is not in *A*. In it the lady states, "I say that it is not at all hers"; the priest asks, "Whose is it then?" and the lady answers, "In faith it's mine."

The claim "I don't care what happens—my fleece will not remain with her" makes a strong ending to the lady's speech. Anything more weakens the force of this conclusion. After that, for her to say "I say it isn't hers at all" is repetitive and weak.

Rychner (R, p. 11) claims that this couplet is necessary to justify v. 427 (R's 429). But it seems particularly obtuse of the priest to be asking, "Whose is it then?" two lines after the lady has called the fleece "ma pel." The priest is anything but obtuse as an interrogator. He has already understood the maid's claim on the fleece, and soon his questioning will force a virtual confession from the lady. It is part of his role as a sharp interrogator to seize on the word *my* in "my fleece will not remain with her" and let the rest of the sentence go.

35. V. 427 († 423). R and MR disagree on their punctuation of the same line. MR punctuates the lines as one quotation: "Vostre, voire! par quel raison?" Given this punctuation, the priest would be saying, "Yours, well! For what reason?" where *voire* would have to be some mild expletive such as *well* or *indeed.* Rychner's punctuation makes for a more exciting line, a rapid exchange between the priest and the lady. (*A,* again, has a punctuation mark after "vostre"):

—Vostre?—Voire!—Par quel raison?

As a whole speech in one word, the lady's *voire* must be translated *yes.*

36. Vv. 428, 429 († 424, 425). There is little agreement here among the manuscripts as to what personal pronoun adjectives to put where. *A* has *our* house on *my* cot and *my* sheets, not a very lively combination. The unvarying repetition of *our* in *H* is a little tiresome, and it indicates a willingness to share the skin with the priest, which is contrary both to the lady's present mood and to the conclusion of the poem. The *your guest* of *C* and *O* makes the lady more aggressive in her arguments than the pronouns in the other MSS: "*You* have had the honor of playing host to this guest, while *I* have had the responsibility and work." But *C* ruins this effect by giving the house as well as the guest to the priest. *O,* however, which we have followed, keeps the strong contrast between the three *mys* and the *your* of *your guest.*

The first letter of line 424 is missing in verse 430 of *T:* "-os." The letter should evidently be either *N* for *nos* (our) or *V* for *vos* (your). If it is *V,* then *T* offers an interesting progression from *your* guest ("don't blame me") to *our* house (you and I together—not she—share the honor of having lodged him) to *my* cots and *my* sheets (the particular responsibilities of seeing to his comfort have been mine alone).

37. V. 469 († 465). Where *C* and *H* have *quant dont* (well, when?), *A* and *T* have *adonc* and *adonques* (then), and *O* simply has *sire.* In *C* and *H* a difference of two words in the middle of a line results in three speeches packed into one line, instead of one speech, and thus dramatically increases the tempo of the interrogation. The pastor's quick questions do not give the lady time to fabricate. If the whole line is given to the lady, the passage might be translated:

No, I was sleeping, unaware
That he had even come in there
Till he was by my pillow. . . .

38. V. 477. *A, T,* and *O* are emphatically redundant: "Ainz plus ne parla ne dist" (He spoke no more and said no more). *C* and *H* are better, for they give *fist* (do) instead of *dist* (say). It makes better sense for the lady to be asserting innocence in deed as well as word. In order to follow *A, T,* and *O,* however, "Not a remark" could be substituted for "Nothing was done" in the translation († 474).

39. Vv. 482, 483. Literally: "And so you have seen in me, thank God, only goodness."

40. Vv. 488–90. "Muer en mue" is a falconry expression referring to the practice of locking a falcon in a cage at moulting time. Therefore, to "imprison, to lock up." "En vo dangier," under your thumb, under your dependency for food or drink.

41. V. 494 (†490). Roy J. Pearcy (CH, pp. 186, 187) demonstrates that obscene language is used when a character discovers the truth about a certain situation. Before that moment, and still under a general atmosphere of illusion, euphemisms and figurative expressions are used. When illusion is replaced by reality, abstract expressions are replaced by concrete obscenities.

42. V. 496. "You should have broken the twig!" The breaking of a twig was a feudal symbol whereby a contract between two individuals was annulled. Here, in the figurative sense, it would mean "to separate oneself from somebody."

43. V. 508. MR chooses *H*'s reading of "vient acourant" instead of *A*'s "tout maintenant." We agree, since *A*'s clause has no verb.

44. V. 513. This line is an extreme example of the complexity of the problem of choosing a text. The variations on this line are so great that they will all need to be quoted:

A Frotant ses hines en meson
H Gratant ses hines en maison
T Frotant ces hueses en maison
O Frotant ses ongles en meson
C Guetant les anglez de meson.

In all but *C,* where the shepherd is "looking in the corners of the house," he is rubbing or scraping or scratching something. In *T* it is his boots; in *O* it is his fingernails; in *H* and *A* it is his *hines,* but the meaning of *hines* is not certain.

Godefroy's dictionary, in a direct reference to this line, defines *hines* as probably the same as *anes* (loins). This might indicate no more than an obscene gesture, but Nykrog (N, p. 161) interprets the line as signifying that the shepherd's hands are sweating for fear and the shepherd is wiping them on his breeches:

> . . . he tramped on in
>
> Wiping his hands upon his hip.
>
> The priest was sitting, biting his lip
>
> And simmering with indignation

This translation is not an altogether happy solution since it requires two anatomical additions to the original text—*hands* for interpretation and *lip* for rhyme.

Rychner's translation of *hines* is more satisfactory, but not necessarily correct. He says *hines* is a "grimacing head," although he admits he does not understand why the noun is in the plural. *Scratching his head* would be, Rychner points out, "a gesture of despair or confusion" (R, p. 104):

> Scratching his head, he came to where
>
> The priest was sitting in his chair. . . .

The "scraping his boots" of *T* would, I presume, be inside the house, where the priest's already bad humor would be aggravated, considering the particularity the priest has already shown about the class of people to be permitted into his house. This version provides better motivation for the priest's outburst of rudeness toward the shepherd.

O's "rubbing his fingernails" is probably another gesture of confusion, to which the modern English "chewing his nails" would be close, although *frottant* does not mean "chewing."

Perhaps the version of *C*, "Guetant les anglez de meson," stems from a mishearing of *O*'s "frotant ses ongles." If so, it is an inspired mistake. The shepherd has become so anxious over his lost sheep that his search continues even to the corners of the owner's house, a delightful parody of the Good Shepherd, who never gives up the search. The parody will continue in the shepherd's lament for the sheep, whom he mourns for like a personal friend. Perhaps this line also says something about the priest, whose shepherd does not trust him even with his own sheep.

These variations on the same line illustrate the fact that changes from the original are not necessarily degradations or misreadings by sleepy copyists. Only one line can be the original, yet more than one can contain deft characterization and motivation, and it is a hard job to decide which is best.

45. V. 518. MR's breaking of the line into three parts makes little sense:

> Qu'est ce? c'on fet? Samblant fez tu?

The last part of the line is difficult to understand: "Are you making a face? Are you playing a role, mimicking?" The line reads better as we have proposed: "What is it? What a face you are making" (*comfet:* what, *samblant:* face).

46. Vv. 533–36 († 528–34). Of the five MSS, only *H* contains the shepherd's complete description of his meeting with the butcher. The fact that he had never seen the butcher before the theft is lacking in *C*, and the butcher's long hard look at the flock, as well as his conversation with the shepherd, is completely lacking in the other MSS. MR, though it generally follows *A*, includes the entire passage. Although unnecessary, it is too much fun to leave out. We have already watched the thief steal away with the sheep. Now we get to see the crime from the victim's point of view.

47. Vv. 543–46 († 541–44). These four lines are not in *A;* MR took them from *H*. It is a judicious choice in that the double use of proverbs enhances the priest's grief and the audience's delight. In that respect, we have also kept vv. 559 and 560, which are not in *A* either: the description of the sheep's worth makes the priest's sorrow even greater.

48. Vv. 562–67 († 560–64). *A* and *O* use two lines for the priest to call the lady, then the maid; then two more lines to tell the maid first to speak when he orders, then to answer when he commands:

> "Come here, my lady," the pastor called,
>
> And answer me as I command.
>
> And you, my girl, come here and stand
>
> And answer when I tell you to.
>
> You claim this fleece belongs to you?"
>
> "Yes, Sir, as I'm a loyal maid,
>
> I claim it all," the servant said.

As Rychner points out (R, p. 11), the four lines of *H, T,* and *C* make better sense, with the priest calling the lady and telling her to speak, then calling the maid and telling her to speak.

49. Vv. 573–78 († 571–76). The priest's justification for keeping the fleece is absent in *A, T,* and *O* and only partially developed in *C* (MR borrowed it from *H*). The priest's justification as a property owner condemns him as a priest, one who interrupts the worship of God for the sake of material gain. Rychner calls the absence of this justification a "fault" (R, p. 12), but it could just as well be a skillful addition by some jongleur.

Despite the quality of the passage, a case can be made for leaving it out, for it does weaken the final joke. The priest thinks he has put one over on the women when he refers the case to the courts, knowing full well that they will not risk their position in his house for a sheepskin. He has the power and he will keep the skin.

However, the joke is that the jongleur, in the last few lines, actually does take the case to the courts, that is, to his audience. And in this court, the odds heavily favor the least unsympathetic of the three, the maid. The jongleur further tips the scale by granting the maid the full length of the last line of the poem, whereas the other two have to share the much less emphatic penultimate line. Even in this conflict, the priest does not get the last laugh.

The joke is stronger when lines 571–76 are absent, that is, when the priest gives *no* reason for keeping the sheep before his sneering reference to the courts, an arena where reason rather than force is the weapon.

> "And you, fair lady, whose should it be?"
> "I swear it should belong to me
> By all that's holy, good and true."
> "It won't belong to her or you
> Without a judgment from the courts."

50. V. 580. *Seignor* in *A, H,* and *T* is better than *vous* in *C* and *O,* because, as Rychner points out (R, p. 12), *seignor* completes the poem as it began at line one, with an address to *lords:* "Seignor. . . ."

2. *De Brunain, la vache au prestre (Browny, the Priest's Cow)*

1. Jürgen Beyer (CH, p. 16) rejects this assumption, pointing to a use of the word *fabliau* as early as 1176 in the Second Branch of the *Roman de Renart.* Whether the author of *Renart* had the present use of the word in mind is still open to question.
2. This fabliau is found only in one manuscript, *A* (fol. 229 vo. to 229 ro.).
3. V. 7. "if one understood right."
4. V. 11. *avoir couvent,* "to promise." Note how the peasant places the responsibility of the outcome squarely on the priest's shoulders.
5. V. 16. *Le donons le prestres,* "That we give it (the cow) to the priest."
6. Vv. 27, 28: Note how the briskness of action is stressed by the rhyming percussion in that couplet, *doing / poing.*
7. V. 59. MR misreads it as *Bon doublere.* JO surmises that the reason for MR's reading is that "They may have thought it curious to find God called a man" (p. 94). Joseph Bédier (*Les Fabliaux,* p. 313, n. 2) also reads it like MR, "bon doubleur." *A* clearly has *hom doublere,* a man who doubles.
8. V. 60. "For Blerain returns, she and another!"
9. V. 68. Compare JO (p. 94): "Allusion to the Parable of the Talents (Matt. XXV: 14–30)."
10. V. 69. *c'est or del mains,* "That is evident," "that is the least one can say" (JO, p. 94).

3. *Des Trois Boçus (The Three Hunchbacks)*

1. The liberties taken in our translation are therefore justified in that they enhance the pathos of the wife's situation (see note to vv. 14, 15).
2. Only one version of the tale exists. It is found in the B.N. fr. 837 (*A*), fol. 238 vo.–40 ro. It has been published by MR (1:13) and JO (no. V). Nothing is known about the author Durans besides what is given in this poem.
3. Vv. 14, 15. It is not the job of a translator to smooth over confusions in the original, and when he does commit this fault, he should at least notify his reader. V. 15, "Que molt ert creüz par la vile," which is translated, "He had some friends who gave him credit," means only, "He was much credited (esteemed) throughout the town." And vv. 49–50: ". . . ont donee la pucele / Si ami . . . " mean ". . . his friends gave the maiden," but are translated as "The father's friends agreed to give / The daughter . . . " († 46–47). In the original text, somebody's friends, *probably* the father's since he is a popular man, seem to appear from nowhere for the purpose of giving the daughter away. He lets his friends sell the daughter into marriage probably because those friends are the very people who gave him credit and whom he cannot pay off now because he has already sold off his properties. In making these assumptions part of the poem, I have overstepped the duties of translator. J. DuVal.
4. V. 36. *encroëes,* "accrochées." "And he had them (his shoulders) fastened up high."
5. V. 76. Apparently this line contradicts the greedy portrait of the husband above (vv. 40–43, 58–59). It can be assumed that his show of generosity, here and at the minstrels' departure (v. 82), is only directed at his own kind and is a very rare occurrence.
6. V. 113. "Near the fireplace was a bed." JO (p. 90) explains that *chaaliz* was a large wooden bed, constructed so it could be carried from place to place and divided into compartments, *escrins* (literally, "a chest, a bin").
7. V. 116. Cooke claims, "This fabliau is unusual in that the poet frequently intrudes upon the story to make personal comments all of which help to maintain a comic attitude on a tale in which three men accidentally suffocate and one is murdered"

(*Old French,* p. 86; compare vv. 7, 42, 44, 46).

8. V. 120. This is an ambiguous line, "who enjoyed his / her pleasures greatly." The antecedent could be *le seignor* or *la dame.*

9. V. 147. *entestez,* "headstrong, determined, stubborn." An important characterization of the porter.

10. Vv. 193, 194. "May you be shamed if you do not come back!" The porter is sure that this time he won't come back and that he will be shamed.

11. V. 202. *Merveille.* Note how the lady plays on the superstitious nature of the porter (see v. 179).

12. V. 207. "By God's holy heart!"

13. V. 242. St. Morant is the patron saint of Douai (v. 8). JO (p. 90) lists several proposed meanings of *röele* (wheel): "round bloodstain" (see v. 229), or "tonsure." The wheel has no apparent connection with St. Morant. An additional possibility is that *röele* should be *böele,* "by the bowels of St. Morant."

14. Vv. 244–46. "I can't carry him far enough that he [the corpse] wants to be unloaded and come straight away back to me."

15. V. 258. The author humorously restates a physical characterization that he has already given (v. 34).

16. V. 271. "Until one sees the woods blooming," that is, "until hell freezes over."

4. *Du Prestre ki abevete (The Priest Who Peeked)*

1. Stith Thompson, *Motif-Index of Folk-Literature,* 4:403.

2. Larry D. Benson and Theodore M. Andersson, eds., *The Literary Context of Chaucer's Fabliaux,* p. 203.

3. For a more detailed account of Picard characteristics, see Karl Voretzsch's *Altfranzösische Sprache,* pp. 320–21.

4. The only available version of this fabliau is found in the B.N. fr. 12603 (*F*) fol. 240 ro.–240 vo. Another possible version, called in the *explicit,* "Du Prestre qui fouti la fame au vilain," is found in the B.N. 1593, fol. 174 ro.–174 vo., but has been erased. A few barely legible parts of lines indicate that it follows our fabliau but with some divergences. The reason for the erasure is puzzling: if a reader or collector has been offended by the crudities of our tale why did he not erase as well the other obscene fabliaux found in that manuscript?

5. V. 3. As is the case in many fabliaux, *courtois* here must be understood as "nice, pleasing." In vv. 6, 7, however, it can be translated also as "of polished manners" in view of the lady's specified honorable lineage. These two lines might well be said as a gratuitous, tongue-in-cheek remark because her background plays no role in the fabliau.

6. Vv. 8 and 9. For *le,* read *la.*

7. V. 10. *F* reads "Et ce le prestre amoit." MR's correction is appropriate (3:54).

8. V. 12. *souspris,* "smitten."

9. V. 21. *tous abrievés,* "ardent, impatient" (Godefroy).

10. V. 23. *i* has been added by MR to make a correct octosyllable.

11. Vv. 29, 30. "What a life her husband is making her lead / (And that) since he enjoys no pleasures with women." The priest not only bemoans the abandonment of the wife by her husband but also accuses him of sexual impotency or deviancy. This should, in his mind, justify his upcoming act (see the comment by the author, vv. 57, 58).

12. V. 38. We have opted for the most obscene English word for *foutre,* because the word is supposed to be shocking in the original. The peasant is shocked by it, more no doubt because he is hearing it from a priest at an altogether inappropriate moment, as far as he is concerned. Part of the humor is that the peasant, to show that he is not offended, politely falls into the priest's own manner of speaking to describe what the priest "seems" to be doing to his wife (v. 75).

13. V. 41. *Je n'en dout rien,* "I have no doubts about it."

14. V. 43. *avuler* ("aveugler?"), "to blind me, to trick me."

15. V. 46. *bien* added by MR.

16. V. 51. "He locked the door with a bolt." "He bolted the door."

17. V. 52. Benson and Andersson's "And then he did not waste his time" is unexplainable. The line must refer to the peasant who "does not like it one bit!" (literally, "he does not esteem it worth a marble!") The direct object pronoun *le* can also be referring to the peasant. In that case, the line would mean that the priest doesn't esteem the peasant worth a marble: once the door is locked, he is on the inside and the peasant on the outside. For other depreciatory formulas, see Robert Harden, "The Depreciatory Comparison: A Literary Device of the Medieval Epic."

18. V. 61. Difficult reading. *F* appears to have *qu'el queroit,* "what she was seeking." MR has it as *que il queroit,* which makes more sense in view of the preceding line, in spite of the fact that we are told that she loved the priest (v. 10).

19. V. 65. MR adds *si.*

20. V. 74. Literally, "If I had not heard you say it before."

21. V. 75. Some sensitive person scratched out

he first syllable of *foutissies*. Somebody else rewrote t above the erasure.

22. V. 81. MR adds *Et, a* to *hans* (v. 82) and leletes the *e* from *encore* (v. 84) to correct the faulty ines.

23. V. 84. The closing couplet in the original is,

> Et, pour ce que li uis fu tuis,
> Dist on encor: *Maint fol paist duis.*

Difficulty in translation arises from the rhyming words: "And because the door was *something,* / People still say: '*Something* feeds or satisfies many fools.' " Benson and Andersson evidently take *tuis* to be a past participle of *trouer* (to put a hole into), and they take *duis* to mean *hole,* with the article *un* (one) understood. They translate the lines (p. 273),

> And because the door had a hole in it
> It is said to this day: "One hole satisfies many fools."

This makes a witty, appropriate conclusion to the bawdy tale, and it can be rendered into verse,

> Since the door had a hole, men still observe,
> "For many fools, one hole will serve."

Unfortunately, Godefroy's dictionary does not give any justification for such a translation of either *tuis* or *duis*. *Tuis* is the old French for *tout* (*all* or *whole*). Godefroy lists another word *tuis* with an unknown meaning, but with a citation that indicates that the word refers to some kind of tree (an interesting reference in view of the *Pear Tree* analogues). In this case, *tuis* may refer to the kind of wood the door is made of. What kind of wood and what bearing it could have on the proverb remain unknown. "Because of the door" will have to do as a vague translation of that line. Godefroy gives *instruction* for the meaning of *duis*. With this meaning, the couplet could be translated,

> Because of the door, men still observe,
> "For many fools, one lesson serves."

But the only example of this proverb given by Morawski in his dictionary of medieval proverbs is "Maint fol pest Deus . . ." (1153). Perhaps, then, *duis* is a corruption of *Deus* or *Dieu*. The word for God relates the moral a little more closely to the rest of the poem than does *instruction* or *lesson,* because it allows *paist* to be translated as "feeds." Thus it reminds us that the peasant, in the eyes of the priest, is a fool to be feeding himself when he should be doing his husband's duty with his wife. But from God's point of view, the priest also is feeding himself foolishly, to the detriment of his priestly duties. In the tolerant world of this fabliau, God feeds the characters what they desire, but they are fools in their desires.

5. De Berangier au lonc cul (Bérangier of the Long Ass)

1. *Orient and Occident,* T.I., p. 116.

2. Roy J. Pearcy, "Relations between the *D* and *A* versions of *Bérenger au long cul,*" pp. 173–78. Pearcy quotes the entire episode of Dagenet on p. 174.

3. Jean Rychner, *Contribution à l'étude des fabliaux: Variantes, remaniements, dégradations,* 1:64–67, reasons that the better motivation in Guerin's version indicates that it is the original, which the anonymous author of *A* had to water down for a bourgeois audience.

4. Raymond Eichmann, "The Search for Originals in the Fabliaux and the Validity of Textual Dependency," pp. 94–96.

5. There are two versions of Guerin's tale. The one we transcribe (*D*) is from the B.N. Fr. 19152 (fol. 54 ro.–55 vo.). The other (*B*), which at times offers better readings, especially at the rhyme, is in the Berne MS 354 (fol. 146 vo.–149 vo.). Jean Rychner (*Contribution,* 2:100–109) published *D* side by side with the anonymous *Bérenger.* Guerin's fabliau has also been translated in Benson and Andersson (*The Literary Context,* pp. 10–25) and by Robert Harrison (*Gallic Salt,* pp. 43–61).

6. V. 11. *Que li avint (D)* must be a scribe's error unless *D* meant that Guerin was somehow a witness to the story, a claim that fableors were not shy of making.

7. V. 58. MR: "Donc li ramentoit son paraige," probably to avoid the homographic rhyming with v. 57. T. B. W. Reid notices the characteristic of repeating the same word in the same sense throughout this manuscript and attributes it to the scribe (*Twelve Fabliaux: From MS. F. FR 19152 of the Bibliothèque Nationale,* pp. xv, xvi).

8. Vv. 71, 72. MR prefers *B*'s reading "Demain me vorrai esprover" (Tommorrow you will see me prove myself), probably to avoid the repetition of *que qu'il ennuit* with v. 77. *D* does not mind repeating expressions, see *prendre à estuper* (vv. 227 and 242). In that case, the repetition might be considered acceptable since it is underlining the carrying out of Bérangier's threat.

9. V. 84. Note Guerin's sarcasm in specifying that the husband's arms are brand new, unused (see also v. 102).

10. V. 91. Rychner: "Qu'avoit molt pres . . ." (*B*). "Qu'il voit . . ." (*D*) seems more correct and more appropriate: the husband has been thinking about how he could deceive his wife into thinking that he is a great knight (vv. 88, 89) and, seeing the woods behind his house, he comes upon the idea of beating on the shield.

11. V. 120. *D:* "traiez vost." MR and Rychner: "vos tost."

12. V. 132. MR corrects the improper rhyme into "Ne set que dire ne que croire" from *B*. It has, however, the disadvantage of having an identical rhyme with the preceding verse.

13. V. 133. MR, to correct a faulty rhyme, suggests "ne l'abace" (from *abastre,* "to combat, to demolish"). MR also prefers *B*'s reading "Le chevalier de ceste guille" (v. 139) for the same reason.

14. V. 149. *recreüz,* from *recroire,* "to become exhausted."

15. Vv. 155–59. MR prefers *B*'s reading probably because of rhyming difficulties in *D*'s vv. 155, 156. (*aparceüe* / *nature*):

> Bien set la dame et aperçoit 155
> Que par la borde la deçoit
> Et panse, s'il i va jamais,
> El bois que ele ira aprés
> Et si verra quanqu'il fera
> Et comment il se contendra,

(V. 156 in our text, *D,* is faulty due to a scribal error. An additional *et* before *est* makes it a nine-syllable line.)

16. V. 181. Literally, "She who does not linger."

17. V. 192. MR corrects *un pou* by *un petit* in order to make an acceptable octosyllable.

18. V. 210. Read *Du poing*. See *Des Tresces,* note 10.

19. V. 218. *B: d'autre renart.* While the allusion to the master trickster is attractive, the insult of calling her husband "Bernart" is much more appropriate in view of his stupidity. To link the husband with Renart in any way would be giving him more credit for trickery and wisdom than he deserves.

20. V. 222. Read *octroi.*

21. Vv. 235, 236. The husband is trying to bluff until the very end, explaining that the shameful action will only be performed by him because of an antimilitant vow he once made.

22. Vv. 249–52. Note in these lines Guerin's utter contempt for the husband.

23. V. 261. Note the insistence by repetition on the term *coard* throughout this episode.

24. V. 264. *B: Au mieus que pot.*

25. V. 265. In view of the company the lady used to keep (vv. 58–62) and to further accentuat the unworthiness of the husband as a knight, th stock character of the lover here is a knight.

26. V. 270. An incomprehensible syllable i noticeable between *Du* and *bois*. Since it adds superfluous syllable, it is best left out.

27. V. 273. *abosmez,* "consternated, disgusted indignant, or frightened." It is quite apropos and in character that the husband quickly recovers fron the clash with Bérangier and reverts to his forme bragging and threatening ways in front of his wif (vv. 278–80).

28. V. 289. *par la vostre proiere?,* "pray tell!" or "To whom will you file a claim against me Through a request from you?" The husband doe not think her capable of initiating a claim in view o the difficulties her family is facing (MS erroneousl has *vostre pere*).

6. *Du Vilain Asnier (The Villager an His Two Asses)*

1. Charles Muscatine, "The Social Backgroun of the Old French Fabliaux," p. 13.

2. Victor LeClerc, "Fabliaux," p. 206.

3. The only version of our tale is from the B.N. 19152, fol. 56 ro. (*D*) and has been edited by MR (5:40), JO (pp. 4, 5), Reid (*Twelve Fabliaux,* pp. 1, 2), and Ménard (*Fabliaux,* pp. 19, 20).

4. Montpellier is famous for its spices and perfumes and has not been chosen simply for rhyming purposes. "The author's choice of this town as the setting for this story is not mere caprice" (JO, p. 86).

5. V. 25. The scribe, confused, wrote *selenne lē.* JO (p. 86) surmises that "the scribe added an *s* above the line to *selenne*" because he forgot that the referent was *l'asne* (v. 24), in the singular form, and not the plural *li asne* (v. 22). Both JO and MR corrected the line appropriately: ("lē" is to be omitted.

6. V. 32. *du son,* some of his (money).

7. V. 40. *a* is lacking in *D*.

8. V. 51. This line does not rhyme with any other and we must suppose that a line is missing either before or after this proverb.

JO claims, "The precise application of this moral to the ass-driver is difficult to see" (p. 86). In light of the allegorical nature of this tale and of the allusion in the preceding line to the prideful nature of the social-climber, the proverb acquires more meaning.

7. *Des Tresces (The Tresses)*

1. Rychner (*Contribution,* 1:92–98) believes

hat *B,* superior in narrative structure and in moti-
ation to *D,* is the earlier one and that *D* has been
eworked in order to "faire . . . plus distingué."
Rychner (*Contribution,* 1:97) considers the re-
vorking an inferior work, which "abimait le
nécanisme de la narration" (spoiled the narrative's
nechanism). We disagree. The lines referring to *B*
re found in *Contribution* (2:136–48).

2. Rychner (*Contribution,* 1:95) berates the pre-
osterous motivation in *D,* stating that the lady
oncocts the whole ruse of the tresses: "*l'engig*
maginé par la dame dès le vers 160 ne peut être
ue celui-là; cette ruse extraordinaire était dé-
à celle des tresses. La dame avait donc tout
révu . . . Cette vue seconde sur l'avenir est tout à
ait invraisemblable" (The trick, imagined by the
ady since line 160 can only be that one: this
xtraordinary ruse already was the one of the tresses.
he lady had planned everything. . . . This amazing
ision of the future is totally unbelievable).

3. Note the numerous ironical usages of the
vords *Oeil, yeux, voir, dévoyé,* and so on, in this
abliau.

4. John T. DuVal, "Les Tresces: Semi-Tragical
abliau, Critique and Translation," p. 7.

5. Vv. 201, 219, 227, 251, 369.

6. *Des Tresces,* found in the B.N. fr. 19152, fol.
22 ro.–123 vo., has been edited by Reid (*Twelve
abliaux,* pp. 23–33), by Rychner (*Contribution,*
:136–48), by Ménard (*Fabliaux,* pp. 95–108),
nd by MR (5:67), which judiciously corrects
ulty octosyllables. The additions have been placed
 brackets.

The confused scribe, after a false start where he
opied the first line, remembered to put the incipit,
Commence des tresces . . . " (*Ci* is missing), then
arted again with the first line, "Jadis avint . . . "

7. V. 28. *Richaut* is a traditional name for pro-
uress or go-between. See the fabliau by that name,
hich Bédier recognizes as such but Nykrog does
ot (*N,* p. 15), edited by I. C. Lecompte in *Roman-
c Review* 4 (1913): 261–305.

8. Vv. 50, 51. "She, the lady who loved him very
uch, never refused him."

9. V. 55. "Who had mastered courtly love." MR
ives *mestroie* the meaning of "to torment" with
n'amor as its subject: "whom courtly love tor-
ented." To arrive at this translation, MR had to
ange *qui* to *que*. Clearly, *D* has *qui*.

10. V. 90. Read *loing: g* may stand for a pala-
zed nasal, as the equivalent of *ng*. See Alfred
oulet and Mary Blakely Speer, *On Editing Old
rench Texts,* p. 78. See vv. 315, 409.

11. V. 104. *D*'s *ont* is incorrect since the subject
 the singular *une cuve* (v. 105). *Ot* or *out* would be
ceptable.

12. V. 113. To correct the faulty octosyllable,
Reid proposes: . . . *et que tost i queure,* while MR
prefers *qu'ele tost queure*.

13. V. 122. Reid proposes *prenrai,* "Never will I
eat another meal if he escapes from here!" instead of
"never will he take another meal . . . " (*prenra*).
Reid's suggestion has the advantage of being
ironic: the lover does escape and the husband,
indeed, will not eat another meal, so to speak, since
he will shortly start on a voyage of pilgrimage and
abstinence.

14. Vv. 124, 125. "Don't show any mercy since
he has been apprehended (on the spot)."

15. V. 130. Reid prefers to add *en* before *envoie*
to make a correct octosyllable because of a similar
expression found in v. 153.

16. V. 157. D: *sa dame*.

17. V. 160. Read as *enging* (ruse, trick).

18. V. 177. *D: i fust son vueil.*

19. Vv. 203, 204. The rhyme *soulaz/laz* is interesting: *soulaz* (joy, divertissement) is essentially a
courtly term, while *laz* (snare, trap) applies more to
fabliaulike situations. They both refer to appropriate circumstances: the first to the lover in bed, in
complete bliss; the second to the lady's friend
trapped in a vulgar situation. (The riding of the
friend by the knight has a sexual connotation: "The
relationship of man and woman has long been
compared to that of a rider controlling a willful
horse." Helsinger, CH, p. 94.)

20. V. 250. An understatement: the lady is very
careful not to wake her husband again in view of his
brutal reaction, which she knows well and which
she is said to remember at that very moment (vv.
252, 253): the tresses that she searches for are a
constant reminder of his brutality.

21. V. 259. *D si les en trait. Ses,* being enclitic of *si
les,* has the advantage of giving a correct octosyllable.

22. V. 268. While most proverbs are located at
the end of the tale, acting like teaching devices, this
one is in the middle at a key moment: the lady is
about to perform her most important deception
and our acceptance of this entire episode is essential
to the climax of the tale. By the proverb, the fabliau
authenticates a bizarre action by appealing to universal knowledge. As Paul Theiner points out, the
use of a proverb is a trick, designed to make us
accept the most outlandish occurrences: "If we all
agree on the truth of the principle enunciated, we
can scarcely find fault with the 'realism' of that
individual feature that does not so much confirm
the saying . . . as provides us with an instance" (CH,
p. 122).

23. V. 272. Read as *joie*.

24. V. 299. Rychner proposes *com* instead of
Qant.

25. V. 363. Rychner and Reid give *se devient,*

the meaning of which in this line is somewhat obscure. MR's *se Dé vient* has the advantage of again involving the Divinity, a clever technique on the part of the lady, as we have already noted.

26. Vv. 375–80. This is a difficult passage. For v. 376, Reid proposes "pas ne s'ensaigne" (*s'ensaigner:* to inform oneself, to inquire) but runs into translating difficulties. We propose: "Then he lifts his hand and crosses himself / But the lady does not cross herself / In view of the things which she had done during the night. / But he would not calm down / Even if somebody gave him the whole of Provence." The lady appears to be superstitious and does not want to cross herself over events she knows are unworthy of God's attention. To trick her husband by implicating the Divinity is one thing, but to use a sanctified gesture that directly involves God is more than she is willing to hazard.

27. V. 381. *apostes,* "placed" (or "replaced").

28. Vv. 427–34. Cooke believes the ending to be an example of the tongue-in-cheek irony that is prevalent in the fabliaux: "The author is ironically implying that all that is necessary in order to keep a wife chaste is to keep her indoors, as though he thinks that we have forgotten that the lover was caught (this time) inside the house" (*Old French,* p. 93).

8. De la Borgoise d'Orliens (The Wife of Orléans)

1. In addition to Bédier's list of the variants of this tale, see W. Henry Schofield, *The Source and History of the Seventh Novel of the Seventh Day in the Decameron.*

2. Compare vv. 104, 105.

3. "When his wife deceives him, it is not necessarily because of some personal faults . . . if he is involved in the import business of luxurious objects our storytellers will treat him favorably; if, on the other hand, he works with his hands or if he is an usurer, he will be treated barely better than a peasant."

4. Later, the author will only refer vaguely to "la vile," vv. 10, 15.

5. "The scene changes more than fifteen times . . . never acquiring any characterization of place except in term of action. Therefore the loft is not dark, nor drafty, nor rat-infested, but '.I. solier dont j'ai la clef,' because the key in question is to be handed over, nearly 100 lines later, to the gang of household ruffians the wife dispatches to cudgel her husband. Even the one-line characterization of the bedroom—'Ou li dras furent portendu'—falls into this category: the room is not so much comfortable as *ready*" (Theiner, CH, pp. 128–29).

6. This very popular fabliau is from the B.N. 83 (fol. 163 ro.–164 ro.) (*A*) and has had the honor c appearing in numerous editions and translation principally MR (1:117), JO (pp. 21–27), Ménar (*Fabliaux,* pp. 21–28), and Rychner, *Contributio* (2:80–99). Among others, Hellman and O'Go man and Harrison have included it in their antholo gies of translations.

Variant versions of this tale are *C* (Hamilto 257) and *B* (Berne 254), which also appear i Rychner's *Contribution.*

7. V. 11. *A* avoids identifying the *clers escoliers* originating from *Normandy,* as do *B* and *C.* Ryc ner speculates that the exclusion of this detail is du to some "susceptibilité provinciale de son publi (*Contribution,* 1:60).

8. V. 17. Godefroy guesses that *ponois* mea "power" or "high position."

9. V. 25. "Whether by action or by words."

10. V. 26. As Rychner points out (*Contributio* 1:60, n. 1), if *le* here is feminine, as is often the ca in *A,* the line would mean "that he would teach her lesson." Furthermore, *il* refers either to the husba or to the clerk: *C* and *B* have *cil* and do refer to th clerk (JO, p. 91, agrees with that interpretation The line would thus be translated: "that the cle would teach her a lesson" (the husband is afraid th the clerk has amorous designs on his wife). Th other interpretation, "the husband would teac him/her a lesson," is also valid.

11. Vv. 59–61. The husband pretends to leav early so as to get a three *lieues* headstart on hi journey.

12. V. 67. Note how *meslee* already predicts th mistaking of the characters' identity.

13. V. 73. This vague and general greeting fo mula is necessary here. Had the lady identified mor precisely the visitor by name, she would have imme diately been caught in her guilt. As it stands now the husband is still uncertain of her actual role i this affair.

14. V. 85. Argus was a mythological giant wit one hundred eyes whose task was to guard Io.

15. V. 120. JO believes the variant in *B* to b superior: *la chanbre demoine,* "the principal bed room," pointing out the contrast with the husban in the uncomfortable *solier.* *A*'s *demaine* might re flect a deformation of *C*'s *le meine* or might be a unusual verb synonymous with but emphatic c *meine.* JO believes *B* to be the original reading. (Se also our note 21.)

16. Vv. 124–27. "Because he would not dee all the others (that is, games) worth an almond, if h had not been there or she not been grateful to him.

17. V. 138. "She hurried them (the househol as much as she could." *B* adds a lot of culinar details in a passage that must have been an additio

o the original: *B*'s v. 138 (like *A*'s) says she is urrying to get the meal over, yet in the lines to ome she is seen unhurriedly preparing a large uantity of varied foods.

18. V. 146. *aportoit* does not rhyme with the receding line. JO proposes *aportot.*

19. V. 161. *A: errer.*

20. V. 164. This line is ambiguous: "now the greement has come to an end" or "now the clerk as come to his end."

21. V. 165. *Perrin* ("room made out of stone," nlikely to be confused with *solier,* "attic, loft"). The se of *perrin* here is puzzling: *C* uses *perrin* hroughout the fabliau to indicate the room where he husband is sequestered, whereas *A* uses *solier* xclusively with this one exception, probably in rder to prepare a rhyme with the next line. But *B* emains consistent in its use of *solier* and provides a lifferent rhyme for vv. 177, 178: *solier* / *setier.* Why 4 suddenly uses *C*'s term when he could have earranged his rhyme like *B* is perplexing, but so is he relationship between the three fabliaux (see Rychner, *Contribution,* 1:59–62). The same curous confusion exists in *La Saineresse* (see below, vv. 33, 47), which is also located in *A:* in all likelihood he confusion originates from the same scribe.

22. V. 227. JO considers the construction *sentir a* to be parallel to *tenir a,* "he feels his wife to be . . ." (p. 92). Also, *a* could be from *avoir:* "he feels he has such a loyal wife."

23. Vv. 242, 243. JO attributes these lines to the husband, but MR and Rychner consider them to be omments of the author. In view of the latter's umerous interventions in the tale, we agree with Rychner (compare vv. 85–87, 102–5, 112, 113, 124, 125, 180, 181).

9. *De Guillaume au faucon (William of the Falcon)*

1. The similarity with Chrétien de Troyes's *Erec* here is evident. Reid, in *Twelve Fabliaux,* (note to vv. 60 and 115) also identifies lines probably borrowed from Chrétien's work. Guillaume's lack of initiative is also reminiscent of Aucassin.

2. "The attitudes expressed in the fabliaux are clearly closer to the nominalist position in the nominalist–realist controversy" (Roy J. Pearcy, CH, p. 195).

3. Placed at both ends of the fabliau, vv. 30–49 and 615–36. See also the fabliau *De un Chivaler et sa Dame et un Clerk* (MR, 2:183). Nykrog (N, p. 94) counted six fabliaux that present a problem to be solved or a delicate judgment to be rendered. We should add our present one to his list.

4. The remainder of the moral is precious: Guillaume is praised for having joined thought to action (*cuer et cors,* v. 628), something he obviously never did. The author ends the tale by asking God's blessings on all lovers (vv. 631–34): if He were to grant them joy, so would the author, provided they were pure of heart (vv. 635, 636).

5. Taken from the B.N. 19152 (fol. 60 ro.–62 vo.), this fabliau has been edited by MR (2:92) and by Reid (*Twelve Fabliaux,* pp. 83–98). A few scribal errors are to be found in the manuscript: v. 184, *tolz* should be *toz;* v. 192, *nen* should be *en* (soupirant); there is a superfluous *f* between *que* and *vos* in v. 207 and a superfluous *ce* between *dit* and *se* in v. 307. *Quant* has been substituted for the erroneous *grant* in v. 619.

6. V. 14. *meri,* "made return for, reward." The *chastelain* owes Guillaume something for his services but has not paid him yet.

7. V. 34. *arragier vis,* "être enragé vif, to go mad." Reid: "even if he were to go stark mad (as a result)" (*Twelve Fabliaux,* p. 119).

8. V. 62. "Faut-il voir dans cet éloge des femmes de la Castille une flatterie à l'adresse de Blanche de Castille?" (Can we see in this praise of Castillian women a compliment directed toward Blanche of Castille?) (MR, 2:320).

9. Vv. 68–77. *acesmee,* "elegant, beautiful"; *jointe:* "elegant, attractive"; *pelee:* "worn out (fur)"; *penne:* "lining"; *sebelin:* "sable"; *chenu:* "gray"; *coulez:* Reid (*Twelve Fabliaux,* p. 119) proposes *oulez* (hemmed), referring us to a similar usage of that word in *Perceval,* v. 1804. The whole description of the lady (vv. 67 ff.) corresponds, according to Reid, with Chrétien's text: v. 68 with *Perceval* 1796; vv. 71–90 with *Perc.* 1797–1816; vv. 91–97 with *Perc.* 1819–21; vv. 112–13 with *Perc.* 1826–27.

10. Vv. 82, 83. "Now I wish that my heart make (guide, lead) me where (so) I will tell the entire truth."

11. V. 88. *sor,* "golden, yellow."

12. V. 97. *synople,* "red."

13. V. 160. This is a difficult line. Reid proposes: "even though I should gain nothing by it, make no headway" (*Twelve Fabliaux,* p. 120).

14. Vv. 161–64. Reid claims that the passage is incoherent and that the lines should be in the following order: 164, 163, 161, 162. The passage as we have it and as it is in the MS represents beautifully Guillaume's uncertainty, hesitations, and lack of articulation. It should stand as is.

15. Vv. 186, 187. "Guillaume gives the lady a sweet look and then salutes her."

16. Vv. 222–24. "If he had enough courage, opportunity, and occasion to disclose his intentions."

17. V. 234. Incorrect octosyllable unless *Ele* is read as a two-syllable word. In v. 246, *estre* must also be considered disyllabic.

18. V. 240. *loerai ge,* "I will advise." See v. 250, "So do I advise him that he tell her."

19. Between vv. 268 and 269, inexplicably, there is this extra line: "Fors vos d'itant me puis vanter."

20. Vv. 272, 273: "Lady, I request that you grant me your love as gift / This is why I am in such distress" (see v. 328).

21. V. 302. *parmi le cox* "is a common qualification of curses in [Old French], perhaps in allusion to hanging or beheading" (Reid, *Twelve Fabliaux,* p. 120).

22. Vv. 312–13. "Bad news bearers always show up too early!" (compare Jean Morawski: "Trop tost vient qui male novele aporte," *Proverbes français antérieurs au XVe siècle,* line 2431). Reid assigns these, and v. 311, to Guillaume. In view of the numerous authorial intrusions, we chose to treat them as such.

23. V. 404. The MS has "Et quant il l'entent toz tressaut." *Et* has been added to the line, in the margin, by a scribe obviously concerned over the faulty octosyllable. In view of the author's propensity for the balanced line (vv. 164, 368) and in view of a similar construction in the next verse, MR's correction by adding *en* seems very appropriate.

24. V. 408. *m'ajue,* "my aid, my help."

25. V. 477. "I believe he will know it soon enough."

26. V. 635. The MS has *si ferai se ne* . . . . Reid proposes *si fera i[l],* referring to God ("thus will He do"). For reasons accounted for in footnote 4 above, we agree with MR, which, respecting the integrity of the verbal form (first person singular), assumes that the scribe left out the inverted subject *je*.

10. De la Saineresse (The Lady-Leech)

1. It is ironic that this misogynist will be duped by two ladies: one in disguise and one real. The *pautonier's* answer to his invitation to come and sit close to him is a putdown, an indication of things to come: "I am not that tired!" he snaps back.

2. Benson and Andersson remark that althoug[h] medieval bawdry is often defended for evoking "healthy and unashamed . . . guffaw," this fablia[u] shows that "our ancestors also sniggered" (*Th[e] Literary Context of Chaucer's Fabliaux,* p. 263). Bu[t] there is more than snigger here. Five lines of copu[-] lating in the attic are the raw material for twenty[-] eight lines of metaphor. It is the verse that lifts th[e] re-creation above the level of the dirty joke. Th[e] lady chants her metaphors. She obviously enjoy[s] speech as something distinct from the reality of th[e] deed. The verse, likewise, is distinct from ordinar[y] language. We may snigger at being allowed to dwe[ll] on a dirty deed for twenty-eight extra lines, or w[e] may indeed laugh out loud at the suddenness of th[e] transformation from dirty deed to art.

3. Nykrog sees in the allegory a triple meaning[:] medical, erotic, and courtly. Nykrog notes that i[n] *Enéas* and in the *Roman de la Rose,* the god of Lov[e] is portrayed with an arrow and a box containing sweet ointment. "In both works the distinguishe[d] poets push their allegory dangerously close to th[e] concrete" (CH, p. 67).

4. B.N. 837 (*A*) (fol 211 vo.–212 vo.). MR['s] text (1:289) is the basis for Benson and Andersson['s] translation (*The Literary Context,* pp. 262–67).

5. Vv. 14, 15. ". . . and seemed half much more lady than a man."

6. V. 18. *posnee,* "bravado, arrogance."

7. V. 33. *solier* and *perrin* (v. 47). See *De l[a] Borgoise d'Orliens,* note 21.

8. V. 57. *sert en manaiè,* "to serve free, withou[t] charge." "Don't withhold anything of what sh[e] deserves, for she served you so freely."

9. V. 75. "on three occasions he took me."

10. V. 77. *peçons,* "lancets."

11. V. 91. "And there is nothing to dislike abou[t] it."

12. V. 94. *forel,* "forest, woods"; or *forre[l],* "straw, forage."

13. V. 98. Benson and Andersson: "You wer[e] not poorly served just now." But *a poi ne* mean[s] "almost," and the line should be translated: "Yo[u] were almost badly handled, badly had," whic[h] enhances the irony of the blind husband's reaction[.]

14. V. 103. *essaucier,* "to exalt."

15. V. 115. *Quant cele,* "When she, just a[s] she. . . ."

Bibliography

The following list contains works that have been cited in the present edition as well as recent important studies. For a complete bibliography of the fabliaux, see Per Nykrog, *Les Fabliaux* (1957), and Thomas D. Cooke and Benjamin L. Honeycutt, *The Humor of the Fabliaux* (1974).

Aquinas, Thomas. *The Summa Theologica of St. Thomas Aquinas. Pt. III (Supplement)*. Vol. 19. London: Burns, Oats and Washbourne, n.d.

Beach, Charles Ray. *Treatment of Ecclesiastics in the French Fabliaux of the Middle Ages*. Kentucky Microcards. Modern Language Series, no. 34. Lexington: University Press of Kentucky, 1960.

Bédier, Joseph. *Les Fabliaux*. 6th ed. Paris: Champion, 1964.

Benson, Larry D., and Theodore M. Andersson, eds. *The Literary Context of Chaucer's Fabliaux*. New York: Bobbs-Merrill, 1971.

Beyer, Jürgen. "The Morality of the Amoral." In *The Humor of the Fabliaux: A Collection of Critical Essays*, edited by Thomas D. Cooke and Benjamin L. Honeycutt, pp. 15–42. Columbia: University of Missouri Press, 1974.

Brunetière, Ferdinand. "Les Fabliaux du moyen âge et l'origine des contes." *Revue des deux mondes* 112 (1893): 184–213.

Chaplain, Andrew the. *The Art of Courtly Love*. Translated by John Jay Parry. New York, 1959.

Chênerie, Marie-Luce. " 'Ces curieux chevaliers tournoyeurs . . . " *Romania* 97 (1976): 327–68.

Cooke, Thomas D. "Formulaic Diction and the Artistry of *Le Chevalier qui recovra l'amor de sa dame*." *Romania* 94 (1973): 232–40.

———. *The Old French and Chaucerian Fabliaux: A Study of Their Comic Climax*. Columbia: University of Missouri Press, 1978.

———. "Pornography, the Comic Spirit, and the Fabliaux." In *The Humor of the Fabliaux: A Collection of Critical Essays*," edited by Thomas D. Cooke and Benjamin L. Honeycutt, pp. 137–62. Columbia: University of Missouri Press, 1974.

Cooke, Thomas D., and Benjamin L. Honeycutt, eds. *The Humor of the Fabliaux: A Collection of Critical Essays*. Columbia: University of Missouri Press, 1974.

Delhaye, P. "Celibacy, History of." *New Catholic Encyclopedia*. Vol. 3, pp. 371–73. New York, 1967.

Dronke, Peter. "The Rise of the Medieval Fabliau: Latin and Vernacular Evidence." *Romanische Forschungen* 85 (1973): 275–97.

DuVal, John. "Les Tresces: Semi-Tragical Fabliau, Critique and Translation." *Publications of the Missouri Philological Association* 3 (1979): 7–16.

———. "Medieval French Fabliaux." *Lazarus* 1 (1980): 8–49.

———. "The Villager and His Two Asses." In *Intro 7*, edited by George Garrett, pp. 273–75. Garden City, N.Y.: Doubleday, Anchor Books, 1975.

Eichmann, Raymond. "The Anti-Feminism of the Fabliaux." In *Authors and Philosophers, French Literatures Series* 6 (1979): 26–34.

———. "The Artistry of Economy in the Fabliaux." *Studies in Short Fiction* 17:1 (1980): 67–73.

———. "The Question of Variants and the Fabliaux." *Fabula* 17 (1976): 40–44.

———. "The Search for Originals in the Fabliaux and the Validity of Textual Dependency." *Romance Notes* 19:1 (1978): 90–97.

Faral, Edmond. "Le Fabliau latin au moyen âge." *Romania* 50 (1924): 321–85.

———. *Les Jongleurs en France au moyen âge*. Paris: Champion, 1910; rpt. New York: Burt Franklin, 1970.

Faral, Edmond, ed. *Courtois d'Arras*. C.F.M.A. Paris: Champion, 1961.

Ferrante, Joan. *Woman as Image in Medieval Literature*. New York: Columbia University Press, 1975.

Flutre, L.-F., "Le Fabliau, genre courtois?" *Frankfurter Universithätsreden* 22 (1960): 70–84.

Foulet, Alfred, and Mary Blakely Speer. *On Editing Old French Texts*. Lawrence: The Regents Press of Kansas, 1979.

Frank, Grace. *Medieval French Drama*, 3d ed. Oxford: Clarendon Press, 1967.

Harden, Robert. "The Depreciatory Comparison: A Literary Device of the Medieval Epic." In *Medieval Studies in Honor of U. T. Holmes, Jr.*, edited by John Mahoney and John Esten Keller, pp. 63–78. Chapel Hill: University of North Carolina Press, 1965.

Harrison, Robert. *Gallic Salt*. Berkeley: University

of California Press, 1974.

Hellman, Robert, and Richard O'Gorman, eds. and trans. *Fabliaux: Ribald Tales from the Old French.* New York: Crowell and Company, 1965.

Helsinger, Howard. "Pearls in the Swill: Comic Allegory in the French Fabliaux." In *The Humor of the Fabliaux: A Collection of Critical Essays,* edited by Thomas D. Cooke and Benjamin L. Honeycutt, pp. 93–105. Columbia: University of Missouri Press, 1974.

Honeycutt, Benjamin L. "An Example of Comic Cliché in the Old French Fabliaux." *Romania* 96 (1975): 245–55.

———. "The Knight and His World as Instruments of Humor in the Fabliaux." In *The Humor of the Fabliaux: A Collection of Critical Essays,* edited by Thomas D. Cooke and Benjamin L. Honeycutt, pp. 75–92. Columbia: University of Missouri Press, 1974.

Johnston, Ronald C., and D. D. R. Owen, eds. *Fabliaux.* Oxford: Blackwell, 1957.

Kasprzyk, Krystyna. "Pour la sociologie du fabliau: Convention, tactique et engagement." *Kwartalnik Neofilologiczny* 23 (1976): 153–61.

Kieson, Reinhard. *Die Fabliaux.* Rheinfelden: Schäuble, 1976.

Lacy, Norris J. "Types of Esthetic Distances in the Fabliaux." In *The Humor of the Fabliaux: A Collection of Critical Essays,* edited by Thomas D. Cooke and Benjamin L. Honeycutt, pp. 107–17. Columbia: University of Missouri Press, 1974.

———. "The Fabliaux and Comic Logic." *L'Esprit Créateur* 16:1 (1976): 39–45.

Lea, Henry C. *The History of Sacerdotal Celibacy in the Christian Church.* New York, 1957.

LeClerc, Victor. "Fabliaux." In *Histoire littéraire de la France,* 23:69–215. Paris: Imprimerie Nationale, 1895.

Livingston, Charles H. *Le Jongleur Gautier le Leu: Etude sur les Fabliaux.* Cambridge, Mass.: Harvard University Press, 1951.

Lorcin, Marie-Thérèse. "Quand les Princes n'épousaient pas les bergères ou mésalliance et classes d'âge dans les fabliaux." *Medioevo Romanzo* 3 (1976): 195–228.

Ménard, Philippe, ed. *Fabliaux français du Moyen Age.* Vol. 1. Textes Littéraires Français 270. Geneva: Droz, 1979.

Montaiglon, Anatole de, and Gaston Raynaud, eds. *Recueil général et complet des fabliaux des XIII*e *et XIV*e *siècles.* 6 vols. Paris, 1872–1890; rpt. New York: Burt Franklin, n.d.

Morawski, Jean. *Proverbes français antérieurs au XV*e *siècle.* C.F.M.A., 47. Paris: Champion, 1925.

Muscatine, Charles. *Chaucer and the French Tradition.* Berkeley: University of California Press, 1957.

———. "The Social Background of the Old French Fabliaux." *Genre* 9:1 (1976): 1–19.

———. "*The Wife of Bath* and Gautier's *La Veuve.*" In *Romance Studies in Memory of Edward Billings Ham,* edited by U. T. Holmes, pp. 109–14. Hayward, Calif.: California State College, 1967.

Noomen, Willem. "Structures narratives et force comique: Les fabliaux." *Neophilologus* 62 (1978): 361–73.

Nykrog, Per. "Courtliness and the Townspeople: The Fabliaux as a Courtly Burlesque." In *The Humor of the Fabliaux: A Collection of Critical Essays,* edited by Thomas D. Cooke and Benjamin L. Honeycutt, pp. 59–73. Columbia: University of Missouri Press, 1974.

———. *Les Fabliaux: Etude d'histoire littéraire et de stylistique médiévale.* Copenhagen: Munksgaard, 1957.

Olsen, Michel. *Les Transformations du triangle érotique.* Copenhagen: Akademisk, 1976.

Olson, Glending. "The Medieval Theory of Literature for Refreshment and Its Use in the Fabliau Tradition." *Romance Philology* 71 (1974): 241–313.

———. "*The Reeve's Tale* and *Gombert.*" *Modern Language Review* 64 (1969): 721–25.

———. "*The Reeve's Tale* as a Fabliau." *Modern Language Quarterly* 35 (1974): 219–30.

Pearcy, Roy J. "Chansons de Geste and Fabliaux: *La Gageure* and *Berenger au long cul.*" *Neuphilologische Mitteilungen* 79 (1978): 76–83.

———. "Modes of Signification and the Humor of Obscene Diction in the Fabliau." In *The Humor of the Fabliaux: A Collection of Critical Essays,* edited by Thomas D. Cooke and Benjamin L. Honeycutt, pp. 163–96. Columbia: University of Missouri Press, 1974.

———. "Relations between the *D* and *A* Versions of *Bérenger au long cul.*" *Romance Notes* 14:1 (1972): 173–78.

———. "Structural Models for the Fabliaux and the *Summoner's Tale* Analogues." *Fabula* 15 (1974): 103–13.

Pitcher, Edward W. "A Note on the Source of *The Child of Snow* and *The Son of Snow.*" *Early American Literature* 13 (1978): 217–18.

Raynaud de Lage, Guy. *Introduction à l'ancien français*. Paris: SEDES, 1966.

Reid, T. B. W., ed. *Twelve Fabliaux: From MS. F. FR 19152 of the Bibliothèque Nationale*. Manchester: Manchester University Press, 1958.

Rychner, Jean. *Contribution à l'étude des fabliaux: Variantes, remaniements, dégradations*. 2 vols. Geneva: Droz, 1960.

———. *Du Bouchier d'Abevile: Fabliau du XIIIe siècle (Eustache d'Amiens)*. Geneva: Droz, 1975.

Schenck, Mary Jane. "Functions and Roles in the Fabliaux." *Comparative Literature* 30 (1978): 22–24.

———. "The Morphology of the Fabliau." *Fabula* 17 (1976): 26–39.

Schofield, W. Henry. *The Source and History of the Seventh Novel of the Seventh Day in the Decameron*. Harvard Studies and Notes in Philology and Literature. Vol. II. Cambridge, Mass.: Harvard University Press, 1893.

Sperry, Earl Evelyn. *An Outline of the History of Clerical Celibacy in Western Europe to the Council of Trent*. Syracuse, N.Y., 1905.

Subrenat, Jean. "Notes sur la tonalité des fabliaux. A propos du fabliau: *Du Fèvre de Creeil.*" *Marche Romane* 25 (1975): 83–93.

Theiner, Paul. "Fabliau Settings." In *The Humor of the Fabliaux: A Collection of Critical Essays*, pp. 119–36. Edited by Thomas D. Cooke and Benjamin L. Honeycutt. Columbia: University of Missouri Press, 1974.

Thompson, Stith. *The Folktale*. New York: The Dryden Press, 1946.

———. *Motif-Index of Folk-Literature*, 2d ed. 6 vols. Bloomington: Indiana University Press, 1955.

———. *Narrative Motif-Analysis as a Folklore Method*. FF Communications, no. 161. Helsinki, 1955.

Togeby, Knud. "The Nature of the Fabliaux." In *The Humor of the Fabliaux: A Collection of Critical Essays*, edited by Thomas D. Cooke and Benjamin L. Honeycutt, pp. 7–13. Columbia: University of Missouri Press, 1974.

Voretzsch, Karl. *Altfranzösische Sprache*. Halle: Niemeyer, 1932.

Wailes, Stephen L. "Vagantes and the Fabliaux." In *The Humor of the Fabliaux: A Collection of Critical Essays*, edited by Thomas D. Cooke and Benjamin L. Honeycutt, pp. 43–58. Columbia: University of Missouri Press, 1974.

Williams, Clem C., Jr. "The Genre and Art of the Old French Fabliaux: A Preface to the Study of Chaucer's Tales of the Fabliau Type." Ph.D. Dissertation, Yale University, 1961.

Index